"YOU'RE GOING TO BE ALL RIGHT NOW," WADE MURMURED. "I'LL MAKE SURE OF THAT."

"Yes," she whispered. "Yes." Julia felt safe with his arms around her.

He gazed at her a moment longer and then gently urged her head to his chest. Feeling a light touch on her hair, she wondered if he'd pressed his lips there. A thrill shot through her at the thought, banishing the remnants of fear. She wanted—what did she want?

Lifting her head from his chest, she gazed up at him, his name trembling on her lips.

"Julia," he whispered and slowly bent his head until his lips brushed hers, a far gentler kiss than any she'd experienced in the past. But, oh, what sensations rushed through her! The kiss lasted all too briefly but continued to tingle through her.

She wanted more.

BOOK YOUR PLACE ON OUR WEBSITE AND MAKE THE READING CONNECTION!

We've created a customized website just for our very special readers, where you can get the inside scoop on everything that's going on with Zebra, Pinnacle and Kensington books.

When you come online, you'll have the exciting opportunity to:

- View covers of upcoming books
- Read sample chapters
- Learn about our future publishing schedule (listed by publication month *and author*)
- Find out when your favorite authors will be visiting a city near you
- Search for and order backlist books from our online catalog
- Check out author bios and background information
- Send e-mail to your favorite authors
- Meet the Kensington staff online
- Join us in weekly chats with authors, readers and other guests
- Get writing guidelines
- AND MUCH MORE!

Visit our website at
http://www.pinnaclebooks.com

LOVELAND

Jane Anderson

Pinnacle Books
Kensington Publishing Corp.

http://www.pinnaclebooks.com

PINNACLE BOOKS are published by

Kensington Publishing Corp.
850 Third Avenue
New York, NY 10022

Pinnacle and the P logo Reg. U.S. Pat. & TM Off.

First Printing: September, 1998
10 9 8 7 6 5 4 3 2 1

Printed in the United States of America

Chapter 1

Clickety-clack! Clickety-clack!

What will he be like? What will he be like? the train wheels seemed to ask.

Time enough to find out when I get to Loveland, Julia Sommers told herself firmly, smoothing a wrinkle from her Nile green skirt. Besides, it really doesn't matter. Not to me.

She leaned toward the window, peering ahead, hoping to catch a glimpse of the Loveland Station but saw only the rolling hills stretching away to the shimmering August heat-haze on the horizon. Texas was so huge, so never-ending. Texas was so hot. Somehow the new and fashionable petticoat with the bustle Great-aunt Polly had bought her for the trip seemed to attract and hold the heat. If only she could open the coach windows without letting in a choking whirlwind of soot and cinders.

The Texas and Pacific locomotive thundered around a curve with black smoke pouring from its diamond-shaped stack. The wheels churned rhythmically, the cowcatcher thrust ahead, and the smoke swirled back past the coaches.

The train was hurtling westward, taking her to a town she'd never seen, to a man she'd never met. A man who was waiting to marry. Not waiting to marry *her*, of course. He expected to marry her sister Emma.

Julia lifted her blond curls up from her nape to try to cool her neck before leaning back against the seat and closing her eyes. Emma's hair was blond, too, even lighter than hers. How surprised she'd been three months before when, as they were walking home from the Wednesday night prayer meeting, her sister announced that she was betrothed to a Texan named Wade Howland, a friend of a friend of the Reverend Josiah Miller, and she would be traveling to Texas to wed him.

"But—but what about Floyd?" Julia had gasped.

"Bother Floyd!" Emma's tone was unusually harsh. "Do you realize I'll be twenty-one years old this month?"

Julia knew very well. Her twentieth birthday was the month after Emma's.

"Floyd Biddescomb's never going to ask me to marry him, and I refuse to become an old maid like Great-aunt Polly," Emma went on. "If I wait much longer no man will want me for a wife."

"Texas is a long way from Massachusetts." Julia put a hand on her sister's arm. "You've never met Mr. Howland. Are you sure . . . ?"

"I've made up my mind." Emma frowned. Her temper was ordinarily equitable, but at times, if crossed, she grew extremely irritable.

Julia could hardly believe her rather timid, follow-the-rules sister had agreed to such a thing. Julia was the rash, impulsive one, not Emma. It seemed you never really knew a person no matter how close you were to them or how long you'd lived with them.

She'd hardly recovered from the shock of her sister's betrothal to a stranger when, three days before Emma was to sail from Boston Harbor aboard the *Enterprise* to begin the long voyage to Galveston, she eloped with Floyd Biddescomb, who'd evidently been galvanized into action when faced with the threat of losing Emma once and for all.

Floyd and Emma, man and wife. Who could have anticipated such an ending? No one, not Julia, not the Reverend Miller, not Great-aunt Polly, and certainly not Floyd's possessive mother. The entire village of Coventry was agog.

"I urge you to take your sister's place," the Reverend Miller suggested to Julia the day after the elopement. She was seated in the parlor of the manse while the reverend, who suffered painfully from gout, limped about the room.

"No, hear me out," he said quickly when she started to protest. He paused in his pacing to stand behind her chair. "Not to marry this man Howland, estimable though I'm sure he is. To explain to him. To assure him the fault wasn't mine. How was I to know your sister would elope with Floyd Biddescomb on the virtual eve of her sailing?"

Julia hated to have him speak from in back of her, but she refused to turn around. "I couldn't go to Texas," she said to the air in front of her.

"The passage is paid for. And surely there's naught to keep you here in Coventry now that Emma's a married woman."

She knew what he meant. On their return from the honeymoon, Emma would never agree to live in Floyd's mother's house, so that meant Floyd would move into the small Sommers house. Great-aunt Polly couldn't be expected to give up her bedroom so Julia would have to offer the room she and Emma had shared to the newlyweds. There'd be no place for her to sleep except the parlor, which would be most awkward with a man in house. Still, that didn't mean she had to go to Texas!

"I've never been farther from home than Boston," she said to the reverend. "Texas is practically on the frontier."

"I've always admired your venturesome spirit," he countered. "I'm surprised at your hesitation."

Julia half-turned before she caught herself. Admired! When he'd forbidden his son Ezra to call on her because of her "forward character." Why didn't he come right out and admit he'd like it just fine if Julia Sommers were to leave town and not come back?

"I sincerely believe you owe Mr. Howland a personal explanation of your sister's untoward behavior," the reverend added. "It's the Christian thing to do."

So for one reason or another, here she was in a Texas and Pacific railway coach rattling across the prairie bound for Loveland. A shiver of panic mixed with excitement and anticipation coursed along her spine. The train whistle wailed and Julia opened her eyes.

She found herself an object of interest to some of the other passengers in the coach. A florid-faced gentleman in a patterned frock coat and wearing a red tie, a drummer she supposed, smiled at her. Julia turned her face from him immediately. She'd had problems with men like him earlier on the journey, men who seemed to think her being a young woman alone made her fair game. She'd learned to protect herself by ignoring them completely.

A sallow-faced woman in a black dress and matching bonnet frowned at her before looking away. What was the world coming to, her frown seemed to ask, when a young woman would travel by herself?

"Loveland's next." The tall, thin conductor consulted the pocket watch attached to a gold chain looped across his black vest.

Julia glanced out the window, trying to make out the buildings of the town among the hills ahead of the train. She saw nothing except the empty rolling prairie with a single, solitary jack-rabbit leaping through the scanty vegetation. Suddenly steam plumed from the locomotive and a few seconds later she again heard the lonely wail of the whistle.

"I'll be right happy to help you with your baggage, miss," the conductor said, reaching above Julia for her carpetbag and her large black valise fastened with leather straps.

With quick fingers, Julia made certain her Dolly Varden

hat sat forward, dipping onto her forehead as it was supposed to. Taking a tiny mirror from her handbag she
grimaced at her reflection, trying to dab away the soot
marks on her face with a handkerchief. The blue eyes
staring back at her held a hint of panic and she blinked
as though hoping to wash it away.

The train slowed abruptly, jerking her forward and then
back as, with hisses and squeals, it ground to a stop. Peering
from the window, Julia saw only the swirl of steam and
smoke.

"This way, miss."

She followed the conductor along the aisle, ignoring the
stares of the other passengers. The conductor manhandled
her bags down the steps to the station platform, then
turned and offered her his hand. Once on the wooden
planks, Julia looked around in bewilderment.

All she saw was an empty platform worn by years of sun
and wind and rain, two benches partially protected from
the sun by a slanting roof, and a rutted track leading away
through the sagebrush.

"Where . . . ?" she began. "Where's Loveland?"

The conductor nodded to a weathered sign at the side
of the track.

LOVELAND.

"This is all there is, miss," he told her.

Julia stood with her carpetbag on one side of her and
the leather valise on the other, staring about her with
dismay. This wasn't a town, not even a village. There wasn't
so much as one single house in sight. Loveland was, well,
nothing at all. Only a speck in the immensity that was the
state of Texas.

"Good luck to you," the conductor said, raising his blue
cap and smiling down at Julia from the top of the coach
steps.

The whistle wailed long and mournfully. Julia reached
for her baggage. She'd reboard the train and ride to the
next town where she'd return to Galveston and the East.

She'd been foolish to come in the first place. It really hadn't been the reverend's words that had put her here but her own impulsiveness.

The train heaved forward.

Julia sighed and let her bags thud to the platform. She raised her chin. In for a penny, in for a pound, as Great-aunt Polly would say. She watched the train gather speed, become small in the distance, and finally disappear in the haze to the west. Around her the empty prairie sweltered beneath the pale blue and cloudless midafternoon sky. Nothing stirred, there was no sign of life except a bird— a hawk, she thought—soaring to the north of the station. She and the hawk were alone in the middle of a dusty nowhere.

Sighing, she carried her carpetbag to one of the splintering benches and sat in the shadow of the roof. Where was Wade Howland? Surely he'd meet the train bringing his bride-to-be from the East. Yet he hadn't. Julia's sense of aloneness gave way to impatience, the impatience replaced by a rising anger, bringing a flush to her face.

She had half a mind to start walking along the dirt trail leading into the hills. Except that would be worse than reckless, it would be foolhardy. She searched the sky for the bird again, deciding it probably was a buzzard, waiting for its next meal. Well, it wouldn't be her. What *was* she to do then? Sit on this bench and wait for the next eastward bound train?

She couldn't see the bird, but far to the west, above the spot where the trail merged with the hazy horizon, she saw what appeared to be a small cloud. No, it wasn't a cloud, it was a rising spiral of dust growing larger and larger as she watched.

Julia waited, her heart pounding as she remembered tales of marauding Indians—weren't there Comanches in Texas—riding out of the west to attack lonely settlements. She sighed in relief when, after a few minutes, a black buggy appeared. The man driving urged on the galloping

horse by snapping a whip against its flanks. As horse and
buggy drew near, Julia saw the animal's gray coat was caked
with dust darkened by sweat.

The driver reined the buggy in beside the platform,
leaped down from his seat, and looped the reins around
a hitching rail. So this was Wade Howland. He was tall and
fair, his hair, from what she could see beneath his Stetson,
was as blond and curly as her own. His blue checked shirt
was dampened by sweat, his red neckerchief was dusty. As
he walked toward her with the rolling gait of a sailor—or
was it a cowboy's gait?—his hand brushed the hilt of the
pistol at his hip and his spurs jingled.

"Miss Sommers?" He swept off his hat.

Who in heaven's name did he think she was? Julia wondered. But she nodded. Seeing him now at close range,
she couldn't help noting his pudgy, reddened cheeks and
his small eyes, as pale blue as the sky. His low-slung belt
struggled to contain the beginning of a corporation
around his waist. Julia controlled her impulse to back away.
She didn't know exactly what she'd expected Wade Howland to look like, but this wasn't it. Why should she feel so
unaccountably disappointed? There was no reason, none at
all, since she was only here to explain about her sister's
defection.

He leaped up the steps two at a time and strode across
the platform toward her. Julia hesitated, then held out her
hand. Even women shook hands in the West, didn't they?

Ignoring her outstretched hand, he gripped her waist
with both of his hands and lifted her into the air. Julia
gasped.

"I'm not—" she began hastily.

Releasing her suddenly, his hands slid up her sides and
around her, drawing her to him. He smelled nastily of
tobacco. Before she realized what he meant to do, he
leaned down and kissed her on the lips.

She'd been kissed before, she wasn't completely lacking
in experience. Hayes Wright had kissed her once on a

dare, and Ezra Miller, the minister's son, kissed her once last winter on a moonlight sleigh ride and once more in her own parlor.

Those kisses had left her more curious than anything else. She'd forgotten what Hayes's kiss was like, but she'd rather enjoyed being kissed by Ezra even if the kisses had been awkward and hasty.

This man's kiss was different—it repulsed her. She tried to struggle free but he held her too tightly, his lips unpleasantly wet on hers. When he opened his mouth and his tongue snaked between her lips, she gagged and managed to jerk her head to one side. He put a hand to her nape to force her to turn back toward him but she ducked her head and broke away, furiously wiping at her mouth with the back of her gloved hand.

She longed to slap his smirking face—how dare he! He reached for her again and she retreated, hurrying across the platform so one of the benches was between them.

"I'm not who you think I am." Her voice shook with anger.

"You said you was Miss Sommers."

"I'm Miss Julia Sommers, not Miss Emma. Emma's my sister."

"Well, I'll be. If that ain't something." Grinning, he started toward her. "You must've come in her place."

She retreated. "No, I haven't. Not exactly. I'm here right enough, but I have *not* come to Texas to marry you, Mr. Howland."

Never in a thousand years would she marry this man. Not even if she remained an old maid all her life. Suddenly she realized that in a far recess of her mind she'd harbored the possibility that perhaps, after a long and pleasant ripening acquaintance, she might consider marrying Wade Howland. If, by that time, she'd fallen in love with him, of course. She'd never believed in love at first sight but now she certainly was ready to believe in what must be its opposite—repulsion at first sight. What she felt was actually close to hatred.

"Sure as shooting we made a mistake, little lady," the man said. "You and me, both. I ain't Wade Howland. My handle's Crain, Jack Crain."

"You're not Mr. Howland?" Julia stared at him in confusion. "Then why did you kiss me?"

"I don't know how it is in Boston and thereabouts. Here in Texas everybody gets to kiss the bride."

She sat on the bench and crossed her arms, still angry, both at him and at Wade Howland for sending a man like this to meet her. "I am *not* the bride, Mr. Crain," she insisted, glaring at him.

Jack shrugged, picked up her two bags and carried them to the buggy where he lashed them down with a length of rope. When he finished he retrieved the reins and looked at her.

"Coming?"

Julia remained on the bench. She didn't want to get into the buggy with Jack Crain.

"You're gonna have a long wait," he drawled. "Next train ain't due at Loveland Station till tomorrow morning along about eleven. If you don't want to spend the night with the coyotes, you'd best come with me."

Coyotes? She hid her involuntary grimace by raising her hand to her mouth. For such a barren land, Texas seemed to have quite a supply of animals.

I suppose I don't really have any choice, Julia told herself, even though he's not much improvement over that buzzard hovering in the sky. She stood and walked to the buggy with all the dignity she could muster, ignoring his offer to help her climb up to the seat. When he sat beside her she edged as far away from him as possible.

Jack snapped the whip and the gray gelding trotted along the barren trail leading into the hills. Riding in silence, they passed a dry streambed coming from a grove of cottonwoods off to their right, the trees a blessed spot of green in the dusty brown. On and on the gelding trotted through what seemed like endless and essentially barren terrain, the buggy jouncing behind him. At last Julia could contain her curiosity no longer.

"Do you mind telling me, Mr. Crain, how far is it?" she asked. "To wherever you're taking me, that is."

"From Loveland Station to the ranch it's a tad more'n an hour's drive." He glanced sideways at her, his gaze lingering, roving slowly and admiringly from her face to the swell of her breasts under the dark green curaisse bodice of her gown. For the first time she found herself wishing the style wasn't so tight-fitting.

Though Julia stared straight ahead, she reddened in annoyed embarrassment. If Mr. Howland employed ranch hands like Jack Crain, what kind of a person must *he* be? Certainly he wouldn't be the kind of a man she could either admire or respect.

"I would've been on time," Jack said, " 'cept Jefferson here"—he pointed to the gelding with his whip—"threw a shoe. Wade got the letter and all from your sister. And the telegram from the harbormaster at Galveston when your ship docked."

I devoutly wish I'd insisted the Reverend Miller send a telegram about Emma instead of coming myself, Julia thought. *Him and his talk of Christian duty. And me and my foolish fancies.*

"Anyhow, that's how come I'm a tad late," Jack finished.

"I'm surprised Mr. Howland didn't come to meet the train himself," Julia said. *How discourteous not to meet a bride-to-be in person. Especially a woman coming from so far away. And sending Jack Crain in his place! But then, maybe all Texans were like Jack, heaven forbid.*

"Wade sure would've," Jack said, "if it wasn't for Sam Bass."

When he didn't go on, Julia looked at him from the corner of her eyes. He was teasing her by arousing her curiosity, she was sure, forcing her to talk to him whether she wanted to or not.

"Sam Bass?" she asked finally, determined to utter as few words as possible.

"Old Sam's a train robber. Been raising all kinds of hell in these parts of late. Rode down from the Dakotas a few months back to hole up in the river bottoms over by Dallas. Sam and his gang get a notion every so often to take some action and then they sashay out of them woods to hold up one of the Texas and Pacific trains."

She remembered seeing two rifle-toting guards in the baggage car on her train. So that was why they were posted there.

"They say him and his cohorts," Jack continued, "got a hankering for two things. One's the gold the railroad's transporting and the other's pretty young fillies the likes of you."

Imagining herself staring down the black mouth of a pistol wielded by a fearsome outlaw, Julia repressed a shiver, glancing quickly at Jack to see if he was still teasing her. He stared straight ahead with a solemn expression on his face, so she couldn't be sure. It was the height of silliness to allow herself to be upset by him when, for all she knew, he was making most of it up out of whole cloth.

"You're the kind of filly old Sam likes best," Jack told her. "He likes 'em with a tad of ginger." He paused, then added, "Or leastways that's what they say."

Julia shrugged. Texas might be as lawless as Great-aunt Polly had insisted it was, but, even if what Mr. Crain said was true, her chances of meeting Sam Bass were few and far between.

Jack reached into his shirt pocket, brought forth a plug of tobacco, bit off a piece, and began to chew, a filthy habit she'd never approved of.

"Anyways, General Steele asked Wade to join the Rangers again to lead the search for old Sam and, being sort of fond of tracking and fighting and suchlike, Wade said okay. So it was me 'stead of him that come to meet the train at Loveland Station.''

She was aghast. "You mean Mr. Howland isn't at the ranch we're going to?"

"Wade's spread, the W Bar H, that's where we're heading. And he's there all right. Today. In the morning him and the Rangers ride west a-looking for Sam Bass."

Julia didn't know whether to be relieved or not. She'd have the chance to explain to Mr. Howland why her sister hadn't journeyed west. On the other hand, would his going leave her alone with Jack Crain on what was certain to be an isolated ranch? She shook her head. Rather than risk that, she'd take the return train tomorrow. The least Mr. Howland could do was see her safely to Loveland Station.

As the wagon crested a low hill, Jack leaned over the side of the buggy and spat a stream of tobacco juice onto the dust. When he sat straight again after this disgusting action, she thought he looked unduly self-satisfied. Resolutely she stared away from him, hoping he'd have the sense to keep quiet. Everything he'd said or done was aimed at unnerving her, she was certain.

The horse struggled up a higher hill and, at the top, Jack reined to a stop. Julia drew in her breath as she looked down into a golden valley where cattle grazed on slopes rising above a cluster of ranch buildings standing in what seemed like an oasis in the prairie. She smelled the acrid tang of smoke from open cooking fires behind the main house. Horses were tethered in a yard near the stables and men and women walked to and fro under the hot August sun, pausing in the shade of tall cottonwoods.

"So many people," Julia said in surprise. "If this were Massachusetts, I'd say they were having a social."

Jack grinned. "You might say so. Or that they're fixing to."

She was determined not to let his teasing provoke her. "I suppose they've all come to the ranch to say goodbye

to Mr. Howland and the other Rangers. To wish them luck
on their mission to apprehend Sam Bass.''

"Well, they wish 'em luck, no doubt about it, but that
ain't the reason they're here.''

Julia felt a lurch of panic mixed with renewed fury at
this repulsive man's behavior. She turned to face him. "Mr.
Crain!'' she exclaimed. "Do stop dragging it out. Why *are*
they here?''

He smirked. "Waiting for us, that's what. I reckon
Wade's invited most everyone in the county including the
fiddler and the preacher. 'Specially the preacher.''

"The preacher?'' Julia echoed in a whisper.

"Wade's been planning this shindig for a long time. As
far as he's concerned, he's getting hitched afore the sun
sets. I reckon he won't mind making do with you 'stead
of your sister.''

Chapter 2

Jack Crain cracked the whip and the gelding trotted down the winding trail leading to the Howland ranch—the W Bar H. The buggy swayed perilously from side to side, forcing Julia to grip the edge of her seat to keep from being hurled to the ground. She suspected he was going too fast on purpose, but her apprehension over what she had to face was so overwhelming she didn't protest.

As they drew closer to the waiting celebrants she smelled roasting meat and pictured a whole side of beef being slowly turned on a spit over one fire, a pig with an apple stuffed in its mouth over another. She tried to keep her mind on that instead of allowing herself to dwell on what else was ahead for her, but found it well-nigh impossible. She gave up completely after a cowhand on the ranch porch spotted the buggy. Waving his hat high above his head, he leaped down, ran to the trail, and raised his voice in a series of ear-splitting rebel yells. She winced when Jack Crain replied with a rebel yell of his own.

Ranchers and their ladies hurried to crowd along the roadside in an informal welcome, the smiling, bonneted women waving handkerchiefs, the men lifting their broad-brimmed hats and cheering.

Julia wanted to jump from the buggy and run back the way she'd come. To escape. She longed to cover her face with her hands, to somehow hide from this happy crowd waiting to greet her. What would they do when they found out she was cheating them out of a celebration? Certainly they'd be angry. Blame her. She could almost see their smiles turn to scowls, their cheers to boos. She began to feel she was little better off than the roasting pig. What was she to do?

Don't be foolish, she told herself, something will happen to save you.

But what? She'd been eager enough to leave Coventry because she felt there was no longer a place for her in the town. When Floyd and Emma returned she wouldn't have a bed of her own, much less a room. Of course, if she took a job in the mill, she could rent a room in a boarding house until she married. If she married. Who was there to marry in Coventry?

Ezra was the only one she liked, but even if Ezra's father hadn't been dead set against his son courting her, Ezra was still a boy, really—a year younger than she was, only nineteen, making no money because he was going to divinity school.

Yes, admit it, she'd leaped at this chance to leave Coventry for the novelty of Texas, and where had it gotten her? Out of the frying pan into the fire.

Something will help me here in Loveland, someone will show me a way out of this, she told herself over and over as Jack reined the buggy to a stop in front of the jostling crowd.

Even a catastrophe of nature would be welcome, like a soaking thunderstorm with violent winds. But there wasn't a cloud in the sky. Finally acknowledging there was no help in sight for her, Julia took a deep breath, straightened her back, and forced herself to smile at the people as Jack jumped to the ground and ran around the buggy to offer her his hand. He smirked up at her, enjoying her discomfort, reveling in the fact that only he knew what was coming. She took his hand without looking at him and climbed to the ground where she stood facing the waiting wedding guests.

She had the impression of countless eyes staring at her. Of women in bonnets smiling politely as they examined her Nile green silk traveling dress with its darker curaisse fitted bodice and especially the bustle. Of men, most of them sporting mustaches or beards or both, nodding approval. When she noticed a cowhand nudge his neighbor, she glanced down to reassure herself no buttons had come undone and saw with dismay that the dampness from the heat caused the silk to cling to the curves of her hips.

She should have realized what might happen with this new style of skirt, flattened in front because of the bustle. At the moment there was nothing she could do to remedy the situation and so she held her head high, willing herself not to blush.

The lowering sun slanted into her eyes and she blinked, looking away, feeling beads of perspiration gather on her forehead. Texas was sweltering. She'd never been so hot before in her life. The heat choked her, worsened by her extreme discomfort due to the circumstances. She could hardly breathe and wished she dared unbutton her collar for relief.

"Here he comes," a man's voice called from the rear of the crowd.

"Let him pass," someone else shouted.

Julia heard a murmur of talk and laughter, a few raucous yells, and slowly the crowd in front of her parted, the men and their ladies stepping to one side until an aisle was formed. Again Julia blinked, momentarily blinded by the sun.

As soon as her vision cleared, she looked down the aisle and drew in her breath. He stood on the porch, a man

dressed all in gray with his shirt open at the neck and a
gray Stetson tilted to one side on his head. Cleanshaven,
he was muscular though not unusually tall. He was dark,
his hair black, his eyebrows black, his face tanned.

He scowled at her.

Julia felt a tremor begin deep within her, a tremor that
spread through her body, a sensation of delicious fear.
She clenched her hands at her sides and tried without
success to control her rapid breathing. Hoping to see the
color of his eyes, she stared at his face but he was in the
shadow of the ranch house so she couldn't be sure. His
eyes are black, she told herself, they must be black.

"Wade," someone called to him, "you lucky devil."

Wade Howland. Julia nodded involuntarily. A man who
looked like that, who held himself as though he owned
the world, had to be Wade. Why did he frighten her so?

Wade started toward her, walking slowly, his gaze never
leaving her face, and as he drew close his scowl softened
and became the beginning of a smile. Julia's hands
unclenched and, without realizing she intended to, she
took a step forward. She stopped, aware only of him. As
he came nearer she saw his eyes, his mesmerizing eyes,
were gray, a light gray, akin to the color of a newly minted
silver coin. She couldn't seem to stop looking into his eyes.

He halted an arm's length from her and, in a voice so
low only she could hear, said, "You're not what I expected,
not at all." He shook his head.

Was he pleased? she wondered. Disappointed? No
longer afraid of him, she pulled off her glove and held
out her hand. Wade removed his Stetson with his left hand
and held the hat over his heart while he took her hand
in his and raised her fingers to his lips.

"Emma," he said softly. The word was almost a caress.

Julia gasped. She'd forgotten. Caught up in the
moment—the excitement of meeting Wade Howland—
she'd completely forgotten he was expecting not Julia Som-

mers but her sister. Julia withdrew her hand and backed away. Wade stared at her.

A murmur of voices rose around her. She breathed in the odor of roasting pork mingled with the pungent smell of the sage. Felt the sun on her face, the searing heat of August threatening to suffocate her.

Through a haze she saw Wade watching her with a puzzled frown on his face, saw a smirking Jack Crain, noticed the crowd pushing closer for a better look at her. What in heaven's name was she to do now?

Her knees felt as though they might buckle at any moment and so she decided to let them. With a moan, she crumpled to the ground at Wade's feet. He reached for her but not in time to catch her. She lay in the dust, eyes shut, trying to close her mind to what was going on around her, wishing with all her heart she could be somewhere other than in Loveland, Texas, or, failing that, at least be able to truly faint so she'd be unaware of her surroundings, at least temporarily.

Strong arms swung her into the air. "Are you all right?" a man's deep voice asked. Wade's voice.

She longed to open her eyes and see him at close range but knew better. She didn't answer. As his boots thudded on the wooden porch, she heard murmurs of sympathy from behind them.

"Poor child" . . . "the heat" . . . "that long trip". . . "Isn't she a lovely girl?"

Julia kept her eyes closed. Keenly aware of Wade's arms beneath her knees and shoulders, she was surprised to find herself wishing he'd hold her like this forever and never put her down. In his arms, she felt protected, out of harm's way.

A door banged and, when Wade shifted her in his arms to walk sideways, she realized they must be entering one of the rooms in the ranch house. An instant later he lowered her gently and she felt a mattress beneath her body and the softness of a pillow under her head. She immediately missed his arms, but it was a relief to be out of the sun and away from the crowd.

A sharp odor startled her into opening her eyes. An olive-skinned older woman was wafting a small bottle under her nose. Smelling salts.

"I'm all right now," Julia whispered. "I'll get up." She raised her head from the pillow, then closed her eyes and sank back once more. "If I could rest," she murmured. "Just for a little while." It was no sham, she'd never felt so drained in her entire life.

"Pobrecita," the woman with the smelling salts said. Through half-closed eyes Julia saw her turn to Wade and shoo him from the room. Then she eased off Julia's shoes before leaving herself.

Julia felt guilty. She'd never fainted in her life or feigned fainting, either. She disliked pretense of any kind. What else, though, could she have done? She couldn't embarrass Wade by blurting out in front of that crowd she wasn't Emma. On the other hand, she certainly couldn't have married a man who thought she was someone else. Couldn't have married a stranger, anyway. Even one who looked like Wade Howland.

Wondering why such an attractive man had seen fit to send East for a bride he'd never met, the exhausted Julia fell asleep.

When she awoke, the room was shadowed and the heat less intense. From far away came shouts mingled with the lilt of a fiddle. Sensing someone watching her, Julia sat up and peered into the shadows near the door.

Wade walked toward her, a tight smile on his lips.

"I was waiting for you to wake up, Miss Sommers," he said.

She tore her gaze away from his silver eyes, frowned and bit her lip. The time had come for the truth. "There's something I have to tell you," she said. "I'm not Emma, I'm her sister, Julia."

"I know that. Now." His voice was flat, neutral, as though

he'd strained out all feeling. "Jack Crain told me a while back, after you'd fainted." The words, which might have been comforting and forgiving, were not. Instead, they were tinged with disappointment and anger.

"Let me explain," Julia said.

"I reckon it's a tad late for that." His eyes were frosty.

"I want to." As quickly as she could, she told him about Emma's elopement and how the Reverend Miller suggested she travel west in her sister's place. Not exactly in her place, but to explain the situation to Emma's intended. As the words poured out, she couldn't help but think how lame it all sounded.

"Emma really loves Floyd," she finished. "At least I think so. She'd just gotten discouraged with him. I'm sorry her confusion inconvenienced you."

"I wouldn't care to marry a woman who loved another man, but there's no need, Miss Julia, for you to apologize for what you and your sister did." Wade's voice was as cold as his eyes.

Julia bridled. He had no right to blame her. "I have no reason to apologize for *my* actions, Mr. Howland. In fact, if apologies are due, perhaps you ought to tender yours. The very idea of having a wedding ceremony on the same day your fiancée arrives from the East!"

He drew in his breath, his eyes warming. Smoldering. As he leaned over her, she could feel his anger. For an instant, she expected him to grab her shoulders and shake her. She stiffened, afraid and yet almost wishing he would touch her.

Wade drew back and she heard the soft release of his breath. "You may be right about that, Miss Julia. I do apologize." Again his voice was flat, all trace of sarcasm or of any emotion absent.

"I hate being called 'Miss Julia,' " she said, knowing her words were irrational but unable to help herself.

"You prefer being called Miss Sommers, then? Is that right?"

Why was he being so infuriating? "I don't care what you call me!" She heard her voice rise and didn't care.

For the first time, he truly smiled. Texans must get a perverse enjoyment from infuriating people, she thought. Actually she didn't want to fight with him, she just wanted it to be the way it was between them before she'd pretended to faint. Or afterward, when he'd carried her in his arms. She wanted him to comfort her, not chill her with cold words.

Unexpectedly, he laid his hand on her forehead. His palm was cool but the tingle caused by his touch wasn't comforting. Far from it.

"Senora Mendoza told me you might have a fever," he said, "and I reckon you do." He removed his hand. "I believe in doing what needs to be done without shilly-shallying around." It was a moment before she realized he was talking about the wedding. "That's why I thought it was a good idea to have the ceremony right away. Jack thought so, too."

"Jack Crain?" Her distaste for Jack showed in her voice.

Wade frowned. "Jack knows what women expect. He was married for five years and a bit back in East Texas."

"I'm sorry his wife died." Julia's tone was softer.

"She didn't die, they were divorced. Jack was a mighty wild galoot in those days." Wade nodded as though he admired him for it.

"I wouldn't say a man whose wife divorced him was an expert as far as women are concerned."

He leaned over her again until his face was only inches from hers. His eyes were the color of rain clouds in a thunderstorm. She couldn't breathe, and her heart pounded so loudly she wondered if he could hear it.

Wade grasped her shoulders, his fingers digging into her arms. He's going to kiss me, she thought, expectant and yet afraid. Somehow she knew his kiss wouldn't be merely pleasant. And it wouldn't be repulsive to her, either. His kiss would be like nothing she'd ever experienced.

His arms fell away but he didn't straighten. His eyes held hers as he gently brushed a strand of hair from her forehead. Her lips parted in anticipation.

Wade pulled back from her. "Whatever happens," he said softly, "try to understand. I had to do it."

She stared at him. "Had to do what? I don't—"

"What you need, Miss Sommers," he interrupted, "is a good night's rest." He strode to the door, closing it quietly behind him.

After Senora Mendoza brought in a tray of cheese, plums, and lemonade, Julia changed into her white cambric nightgown with its tucked yoke and broderic anglaise frilling. Later, she lay awake listening through the open window to the sounds in the night, the rise and fall of the music, the shouts and laughter of the dancers, the nickering of restless horses—a party going on without her. A sense of loneliness swept over her and she wished—what did she wish? To be home again?

In Massachusetts katydids chirped on a summer evening while fireflies danced. Coventry, the dull village she'd longed to leave, held a nostalgic fascination for her now. She wanted to be walking across a field of wildflowers in the spring or to be crossing the village square as brilliant autumn-hued leaves twirled to the ground around her. Or to hear the choir of churchbells pealing on a cold Sunday morning in December and awaken to the hush of a deep snow that had, overnight, transformed the drab village into a strange new world.

Texas offered few if any of those things. Texas had nothing to offer. Why had she come here?

Wade Howland walked toward her through a field of blue wildflowers, his smile warm, his eyes glowing . . .

With a start, Julia sat up in bed. She'd been dozing, for the room was now dark and the night quiet, the dancing over, the revelers departed.

Something had awakened her, though. What?

Pulling the single sheet up over her thin nightgown, she

peered into the darkness of the room but saw nothing except the black of the night. She held her breath, listening. There. A sound, the rustle of clothing from near the door.

"Who is it?" she whispered, trying to keep her alarm from her voice.

There was no answer. Yet she knew with a dread certainty there was a presence in the bedroom with her. Someone. Who was it? Why were they here? If it were Wade, surely he would have answered. But if it wasn't Wade, whoever waited in the dark meant her ill, as the lack of response indicated. A footstep, close to the side of bed. The intruder was coming toward her, coming for her.

Easing the sheet from her body, careful to make no sound, Julia slipped from the far side of the bed and crouched on one knee. As her eyes grew accustomed to the darkness, she saw a form on the far side of the bed, a form outlined in the dim light coming through the window. A man? She breathed in the faint fumes of whiskey and nodded. Yes, a man.

Tense with fear, she watched as he leaned to the bed, his hand seeking along the sheet. Finding her gone.

"Well, I'll be," he muttered under his breath.

Jack Crain's voice? Hadn't he spoken those very words earlier in the day? She was almost certain it was Jack. Now drunk and dangerous. Frightened as she was, anger shored her up. How dare he!

"Get out." She spoke between clenched teeth. "Get out of my room. I'll scream."

He didn't reply, his bare feet padding on the floor as he hurried around the bed to where she crouched. Julia reached behind her for the pitcher on the nightstand beside the bed. Her hand touched the handle. She gripped it and stood up, the half-filled pitcher heavy in her hand. He was almost upon her when she flung the pitcher with all her strength and heard it strike him. The man grunted.

Water splashed as the pitcher thudded to the floor without breaking.

She screamed, her voice high-pitched with terror. Silence. Had no one heard her? Desperate, she screamed again. The intruder seemed frozen where he was. Footsteps pounded far away, footsteps rushing along the hall to her room. The intruder swung around and ran to the open window where she saw his form silhouetted black against the pale light.

Her bedroom door banged open and a man paused just inside the room. She looked from him to the window. The curtain fluttered, the intruder was gone. Lamps flickered down the hall and by their light she saw it was Wade Howland in her doorway.

"Miss Julia?" Alarm and concern threaded through his voice. "Miss Julia, are you all right?"

She flung herself at him and clung to him. Wade's arms closed around her, strong and reassuring.

"A man," she gasped. "In my room."

"Are you all right?" he asked again.

"Yes." She nestled her face against his chest. "He—he went out the window."

Wade thrust her aside and strode to the window. Leaned out. "He's gone."

She hurried to his side and peered into the night. Saw nothing. "It was . . ." She hesitated. Was she sure? The intruder had only spoken three words. Could she really be positive it was Jack Crain?

"I—I don't know who he was," she told Wade. "I couldn't see him very well in the dark."

He turned to her. "A nightmare, maybe?"

"No, no, he was in here. I could smell whiskey." She shuddered.

Wade's arms went around her and he looked down into her eyes, his lips a breath from hers. She clung to him, still unnerved.

"You're going to be all right now," he murmured. "I'll make sure of that."

"Yes," she whispered. "Yes." She felt safe with his arms around her.

He gazed at her a moment longer and then gently urged her head to his chest. Feeling a light touch on her hair, she wondered if he'd pressed his lips there. A thrill shot through her at the thought, banishing the remnants of fear. She grew conscious of the hardness of his body against hers, the intimacy starting a strange and disturbing warmth deep inside her. She wanted—what did she want?

Lifting her head from his chest, she gazed up at him, his name trembling on her lips.

"Julia," he whispered and slowly bent his head until his lips brushed hers, a far gentler kiss than any she'd experienced in the past. But, oh, what sensations rushed through her! The kiss lasted all too briefly but continued to tingle through her. She wanted more.

Wade lifted his head and seemed to be listening. She stiffened. Was the intruder returning?

Chapter 3

Senora Mendoza hurried into the room holding a lighted lamp. Wade released Julia, stepping back and turning to the Mexican woman.

"The senorita had a nightmare," he said. "A bad dream."

"I didn't," Julia protested. "I wasn't dreaming. There was someone in my room. A man who smelled of whiskey."

He glanced at her and she crossed her arms over her breasts, blushing as she realized her body was covered only by the thin cotton of her nightgown. Wade looked quickly away.

"None of my guests or my ranchhands would enter a lady's room," he said flatly.

"Not even under the influence?" she asked tartly, annoyance replacing her tender feelings of moments before.

"No one was that drunk." Grasping the back of a straight wooden chair, he set it on the hall floor outside her door. "Just the same, I'll do picket duty here for the rest of the night so you'll be able to sleep."

After Senora Mendoza left, closing the door behind her,

Julia stared at the open window and shook her head. If she closed it, the room would be stifling. But if she left it open whoever had gotten out that way could also get in. Finally she rose from the bed and balanced the empty pitcher on the window sill so it would fall if any intruder tried to crawl inside, then got back into bed where she lay wide awake.

Why didn't Wade believe her? There *had* been a man in her bedroom—Jack Crain, she was almost certain. What would Wade have said if she'd accused Jack? Did Texans stick together no matter what?

She heard Wade's chair thump against the wall outside her room and pictured him leaning back and closing his eyes. She didn't understand the man at all. When he'd held her in his arms she'd felt a current pass between them, an awareness she was sure he must have felt as well. Then when his lips brushed over hers she was certain they shared a closeness. Yet he'd rejected her truth of a man in her room, he wouldn't believe her. At the same time he'd asked her to be understanding—about what, she had no idea.

Puzzled as well as irritated, she shook her head, finally hugging the pillow as she searched for sleep. A sound from outside, from the direction of the corral, made her jerk straight up in bed. A horse whinnied but nothing more happened and she quelled her impulse to call to Wade. I don't need a man who won't believe me, she assured herself. I'm better off looking after myself.

Though she hadn't expected to sleep a wink, she woke to a room bright with sunlight. From outside she heard the neighing of horses and the shouts of men. Julia threw back the sheet, sprang from the bed, and ran to the window to peer between the curtains. She eased the pitcher from the sill, gripping it her hands as she watched Wade and four other armed horsemen ride past the ranch house, no doubt on their way to the trail.

Wade turned toward the house, and for an instant she

thought he'd noticed her in the window so she drew back but then she saw he was looking to her right at something or someone hidden from her view. He swung down from his gray, strode toward the house, and disappeared.

She glanced at the other riders and noticed Jack Crain. Thank heaven he was leaving with the the Rangers in pursuit of the train robbers. The day before he'd led her to believe he wasn't involved in the hunt for Sam Bass.

The possibility that Wade had entered the house to say goodbye to her made her pulses pound. She was about to leave the window and pull on a robe when he appeared again, dashing her hope. He walked swiftly to his horse without looking back, mounted, and joined the other riders waiting for him on the trail. He sat his horse easily, the gray and its rider seeming to be a part of one another, moving as one, responding instantly to one another.

Julia sighed, watching the horsemen until they disappeared over the first of the hills, troubled by an emotion she couldn't quite identify—it was almost a feeling she'd been deserted. By Wade. But that was foolishness. He'd been planning to ride after Sam Bass even before she arrived.

After washing, she chose a day dress of pale blue muslin with a modified bustle from where Senora Mendoza had hung her clothes on pegs along one wall. She limited her petticoats to one because of the heat. Once she was dressed, she began brushing her hair in front of a small mirror hung on the wall above a dressing table. Actually it was a pleasant enough bedroom even though lacking a woman's touch.

The door inched open behind her. Startled, Julia swung about but saw no one. The sound of giggling came from the hallway. Children? She hadn't seen any the evening before. Perhaps Senora Mendoza had children but had kept them out of the way during the party.

As Julia turned once more to the mirror, the door

opened a few more inches. Looking in the mirror, she saw two small girls peeping around the side of the door.

Both were about four years old, the same height, and both were black haired with gray eyes and lightly freckled faces. Twins. Julia drew in her breath. Definitely not Senora Mendoza's—the twins all too strikingly resembled Wade Howland. As Julia turned to face them, one of the twins pushed her sister into the room. The girl looked back, all the while shaking her head.

"Nancy, you promised," the girl who was doing the pushing said.

Nancy drew in her breath and hurtled across the room, flinging herself at Julia and burying her head in her lap.

"*Madre,*" Nancy mumbled.

Julia didn't know much Spanish but she knew what that word meant. Her heart twisted in her chest as she leaned over and hugged the child. "I'm not your mother, Nancy," she said as gently as she could, "but I'm glad to meet you."

Nancy's gray eyes widened in puzzlement.

From the doorway the other twin said, "You are, too. You're our new mama."

Julia smiled at her. "What's your name?" she asked.

"Susan." The girl smiled shyly.

"Who told you I was your mother, Susan?" Julia asked with her arms around Nancy.

"Papa Wade said so. He said you sailed on a big ship and rode on a train. He said you came here to be our new mama."

"Wade? Mr. Howland told you that?" Julia looked from one twin to the other. There was no doubt they looked like Wade. "He said I was to be your new mother?"

Susan nodded vigorously. "Our real mama's in heaven," she said solemnly. "Papa Wade said the angels sent us a new mama to take her place."

Anger rose in Julia. How could Wade have been so cruel to these two adorable little girls? And so deceitful to Emma? Certainly neither Emma nor the Reverend Miller had known anything about a previous wife who'd passed away or twin daughters. No wonder Wade had wanted the wedding held the moment Emma arrived in Loveland. He had no intention of giving his bride-to-be time to discover she was gaining not only a husband but a ready made family as well.

"Susan," Julia said, feeling like a monster but knowing the girls had to be told. "Nancy. I'm sorry I'm not going to be your new mother. You see, I came here in place of my sister so Mr. Howland and I aren't going to be married. I can't be your mama."

Susan, still clinging to the door, lowered her head, tears glinting in her eyes. Nancy clutched at Julia and began to sob. Julia held out her hand to the other twin. Susan hesitated, then ran to Julia and she held both of the girls, hugging them as she fought back her own tears. For the moment, she wished she could promise she would be their mother.

"Susan. Nancy." The voice from the doorway startled Julia. Looking up, she saw Senora Mendoza standing with her hands on her hips. *"Vamos,"* the Mexican woman told the twins. "Pronto."

The girls ran off, squealing in mock fright.

"Such pretty little girls," Julia managed to say after swallowing the lump in her throat.

"Muy bonito." Senora Mendoza smiled indulgently. "They are here, they are there. Into everything."

"They told me their mother is dead."

"Muy triste. Very sad what happened two years ago." She crossed herself. "It was God's will. Now, come with me. You must eat."

Julia hastily arranged her hair, then followed the older woman along the hallway and through a door into the kitchen where the biggest black woodstove Julia had ever seen dominated the room. Pots, pans, ladles, and a variety of other cooking utensils hung from nails on both sides of the stove. Inviting odors of fresh coffee and cooking meat filled the air.

"May I help, Senora Mendoza?" Julia asked.

"I am Adelina," the Mexican woman said.

"I'm Julia. And I'm really quite handy in the kitchen."

Adelina shook her head. "You are a guest. Senor Wade would not approve." She indicated a bench next to a long plank table. "I have the food ready for you."

Julia sat down on the bench. Through an open window at the rear of the kitchen she saw a buggy leading a tethered horse jounce past the ranch on its way to the trail. A rancher flicked the reins, calling to the palomino drawing the buggy. He smiled at the woman beside him, she leaned to him, and the man put his arm around her shoulders, drawing her close. The last of the guests from the festivities of the night before, Julia supposed, more than ever feeling deserted.

By Wade? A man she now knew better than to trust?

Adelina placed a full tin plate in front of her. Julia stared down at steak and eggs. "Good heavens, I'll never eat this much," she said.

Adelina's only reply was to pour coffee into a mug, then return the coffeepot to the back of the stove. Julia shrugged and started to eat. The eggs were exactly right, the steak was delicious. Before she knew it her plate was clean and she was sipping the last of her coffee. Getting up, she took the pot from the stove and poured herself a second cup.

Adelina, who was washing pots and pans in a sink next to a pump, began to talk to her once she saw Julia was through eating. As far as Julia could make out from the older woman's mixture of Spanish and English, Adelina preferred Nancy, though she praised both girls. Maybe that was why Nancy had spoken to her in Spanish while Susan used English, Julia decided.

"Me, I have a daughter in Austin who is married," Adelina went on. "She is sick and has two *muchachos*. I must go to her soon, she needs me. A mother should be with her children when they need her.''

Julia nodded, thinking of the twins. She ached for the girls, knowing the heartache of losing her own mother when she was young. But not as young as these poor little ones. Nancy and Susan should have a mother of their own and soon. She pictured herself tucking them into bed at night, making dresses for them, teaching them to read and write, to sew and cook and ride. Or maybe their father should teach them to ride. Their father. Wade.

Stop it, Julia ordered herself. You want no part of that devious man. His children are not your responsibility, no matter how sweet they are. Despite herself, she remembered Wade taking her in his arms, remembered the sudden strange excitement she'd felt when he kissed her. She closed her eyes, shaking her head violently. No, she didn't want Wade Howland or his kisses, she didn't want the man who'd lied to her and to Emma. If she had any sense, she'd leave Loveland at once.

Yet how could she leave those motherless little girls? Maybe, she told herself, she might stay on as their caretaker until Wade could make other arrangements. While he searched for another woman to marry? She sighed.

Hearing the steady clip-clop of a horse grow louder, Julia opened her eyes. Wade? She drew in her breath. No, it couldn't be. Seeing no one through the window, she hurried to the open door and looked across the yard where a horseman rode along the corral fence heading toward the barn. When he swung his mount away from the barn and began climbing the hill behind the ranch, she recognized the rider as Jack Crain. A shiver of distaste ran along her spine.

She turned to Adelina. ''I thought Mr. Crain left with Mr. Howland and the Rangers this morning, but he's back.''

''Of a certainty. Senor Jack cannot ride after the *bandidos* while Senor Wade is gone. He is the *jefe*—what you call the foreman—of the rancho so he remains here.''

Wade had left her alone at the W Bar H with Jack Crain! Surely he must know what the man was like. She might not be positive Jack was last night's intruder but she felt in her bones he had been. And now there was no one here to protect her from him.

She'd been swayed by the plight of the motherless twins into contemplating remaining at the ranch, at least until Wade returned so they might discuss the matter. Now, though, there was no question about what she must do. Her mind had been made up for her.

She thanked Adelina for the breakfast and left the kitchen, walking quickly to her room. Since she had little time if she wished to catch the train, she hurriedly changed into her Manila brown riding costume, then packed as much as she could squeeze into her carpetbag, putting the rest into the large leather bag and leaving it beside the door of the bedroom. She couldn't carry it, they'd just have to send the valise to her in Coventry, that's all.

Should she tell Adelina what she intended to do? She'd have to because of the horse she meant to borrow, but she wouldn't say a word until it was too late to try to stop her. Of course, she must let Wade know what she intended to do. Sitting at a small desk, Julia found note paper in its drawer. Dipping the pen into an almost dry ink bottle, she wrote a brief note to him, leaving it on the bed.

Taking the carpetbag, she walked slowly to the front door and looked out. She saw no one. She hesitated, glancing back into the house, then faced the door again. Nothing was going to change her mind. Other considerations aside, she had no intention of remaining on this ranch with Wade gone and Jack Crain here.

Placing the bag on the porch just outside the door, she went down the steps and made her way to the corral. The ranch seemed deserted, the only evidence of the wedding party was a heap of ashes in the barbeque pits behind the kitchen. No doubt all the ranch hands were riding with

Wade. Or maybe some were out on the range—isn't that what they called it?

Julia found an old but usable sidesaddle in the tack room of the barn. Selecting a chestnut mare who appeared to be the best-mannered horse of the five in the corral, she slipped a bridle over the mare's head and led her from the enclosure. After saddling the docile chestnut, she walked the horse to the front of the house and tied the carpetbag to the saddle. As she finished, Adelina Mendoza came onto the porch.

"You are leaving?" the Mexican woman asked in astonishment.

"I must catch the train," Julia told her. "I'm sorry, but—" She broke off. "I'm sure the mare will find her way back safely."

"But, senorita—"

"My mind is made up." Julia stepped to the top of the mounting block and pulled herself up onto the saddle. *"Adios,"* she said. "Thank you for everything."

She rode away from the ranch, vowing she wouldn't look back. When she reached the main trail, though, she turned in the saddle. Adelina still stood on the porch. A flick of movement in one of the front windows caught her eye and, looking more closely, she saw two small faces pressed against the pane. The twins, Susan and Nancy. She felt a pang of regret. Was she doing the right thing by leaving?

Of course, she was. There was nothing for her at the W Bar H, nothing at all. Except the danger Jack Crain represented. But her heart remained heavy.

Tears in her eyes, she raised her hand and waved to the two girls and thought she saw them wave back, but she couldn't be sure. Sighing, Julia turned once more and urged the mare into a lope up the trail leading over the hills. If she remembered correctly, the next train was due at eleven this morning. She ought to just make it nicely. Soon she'd be far away from Texas, and Loveland would be forgotten. All but forgotten, anyway. She'd only been here for a day. The longest, most complicated day of her life.

She would not think of the little girls she'd abandoned. She would not think of Wade's arms around her or the feel of his lips on hers. Not now, not ever again.

When Julia reached the crest of the first hill she looked around her at the puffs of clouds drifting across a magnificent blue sky. Though the sun was hot, a breeze from the north tugged strands of her hair from under her riding hat and kept her comfortably cool. She breathed deeply of the heady tang of the sage. If she hadn't been so despondent she'd almost enjoy the ride. Yet there'd been no other possible decision.

As she followed the trail south over the hills, the ranch lost to sight behind her, she discovered that the mare, seemingly so docile in the corral, was a stubborn animal who insisted on traveling either at a steady lope or a walk. For a time they rode beside the dry creek she'd noticed the day before and then, after leaving the creek, climbed into the low hills.

The route looked very different now that she traveled in the opposite direction and was on her own rather than a passenger in a buggy. Luckily, the trail was clearly marked. She topped a hill, rode across a saddle between two more hills, and suddenly the trail divided. One branch veered to the right and the other slightly left.

Julia reined in the chestnut and studied the two forks of the trail. They seemed very much alike, the rocky ground giving no clue which was the most used. She was certain she'd noticed no such juncture on her way to the ranch so she decided it must have been on Jack's side of the buggy. That would make the left-hand branch the main trail. She urged the chestnut in that direction.

She rode with the sun rising above her. As she crested each new hill she expected to see the railroad tracks ahead of her but instead she saw only another series of hills. The trail twisted snakelike to the south and, as the sun climbed higher, the morning became hotter. Suddenly the day darkened and, looking up, Julia saw a cloud covering the sun. Behind her more clouds piled like massive mountains above the northern horizon.

The trail came to a dry basin that must, at another time of year, hold water. She rode past the depression only to see the trail peter out in a jumble of rocks and brush. Biting back an exclamation of dismay, she was forced to admit she'd taken the wrong turning and that there was nothing to do except retrace her route and follow the other fork.

She tried to hurry the chestnut, but the mare refused to respond, loping along the trail as shadows alternated with sunlight. Surely it must be almost eleven, Julia thought. At last she reached the fork and turned onto the other branch. This must be the right way, even though the hills around her all seemed the same, one following the other with monotonous regularity.

She crested a rise and heard, far ahead, the wail of a train whistle, a long, shrill scream. Silence followed and then the whistle called again, the sound echoing from hill to hill. Unable to see either track or train, she rode into a valley and up another slope.

There. At last. The train, a mile ahead and below her, was stopped at Loveland Station. Could she reach the coaches before the train pulled out? She had to!

Leaning forward over the mare's mane, she urged the chestnut past a grove of cottonwoods. When she glanced up she saw the train, smoke billowing from its black stack, still sitting at the station. Good. Perhaps they'd seen her and were waiting. For the first time she noticed horsemen raising dust as they rode away from the train toward her. She counted four men, all riding hard.

Wade Howland and the Rangers? Her heart began to beat crazily, then she shook her head. No, it couldn't be, they'd ridden in the opposite direction. Suddenly cautious, she reined in and studied the approaching riders. They wore dark clothing and broad-brimmed hats. Neckerchiefs covered their faces. Masks.

"Dear God," Julia said under her breath as the truth hit her. "They must be the outlaws. They've robbed the train and now they're escaping."

Had they seen her? They must have. There was no way she could ride past them toward the train, but she still had a chance to get away. Julia wheeled the chestnut, looking back apprehensively over her shoulder, Jack's comments about Sam Bass liking his women feisty drumming in her ears. Kicking her heels into the mare's flanks, she called to the horse and, as though sensing danger, the mare responded and broke into a gallop, heading back along the trail.

Looking over her shoulder she saw to her dismay that the bandits were pounding after her. Why, oh why, had she chosen this particular day to try to catch the train? Alone, at that. At the moment, even Jack Crain's company would be welcome.

"They won't catch me," she muttered. "Never!" But she had trouble believing her own words, since it was clear that two of the men, riding ahead of the rest, were gaining on her.

Fear crawled along her spine. What would happen if she fell into the hands of Sam Bass? Nothing good, she was certain.

Chapter 4

As Julia pounded ahead of her pursuers, the chestnut mare decided she was tired of maintaining such a fast pace and, no matter how furiously Julia urged her on, stubbornly slowed to a walk. In a matter of minutes, the two masked bandits leading the pack caught up, one riding to either side of Julia.

The bandit to her left pulled down his dirty red bandana revealing a bewhiskered face. "Well, well, little lady," he drawled, "seems you got a hankering to meet up with us."

"My horse may have, but I certainly do not," Julia snapped, keeping her voice from quivering by pure will. She was scared to death. Was this Sam Bass?

The man to her right chuckled and cut his horse ahead of her mare. The chestnut stopped obediently.

"Sir, you are keeping me from my destination," she said, hearing the tremor in her tone with dismay.

The man who'd stopped her pulled down his kerchief and grinned at her. He sported a ragged-looking red mustache. "Who do I have the pleasure of addressing?" he asked with exaggerated courtesy, which was, she knew, as worthless as a Confederate dollar.

Certain her plight would worsen if she openly showed her fear, she said as crisply as she could, "My name is Miss Sommers and I am headed back to the ranch, if you will be so kind as to let me pass."

"Can't rightly do that, miss," he said. "Not when we got our necks to consider."

By that time the other two riders had caught up. She was surrounded by bandits!

"This here's Miss Sommers, Sam," the bewhiskered man said, addressing the only clean-shaven man in the group. "Les done asked her ever so polite, but she don't seem to want to come along with us."

The dark-haired, dark-eyed man addressed as Sam— no doubt the infamous Mr. Bass, himself—said, "What a shame. I can't think why she wouldn't want to join us— can you, Seeb?"

Seeb, the fourth man of the group, bore a neatly trimmed dark mustache along his upper lip. Evidently a man of few words, he merely grunted.

In the next jocular exchange among the men involving what was to be done with her, she learned the bewhiskered man was Frank.

"So it seems," Sam Bass said to her, "you'll be riding with us, after all, Miss Sommers. We trust you'll enjoy our company as much as we will yours."

A captive of bandits, of the notorious Sam Bass—this was where her impulsive behavior had landed her. She'd leaped out of the frying pan into the fire for sure! Stiffening her spine against her impulse to give way to gibbering terror, she said, stretching the truth, "I must protest, sir. I'm needed at home."

Sam shook his head. "Our need comes first. You're our ticket to safety in case of pursuit, plus giving us the pleasure of your company in the meantime." He turned his attention to the man with the red mustache. "Les, you escort her. Let's git!"

Grinning, his teeth under his mustache crooked and yellow, Les reached over and grasped the chestnut's reins from her nerveless hands, pulling her horse along with him as he kicked his mount into a trot. Willing or not, she was riding with Sam Bass and Company, as Jack Crain had labeled the bandits.

At first her mind darted in all directions, concocting futile plans for escape but, gradually, as one hill gave way to another, her thoughts became concentrated on her immediate discomfort. She hadn't thought it possible to be hotter than she'd been yesterday but she rapidly discovered she was wrong. Furthermore, she wasn't accustomed to riding long distances. Where was she headed? Would they never stop to rest?

"Dust," Seeb announced, pointing behind them.

Julia didn't take in his meaning immediately. Of course there was dust, she thought crossly. Texas was full of dust. Not until Sam Bass spoke did she understand.

"Think they got us spotted?"

"Can't tell," Seeb said.

"We heard the Rangers was hunting us," Les put in. "Could be they got flagged down by the train crew so they know we're around here somewhere."

Julia's heart lifted. Wade! Surely he'd rescue her.

"Calls for a switch in plans," Sam said. "They never did locate Hank's place. Too hard to find. We'll head there and hole up for the night."

They changed direction and rode on. Julia watched and waited in vain for any sign of pursuing Texas Rangers. Eventually she gave up. By the time they came to what looked to be no more than a narrow gully, her nether regions had grown quite numb.

To her surprise, Sam led his crew into the gully, through which a mere trickle of a stream ran. At last they emerged into a tiny valley thick with cottonwoods. A rough cabin huddled under the trees. A scruffy brown dog ran toward them, barking.

"Suppose old Hank's still hanging on?" Frank asked no one in particular.

"Me, I'd never get well if I had a good-looking nurse like he got," Les said. "Just lay there and have me a good time, that's what I'd do.

"Silver Wing's his daughter." Sam's voice held a warning note. "Hank's fixed more than one man for looking sideways at her."

Seeb spoke for the first time since Julia had been captured. "Old Hank kin be deader'n a calf in a sink-hole, Les, but that don't mean nothing far as she's concerned. Don't be in no dang rush to climb onto her blanket—she got Apache kin. Bad medicine, them Apache."

Tired and sore as she was, Julia couldn't help wondering if the long, disfiguring scar along Seeb's left cheek had anything to due with the Apache. She gathered there was a sick man and his daughter inside the hut, and she was Indian but her father wasn't.

Les dismounted and slung a rock at the barking dog, sending it slinking away growling before he helped Julia off the mare. She bit back a cry of pain when her feet touched the ground. From her waist down, every part of her body ached. Since she'd rather die than show any weakness in front of her captors, she forced herself to walk normally instead of hobbling along the way her legs wanted to do.

The hut was dark inside, the one window covered over with a newspaper rather than glass. Though stuffy, the shade from the trees made the interior cooler than outdoors. When her vision adjusted, Julia saw a white-haired man lying on a mat in one corner of the room. Standing beside him was a young woman—a girl, really—dressed in a long cotton skirt and what appeared to be a buckskin tunic.

"Who she be?" the old man named Hank asked

hoarsely, his rheumy gaze on Julia. The effort caused him a coughing spasm that continued on and on. It hurt Julia to watch the way his thin frame convulsed with each and every cough.

"Whiskey and honey," she said without thinking, Great-aunt Polly's renowned cough remedy. As a child she'd suffered through enough nasty-tasting doses to know it really did help.

"You think so?" Sam asked. "Got a bottle of rotgut with me. No honey, though."

"I have honey." Silver Wing's voice was so soft Julia strained to hear her.

Hank continued coughing while the whiskey and honey was fetched, on through Julia's combining the two ingredients in a large spoon carved from an animal horn. "I hope you don't mind me using my finger to mix it," she said to Silver Wing. "I didn't know what else to do."

The Indian girl shook her head, accepted the spoon and, lifting her father's head, held it to his lips. Between spasms he managed to swallow it all, licking his lips afterward.

Julia worried that the dose would be too much for him—the spoon Great-aunt Polly used was a lot smaller. But at least the remedy seemed to be working, for his coughing lessened and then stopped entirely. He closed his eyes. He was, Julia realized, a very ill man. Could he be one of Sam Bass's gang?

It was clear they all knew him—and Silver Wing as well. Recollecting her own plight, Julia turned to look at the Indian girl, thankful she understood and spoke English. "Is there water for me to wash in?" she asked.

Silver Wing took her behind a curtain hung across another corner of the cabin—obviously where the girl slept. "Wait, I bring water from creek," she said.

When she emerged from behind the curtain, having washed her face and hands, removed her riding hat and tidied her hair as best she could, Julia felt more like herself, though she still ached from the long ride. Nothing had changed, her danger was no less, but her mind had begun to work again.

So far no one had offered her actual harm, despite Jack Crain's snide remarks about Sam Bass's preference in women. How long she'd be safe was the question. She must find a way to escape before things changed, though she cringed at the idea of mounting a horse again. She couldn't count on Wade and the Rangers locating this well-hidden cabin, so she had to depend on herself. Was Silver Wing a possible ally?

At the moment, the girl was nowhere in sight. Her father lay quietly on his mat, apparently sleeping. The four bandits were huddled around a table, arguing about what Julia finally figured out was the distribution of their loot from the train robbery.

"Look at old Hank," Les complained. "He ain't gonna last long enough to spend a cent of his share. 'Sides, he didn't take the risk we did. Once he's gone, that Injun gal of his'll likely go back to her ma's folks—them Apaches sure as hell don't deserve his share."

This sentiment brought an affirmative grunt from Seeb.

"What do you think, Frank?" Sam Bass asked.

"Hank rode with us when he could," Frank reminded them. "If he don't deserve a full share, we oughta kick in a little for the poor old bastard."

"That gets my vote," Sam said.

Grumbling, the other two finally agreed.

Though they paid her little heed, one or the other of them glanced her way often enough so Julia realized they knew where she was. She had no chance to slip past them and try to escape. Even if she did manage to get away, she couldn't trust the chestnut mare to outrun any pursuer. And she had no idea in what direction to go in the first place.

The brown dog stuck his head in the open door but

retreated when Les yelled at him. Julia heard Silver Wing calling to the dog from somewhere outside.

"Did you tell that gal no fire?" Sam asked.

Les nodded. "Yeah. She's pretty savvy about not calling attention to the cabin. I said she had to keep the dog quiet and she swore he never barks except when strangers ride up the draw. Makes the mutt useful to us. Might even be able to catch some sleep tonight."

"Gotta draw for sentry duty just the same," Sam said. He glanced at Julia. "Go help the gal fix us some grub," he ordered.

She stared at him. Was he actually going to let her leave the cabin by herself?

Sam smiled. "Les hid your saddle. You wouldn't get far anyway. That mare of yours ain't built for speed. Not like my Denton mare. Won every race I ever entered. I miss that horse."

Julia hurried from the cabin and glanced around to locate Silver Wing, who was crouched by the nearly dry stream bed digging in the dirt with a pointed stick. She walked over to the girl, saying, "I came to help. What's that you're doing?"

"I dig up what my father calls Indian turnips to roast in fire pit with three rabbits I catch in my nets."

"I thought you weren't supposed to build a fire."

Silver Wing shrugged. "Fire burns slow and small in hole in ground. No smoke. Turnips and rabbits go in, I cover pit and fire goes out, coals stay hot, food roasts."

"Like an oven," Julia said. "I'll help, if you tell me what to do."

Silver Wing smiled at her. "You help my father, no more needed. You walk like you hurt, you rest."

"Too much riding," Julia admitted. She hesitated, then decided to go on. Silver Wing might be the daughter of a bandit, but she was also a woman. "Sam Bass took me captive because I saw them rob the train. He plans to use me as a hostage if the Rangers track them down. I don't know what else . . ." She faltered and didn't go on, unable to put in words her fear of what might happen to her.

"You sleep with me tonight," the girl said. But she sounded uncertain, as though she knew, as Julia did, that she couldn't really protect Julia from the men.

Julia eased down near her, bracing her back against the trunk of a cottonwood. "Your father is very ill," she said.

"His time to die." Silver Wing spoke calmly. "When time to die come, my mother's people know to offer their spirit to Great One and they die. My father don't know to do this. He suffer."

Julia considered her words and decided the Apache way might save a lot of pain and suffering.

"I can't help you escape," Silver Wing told her.

Julia sighed. "I know."

"I see, I don't tell," the girl added. "Brownie won't bark, not at you leaving. Only at stranger coming."

Julia smiled her thanks, happy to have an ally, even if Silver Wing couldn't see any way to actively help her. "You speak very good English," she said.

"My father teach me when he take me with him after my mother die." She fingered her buckskin tunic. "He wish me to dress like his people. I try. Not easy for me."

"How old are you?" Julia asked.

"Sixteen winters."

Les had called Silver Wing good-looking and she was a pretty girl in her own fashion. Slim and lithe, she moved with grace. Her dark hair hung in two braids, Indian fashion, but strands curled around her face, curls that must be inherited from her father. Her skin was no darker than Wade's suntan and her eyes eyes were a soft, appealing brown.

Sixteen was young. What would happen to her after her father died? Impulsively, Julia said, "If you ever need help, go to the W Bar H ranch. If I ever get out of this mess, I'll be there for a while at least."

"I hear what you say." Silver Wing gathered her tubers into her skirt and rose from her knees.

Julia watched her carry them to what must be the fire pit. She saw no rabbits, perhaps they were already cooking. Without her willing it, her eyelids drooped and she fell into a doze.

She woke abruptly from a dream of rescue by Wade, to find Brownie gazing into her face, his presence reminding her Wade was not here and she remained unrescued. Despite this, and though he had to be the mangiest mutt she'd ever seen, and smelled bad besides, Julia liked dogs and held her hand toward him. He sniffed her fingers warily but came no closer.

Silver Wing was standing in the creek, painstakingly filling a gourd with water. Julia had no idea of how much time had passed. Had she slept for ten minutes or an hour? In any case, it was time for her to get up and make herself as useful as she could to Silver Wing.

Rising to her feet proved to be a painful maneuver. How could she manage to sit a horse even if the Rangers arrived in force to free her? Which wasn't likely to happen. Other than the dust Seeb had seen, there'd been no indication Sam Bass and Company were being pursued by anyone.

The evening meal was welcomed by all. Besides the roasted tubers and rabbits, Silver Wing had soaked dried berries in water and mixed them with honey until they made a delicious sauce. Even Hank managed a few mouthfuls. Julia ate more than she'd intended to.

When night overtook evening, Silver Wing lit a candle, apparently the only source of illumination. Frank pulled a deck of cards from his pack and the men gathered around the table. After giving her father another dose of whiskey and honey, Silver Wing took Julia's hand and led her to the curtained off sleeping area they'd be sharing. At any moment, Julia expected to be ordered to stop, but the command didn't come. Minutes later, fully clothed except for her riding boots, she stretched out beside the girl on what seemed to be a reed mat and tentatively closed her eyes.

But she couldn't relax, fearful of what might await her in the depths of the night. Somehow, to be surprised from sleep by unwelcome advances was far more terrifying to contemplate than being awake when approached. This would be nothing like being able to rout Jack Crain with a pitcher of water while she screamed for help. There was no help for her here, and she was far weaker than any of the bandits.

At last, though, exhaustion overcome her anxiety and sleep claimed her. She was working her way through a confused and jumbled dream when something touched her arm, rousing her. She started, her heart pounding in fright.

"Ssh," a man's voice whispered. "Don't yell."

As if screaming would do any good. As she was making up her mind to fight him as long as she could, he whispered, "I'm gonna help you. Meet me outside."

Listening to the soft sounds he made as he eased from behind the curtain, Julia wondered what to do. Which man was it? How could she believe he intended to help her? Yet what did she have to lose by doing as he asked? If it was a trick to get her outside—well, how was that worse than being attacked inside?

Grabbing her boots from the foot of the mat and finding her hat by groping for it, Julia, carrying boots and hat, started to leave. Silver Wing's whisper made her hesitate.

"I ask Great One to aid you."

Warmed by the girl's well-wishes, Julia jammed her hat on her head and tiptoed from the cabin, her progress helped by moonlight slanting in through the partly open door. She slipped through and carefully closed the door behind her.

"Psst." The signal led her to the corral.

A dark shape crossed in front of her, scaring her until she realized it was Brownie. "Your mare's ready," a man said in a low tone. Brownie growled, apparently at the man, whose voice she recognized as Les's. "Got a man's saddle on her."

Maybe the dog, still growling, remembered the rock Les had slung at him. She put that thought aside as trivial and concentrated on what Les had said about the saddle.

Since her riding skirt was divided, she shouldn't have a problem. When she was younger, she'd ridden astride several times, upsetting Great-aunt Polly and shocking the neighbors. It might even prove to be be a boon as far as her sore muscles were concerned, she told herself as she struggled into her riding boots.

The mare loomed before her, Les hoisted her into the saddle and, after a few minor adjustments, she settled herself as comfortably as possible. He swung onto his own mount and told her to follow him. As if she had any choice. How would she know which way to go?

He had, she found, retrieved her carpet bag and attached it to this saddle. The waning moon was low in the sky, near setting. Already the sky had lightened in the east.

"Ain't never fooled around with them sidesaddles," he said after they'd maneuvered through the draw. True to Silver Wing's prediction, there hadn't been a sound from Brownie.

"I'm perfectly all right this way," she assured him. "Why did you come to my rescue?"

"Didn't think a pretty young filly like you oughta be mauled by them bastards back there."

A chivalrous bandit? Les hadn't struck her like that in the least. "I thought they were your friends," she said.

"Yeah. But you deserve better'n them."

Something in his tone unnerved her, but she ignored it for the moment. "I'm afraid I can't direct you to the W Bar H ranch," she said. "I don't know where it is from here. "If you can take me to the Loveland Station, though, I think I can find the way from there."

"Honey," he said, "that ain't where we're headed."

She should have suspected there'd be a catch in it. Putting her fear firmly aside, she demanded, "Where *are* we going, then?"

"I recollect a little hotel in Austin where no questions are asked. I reckon you and me can have ourselves a good time there. The way I figure it, one man like me's worth the three we left behind."

"You and Jack Crain," she muttered, anger mixing with her fear. She couldn't decide which of the two was the more despicable. What she did know was that she'd rather die than continue on with Les to Austin.

Dawn wasn't far off. Before the sun rose, she had to make a break for it, to escape him while she had darkness on her side. Never mind that she hadn't the slightest idea which way to ride—away from Les was good enough for now.

"Jack Crain?" he said. "Who's he? What's he got to do with it? My name's Slocum, not Crain. Me and my two brothers, we're proud to be Slocums."

She didn't bother to answer, busy calculating which direction to choose. By cudgeling her brain for clues, she recalled where the sun was yesterday after the bandits captured her. If she remembered right, they'd ridden to the southwest, more south then west. She could figure the directions now by where the sky was lightening. If that was east, as it must be, they were still heading south. That meant she should go north and east.

The moon had set, night was losing its grip—she could see hills outlined against the sky. Judging by yesterday, she couldn't trust the chestnut to break into a gallop just because she dug in her heels, so she surreptitiously removed the hatpin that held her riding hat firmly in place.

Jerking the chestnut's head abruptly to the left, she used her other hand to jab the pin into the mare's rump. With a snort of surprise, the mare took off to the left, running flat out. Julia hung on as best she could, glad she was astride so she could grip with her knees.

Leaning forward she murmured, "Go, girl, go," to the chestnut. Elated because she'd gotten away, temporarily at least, it took her a few minutes before she realized that, despite her careful planning, she'd turned the mare's head the wrong way. They were headed west instead of east and, at the speed they were traveling, she didn't dare try to alter course.

She tried to glance behind her to see if Les was pounding after them but was afraid to turn around far enough to see, lest she lose her seat. A stray thought flickered across her mind as the chestnut, without any more encouragement from her, galloped on and on. Sam Bass had mentioned his racer, the Denton mare. Perhaps this mare was related to that one after all.

Moment by moment, the sky brightened. When she finally risked a look to the rear, she drew in her breath. Not only was Les pursuing, but he was far closer than she liked to see. She'd failed.

Wade Howland, riding in scout position, ahead of the Rangers, glanced up at the reddening sky. He'd hoped to be able to lead the company into that draw before dawn but they weren't close enough yet. It'd be fully light by the time they reached the hidden cabin he'd spotted last year while trying to reach a calf caught in a mud hole. He hadn't gone near the place at the time, intent on rescuing the calf.

When the T&C train men had flagged down the Rangers yesterday, and he'd heard about the robbery, that cabin flashed into his mind as a perfect hideout for Sam Bass and Company. The major leading the group had agreed. They'd had to camp for the night, and now his theory was about to be tested.

His gray snorted, throwing up his head, ears perked, as though aware of something beyond Wade's ken. Alerted—he was alive because he'd paid attention to this horse in the past—he scanned ahead and to to both sides.

"What do you see, Thor?" he whispered.

Thor's ears stayed forward. Ahead, then. Wade had been about to give a signal to turn to the south, instead, he halted. When the major rode up to him, Wade said, "Go due south here about a mile and watch for that draw I told you about—it's narrow and hard to spot. Probably not much water left in it this time of year."

"What about you?"

"Thor thinks there's something straight ahead. I want to take a look."

Luckily the major had been part of the posse when Thor's keen hearing had saved all their necks. "Go reconnoiter," he said. "We'll find the draw."

Wade urged Thor into a lope west, while the rest of the Rangers turned south. He saw nothing remarkable until he crested the next hill. Below him, two horses galloped, the second rider seeming to be in pursuit of the first. It wasn't yet light enough to make out details so he paused, watching, trying to decide if either man or both could be the bandits.

The sun edged up behind him flooding the earth with light, giving him a clearer view of the riders below. He frowned. Something about the first rider wasn't right. As the second rider was overtaking the first, a hat blew off, tumbling behind the horses. Long blond hair streamed in the wind. A woman!

She swerved this way and that, obviously attempting to avoid her pursuer. Time to intervene. Wade urged Thor down the rise toward the pair. He was reluctant to shoot at the man in case there was some legitimate reason for his pursuit of the woman, but as he came closer, he spied the man's bushy red mustache. Had to be Les Slocum, one of Sam Bass's men. But who was the woman?

It didn't matter. Slocum was one of the bandits the
Rangers were out to capture if possible, kill if necessary.
Rescuing the woman was secondary—for all he knew she
might be one of the Bass gang followers. He pounded
after the pair, Thor's powerful stride closing the distance
between them.

The woman was the first to see him. Changing direction,
she galloped toward him. Slocum turned to follow, saw
him, and reined in his horse so abruptly it stood on its
hind legs. Wade's Colt was already in his hand and he fired
when he saw Slocum reach for his. Then the woman rode
between them and he didn't dare snap off another shot.
Wade cursed. The little fool! A good way to get herself
killed.

Wade swerved Thor to avoid her. As he passed her, intent
on reaching Slocum, she called to him. "Wade! Wade!"
He recognized that voice.

Slocum, slumped to one side of his mount, rode steadily
away from him. Wounded? Wade thought so, but instead
of pursuing him, he turned back to the blond woman,
who'd halted her horse. Scowling, he reined in beside her.

"What in the devil are you doing here, Julia Sommers?"
he demanded.

Chapter 5

Julia stared at Wade, her gratitude fading in the face of his obvious angry disapproval. A moment ago, in her intense relief at his timely rescue, she'd been ready to fling herself into his arms. Even if she still felt that way, and she decidedly did not, he'd made it impossible by remaining on his horse and not offering to help her off hers.

Les Slocum had disappeared over a rise and she fervently hoped she'd never set eyes on him again. As for Wade, she still owed him her thanks. "Uh—I'm grateful to you," she began, only to have him cut her off.

"Thanks to you, I've lost the chance to capture Slocum," he snapped. "Winged the bas—him, but he got away. If you hadn't stopped me I'd have nailed him."

"I didn't stop you!" she cried.

"You called my name. Until then, I had no idea the woman I saw him chasing was you. The last I knew, you were safe and sound at my ranch. Sam Bass wasn't anywhere near the W Bar H, not if he was robbing the T&P, which he was. Means you rode away from the ranch. Whatever got into you?"

"You left me with Jack Crain," she said crossly. "I don't trust him, not at all. How could you leave me alone there with such an obnoxious man? Naturally, I left."

"To take up with Sam Bass and Company?"

"They robbed the train I was trying to catch." She blinked back angry tears. "You don't care one whit what happened to me or what I've been through, all you care about is capturing Sam Bass."

Wade blinked. His expression changed from furious to stricken. "Are you all right? I mean, they didn't . . . ?" His words trailed off in obvious embarrassment.

Julia raised her chin. "I have not been violated, if that's what you mean. Although Les Slocum did inform me he had that very thing in mind. I never would have ridden off from the cabin with him if I'd known what he intended. I thought he meant to—to rescue me." Her voice broke and, despite her effort not to dissolve in tears, she did.

Wade slid from his horse, pulled her down from the mare, and wrapped his arms around her, patting her back awkwardly while she sobbed into his chest. For the first time in God only knew how many hours she felt safe.

"I couldn't even pray," she confided through her tears. "All I could remember was Great-aunt Polly telling my sister and me that God helped those who helped themselves and so I tried to help myself. I really did."

"There, there," he murmured. "It's all over. You don't have to worry about the bandits any longer, you'll soon be back at the ranch and—"

She pulled free of him. "The ranch!" she cried, remembering what was there besides Jack Crain. She searched frantically for her handkerchief until he produced a clean bandana from a pocket. Taking it reluctantly, she dried her wet face and then glared at him.

"The twins," she said accusingly. "You kept them a secret from Emma. You didn't ask my sister if she wanted to become an instant mother as well as a wife. How deceitful."

He spread his hands. "I didn't think of it that way. All

that came to me was how badly I needed a wife to take care of my brother's orphaned little girls. You're right, though. Next time I look for a woman to marry I'll say so right out.''

"You needn't think I intend to take my sister's place," she snapped.

"I didn't plan on asking you to." His tone was cool. "Now, if you don't mind, I'd like to get on back to the ranch with you so I can rejoin the Rangers."

She wished she could say haughtily that she'd find her own way there, thank you, but she wasn't an idiot. If he left her alone out here in this nothingness, she'd be hopelessly lost, besides risking being recaptured by Sam Bass.

She'd come to the wrong conclusions about the twins— they weren't his, but his dead brother's. Still, that didn't— excuse his omission—he should have told Emma about them. As for him losing Les Slocum, she started to admit she was sorry she'd interfered with his pursuit of the bandits. After all, she was as eager as anyone to see them behind bars. Before she got out the first word, though, a spatter of gunshots sounded—not too far away, from the sound.

"Bass *was* at the cabin," Wade muttered.

"Didn't I say so? If the Rangers were headed there, Brownie would have given the alarm while they were riding up the gully—I mean draw."

He looked confused. "Brownie?"

"Silver Wing's dog."

"Never mind, I'll sort it out later. Best find some cover in case any of the gang gets away. It doesn't pay to be easy pickings."

Like me riding toward the train, she told herself. Real easy pickings. She didn't intend to make a mistake like that again.

Once they'd remounted, he chose a niche part way up a rise to leave the horses. After he warned her not to get out of his sight, the two of them made their way cautiously to the top—crawling the last few feet. On her stomach, Julia peered over the crest of the rise. Two riders pounded across the flat land below, one veering to the right, the other to the left.

"That's him," she hissed in Wade's ear. "Sam Bass. I think the other's Seeb."

Wade cursed, muttering something about leaving his rifle with the horse. A scattering of riders came into sight, following the two outlaws. The Rangers, no doubt.

A single rider way off from any of the others caught her eye and she pointed him out to Wade who swore again. "Splitting up," he said. "Sam's outfit is good at that."

"That must be Frank."

"The train men told us four men. You've accounted for Slocum, Bass, Seabourn, and Frank Parker. Were there any more at the cabin?" he asked.

"A dying old man named Hank and his daughter—she's just a girl. Plus the dog."

"Who evidently barked in time to give Bass and his boys a chance to escape the Rangers."

When the last of the riders was out of sight, Wade said, "Time to git."

"You sound like Sam Bass with your 'git,'" she told him. He wasn't pleased.

When he boosted her onto the mare she couldn't help wincing as she took her seat. Astride was better, but she still ached.

He noticed and started to say something, evidently thinking better of it. *Probably going to tell me I deserve to hurt,* she thought resentfully.

When they were underway, he said, "The sooner I get you back to the ranch the better."

Julia reined in the chestnut. "Wait," she said, remembering the gun shots they'd heard. What if Silver Wing had been wounded? There'd be no one to help her. "We have to go and check the cabin first."

He looked at her as though she was off her head. "What for?"

"I heard that shooting. I'm not going to the ranch until I make certain Silver Wing isn't hurt. Her father is dying, he'd be no help."

Wade rolled his eyes. "She's the daughter of a bandit and, like as not, one of Sam Bass's lady loves."

"She may be the daughter of a bandit, but she's not Sam Bass's anything," Julia said heatedly. "The girl is only sixteen. I insist we go."

She translated Wade's sigh as a masculine protest against the foolish notions of stubborn women, but she didn't care because it meant he'd given in.

The cabin was nearer than she realized. As they entered the draw, she heard Brownie start barking. When they came in sight of the cabin, he stood at the bank, carrying on something fierce. "Shush, Brownie," she said. "You know me."

Somewhat to her surprise, he stopped. When Wade helped her from the mare, the dog's stump of a tail began to wag. "He remembers me," she told Wade.

Wade's glance at the dog showed he had the same first opinion of the mutt that she'd had. True, Brownie was no beauty. Wade, she noticed, kept one hand on the butt of his holstered Colt.

"Silver Wing," she called. "Are you all right?"

The girl appeared in the open door. "Julia? You come back?" Her gaze took in Wade.

"He's a friend," Julia assured her. "We wanted to be sure you hadn't been hurt."

"My father is dead."

Julia hurried toward her, jerking away from Wade's attempt to hold her back. He couldn't help being suspicious, she supposed.

Entering the cabin, with Wade at her heels, Julia saw that Silver Wing had started to wrap her father in a blanket.

Wade stepped closer and stared at the dead man. "Hank

MacDonald,'' he said. ''Thought it might be him. Rode with Sam a couple years ago, then faded out of sight.''

Silver Wing nodded as she pulled the blanket over the old man's face. ''You say his name. He want to be buried.''

Wade looked from her to the blanket-shrouded man and back at her again. ''Got a spade handy?'' he asked resignedly.

Hank was interred in back of the cabin in as deep a grave as Wade was able to dig. Once the hole had been filled in and covered with rocks and fallen cottonwood branches, they stood beside the grave with bowed heads, Wade holding his hat over his heart.

''Rest with God, beyond pain and suffering,'' Julia murmured.

''May the Lord keep your soul, Hank MacDonald,'' Wade said, surprising Julia, who hadn't expected him to participate.

''My father, you are one with wind and rain,'' Silver Wing chanted. ''Great One welcomes you to his sky lodge.'' She switched to another language, one Julia knew must be Apache, and continued intoning the unfamiliar words.

When she finished, Brownie, who'd approached unseen, threw back his head and howled, the eerie sound raising the hair on Julia's nape.

Wade glanced at the sun, past the zenith, and frowned. ''Can't make it to the ranch before dark. We may as well spend the night here, where there's water and shelter. With the Rangers after them, odds are none of the Bass gang will show up again. They have no way of knowing a man or two wasn't left to give them a warmer welcome than they want.''

''Cabin must burn,'' Silver Wing announced. ''If not, my father's ghost can't leave.''

''I'll take my chances with his ghost tonight,'' Wade said. ''We'll burn it in the morning, if you insist. But then where will you go?''

''She's coming to the ranch with us, of course,'' Julia

said before Silver Wing could open her mouth. "She and Brownie both."

"I could go back to my mother's people." Silver Wing sounded so uncertain that Julia understood she wasn't happy about doing that.

"You're no longer accustomed to Apache ways," Julia insisted. "Please come with us."

"Apache," Wade repeated. "That what you are?"

"My mother was Apache. She no longer lives."

"And neither does your father, who was white." Wade ran a hand through his dark hair. "You'd best come with us for now." He glanced at the dog. "I guess we can't leave Brownie here to fend for himself."

Silver Wing cooked fry bread for their meal and Wade shared his rations with them. Afterward, he roamed the small property while Julia helped Silver Wing pack her few belongings, which the girl promptly removed from the cabin, along with her sleeping mat and blanket.

"I sleep under the trees," she announced. "Alive, my father was good man. Dead, he is ghost. All ghosts bad. Ghost will stay till we burn cabin. Don't sleep in cabin tonight."

Julia had never thought she believed in ghosts, but as long shadows came creeping with evening, she eyed the dark maw of the open cabin door and admitted she didn't want to go inside.

"What do you mean you don't want to sleep in the cabin?" Wade said when she told him. "You can't be afraid of the girl's story about a ghost—she's just repeating some Apache superstition."

"I don't have good memories of the cabin," Julia countered. "Prisoners aren't fond of their jails."

"You'd feel differently if it was raining."

"But it's not. I have difficulty believing it ever rains in Texas."

"Floods the draws when it does," Wade said. "A sight to see."

A sight she wasn't going to stay in Texas long enough
to see. If she could train Silver Wing to be a nursemaid
for the twins, there'd be nothing to keep her at the ranch.
Certainly not Wade. Why, he hadn't been intending to
rescue her at all, his purpose had been to capture Les
Slocum. If she hadn't called his name, he might have
ridden right past her.

Grumbling, Wade retrieved his gear from his saddlebags.
Another night in the open didn't bother him, it was more
Julia's wrong-headed stubbornness. Ghosts. Jails. The half-
breed gal couldn't help her Indian beliefs, but Julia should
know better. He felt it his duty to stay outside the cabin
to protect them from any danger—and he didn't mean
ghosts.

He'd agreed to bring Silver Wing back with them
because he figured she'd never get through to her mother's people. Too many Comanche villages lay between this
place and Apache country, and they'd either kill a young
girl traveling alone or make her a slave. He'd try to find
a way later on to get her safely back to her people.

Not that he had bad feelings about half-breeds, on the
contrary, Jamie, his best hand, had Mexican Indian blood.
But a girl was different. He knew she wouldn't fit in at the
ranch, especially since she was a pretty little thing. Not all
the men in these parts felt the way he did about breeds,
and they'd consider her fair game. She'd be better off with
her blood relatives. With the Apaches.

Come to think of it, she could claim whites as blood
relatives, too, on account of old Hank MacDonald. He
hadn't happened to think of it that way before and he
didn't figure many people did. At least none he knew.
Julia might, though. She had strange ways of looking at
things.

As he spread his sleeping blankets under a cottonwood,
he wondered how he would have liked Emma, if she'd
come as she was supposed to and he'd married her. The
minister back East had called her a "biddable girl." That

term didn't apply in any way, shape, or form to her sister Julia.

Imagine her haring off to the train all alone when she knew Sam Bass and Company might be in the vicinity. Talk about reckless behavior. He shook his head. God preserve him from unbiddable females.

He saw that Julia was laying a sleeping mat near where Silver Wing was already stretched out, the dog at her side. Of all the ugly mutts he'd ever seen, Brownie took the prize. "Good night," he called.

Silver Wing didn't stir but Julia's soft "good night," settled over him like a blessing. He had to admit she was as attractive a gal as he'd ever seen. Even beat Monette down in Austin for looks, and Monette was the prettiest gal in that town. He wished he could think of Monette's red hair and seductive brown eyes now instead of Julia's silken blond tresses and her wide, innocent blue eyes.

Back there at the ranch, touching her lips with his, brief as it had been, stirred him in a way Monette never had, for all her expertise. If he faced the truth, he'd have to admit he wanted Julia. But she was the last woman in the world he'd ever marry. Any man who got tied up with her was asking for trouble for the rest of his natural life.

Being an honorable man, he shouldn't take advantage of her innocence, either. Wade turned over in his makeshift bed and smiled wryly. Not that she was likely to let him. She'd made it clear she wanted no part of him.

He fell asleep quickly.

Wade watched in disbelief as a misty white shape, as insubstantial as cottonwood down, drifted among the trees, moaning—or was it howling? The hair raised on his neck as the shape drifted ever closer, yet he couldn't move so much as a finger. Soon it hovered above him, eerie and frightening. What did it want?

"Wade," it whispered between moans, "Wade . . ."

He woke abruptly. Something white *was* hovering over him, and he sat up, his heart thudding in his chest, staring in the slant of moonlight coming through the branches at—Julia.

"What's that awful howling?" she whispered. "Is it wolves?"

Calming himself, he listened to the not-so-distant wail of coyotes and told her what they were. "Harmless," he added.

"They're making Brownie restless," she said. "And besides—he stinks. I had to move."

He noticed she was carrying her mat and a blanket. Gesturing to the space to either side of him he said, "Be my guest. You're right, Brownie's not the best-smelling dog in the world."

"He needs a bath." She plopped the mat down near his right side but not too close.

"Granted. I also have no intention of bathing any dog in the middle of the night."

"It's not that I'm scared," she said. "I've slept outside before, back in Coventry, with my sister. It's just that this country is so open, so lonesome. And I wasn't sure if whatever howled was dangerous."

He smiled to himself and lay back down. "You figured I'd be more help than Silver Wing and the dog if danger threatened, is that it?"

"Something like that, yes," she admitted. "Besides, you don't smell bad."

He chuckled. "Thanks—I guess."

Something rustled in a nearby tree.

"What was that?" she asked. He could hear tenseness in her voice.

"Probably a roosting bird."

"Oh." She was quiet until something dislodged a stone in the draw and it rattled against another stone. "That wasn't a bird!"

"No. Most likely some small night critter foraging for food. Brownie will let us know if any strange men show up."

"I wasn't thinking of humans. Aren't there any danger-ous animals in Texas?"

"Sure, but not around here." He decided not to men-tion rattlesnakes. "Look, would you feel safer if I held your hand?"

"I think so," she admitted in a very small voice. Shifting her mat a little closer, she reached for his hand.

How small and delicate her hand felt in his callused palm. He savored her trust as a precious gift. No matter how unhappy she was with his behavior, she'd come to him to shield her against the terrors of the night, imagined by her, but no less real to her for being nonexistent.

Her hand was soft in his grasp. He imagined the rest of her skin would be even softer, soft and smooth as the finest silk, and immediately tried to banish that thought as it stirred a part of him that was better left quiet.

He hadn't thought beyond returning Julia to the ranch where she'd be safe. He realized now, though, that he'd better do some thinking. Did she mean to stay? He didn't think so. Did he want her to stay? Despite his feeling that the sooner she returned to Coventry the better, the truth was he didn't want her to go. Not right away, at least.

Not just because of the twins, either, though they were a factor. They needed mothering. Adelina did what she could, but she had enough work without being saddled with two lively four-year-olds.

For the twins' sake, yes, he wanted her to stay. But also for himself.

Julia, her hand snug in Wade's safe grasp, began to relax. How comforting the touch of another person could be. Especially when she had to sleep outside in a strange place, in a strange country like Texas. Especially when the person who held her hand was larger, stronger, and a man she knew could and would protect her. Especially if he hap-pened to be Wade Howland.

His touch was not only comforting, she realized as warmth began to seep into her from the handclasp, settling low inside her, making her want to edge closer to him, to actually snuggle up against him.

She wouldn't do such a thing. Never. Why she felt that way was a total mystery to her. Perhaps it had something to do with feeling she needed his protection. Just because the sensation reminded her of when he'd brushed his lips across hers had nothing to do with the present circumstances.

If she had the courage of her convictions, she'd pull her hand from his, turn her back to him and go to sleep. Yet she didn't want to give up his touch. All right then, she'd stay as she was, except she'd stop thinking about him and all these errant feelings and go to sleep.

A rustle on a branch directly over her head jerked her from a doze. She stared up into the tree where, to her horror, something large and white was rising into the air with a soft swoosh. Biting back a scream, she flung herself at Wade.

"A ghost," she babbled. "In the tree. I saw Hank's ghost."

His arms went around her, holding her close to his body. "You're shivering," he murmured. "Don't be frightened. Whatever you saw wasn't a ghost."

"It was," she whispered, her lips near his ear. "It was on a tree branch when I looked up, big and white and it floated into the air and disappeared."

"Did it make any noise?" She could feel his warm breath against her neck as he spoke, a strange, exciting sensation that cut through her fear.

"A sort of swooshing sound," she said.

"What you saw was an owl, what we call a great white in these parts. They usually go north in the summer but sometimes, if they find a cool spot with water, like in this draw, they stay around." As he spoke, his hand stroked her back, increasing the warmth deep inside her.

"An owl," she repeated, realizing it could have been.

"Julia," he said with a deep, hoarse tone to his voice

that settled like fire into her bones. "Julia, Julia, what am I going to do with you?"

Before she could even begin to ponder his meaning, he kissed her. No mere brush of lips like before, a real kiss, like none she'd ever experienced. A kiss that took away her breath and her mind. All she could think was that she never wanted this kiss to end.

He urged her lips apart and, when she felt his tongue tasting her mouth, everything inside her turned to liquid. She wanted more, needed more, even if she wasn't sure exactly what it was she wanted. Her fingers tangled in the hair that grew long at his nape, urging him closer and closer, even though he already held her tightly against him.

Brownie chose that moment to start barking.

Chapter 6

Wade released Julia and sprang to his feet, grabbed his gunbelt, stashed at the head of his bedding, belted it on, and pulled out his Colt. Silver Wing, he saw, was on her feet, hurrying toward him. Brownie, a dark shape on the bank of the wash, barked up a storm.

"Who is it?" Julia asked from beside him.

"Who knows?" he muttered. "You and Silver Wing hunker down behind the trunks of those big cottonwoods."

The best he could hope for was one of the bandits taking a chance on returning. The worst was a word that struck dread into any Texan. Comanche. Or as bad, Comancheros, desperados as fierce as any Indian.

Because he thought it was unlikely, he hadn't bothered to ask either of the women if they could use a gun. His rifle was with his saddle and old Hank must have had a Colt, at least, if not a rifle, but extra guns weren't of any use without someone who knew what they were doing pulling the trigger.

With the racket the dog was making, he couldn't hear how close the intruders were. The moon had shrunk some from a couple nights ago but still shed enough light so he had a fair view of any rider coming along the draw. He lifted the Colt and waited. One man against—how many?

"Damn it, dog, shut the hell up!" a man's voice ordered.

Wade, his Colt aimed at the rider just now visible, froze in place. There was no mistaking that voice. "Major?" he called.

"Howland, that you? Been looking for you."

Wade slid his gun back into the holster. "I'm here. Got two women with me. Just buried the father of one of them—Hank MacDonald."

As the major and two other Rangers rode toward Wade, Silver Wing called to the dog and Brownie left off barking.

"MacDonald," the major repeated, dismounting. "Sounds like one of Sam Bass's boys."

While Wade was telling him the circumstances of old Hank's death, Julia and Silver Wing emerged from the cottonwoods, coming to stand nearby. When he finished, Wade introduced them to the major and the other rangers, adding that he intended to escort them back to his ranch where they'd stay for the time being.

"Miss Sommers had ridden away from the W Bar H," he explained, "and was taken prisoner by Sam Bass and Company. I managed to rescue her."

"I wouldn't want you to get the impression Texas is overrun with desperados, Miss Sommers," the major said. "Just the same, it's best to remember you're not back east."

"I've learned that lesson, sir," Julia replied.

By mutual agreement, Wade and the two women decided to return with the rangers to their night camp, Silver Wing on her Indian pony, leading her father's buckskin gelding. Before they left, Wade fired Hank's cabin for Silver Wing. The brittle, dried wood burned fiercely but, with little wind, didn't catch any of the trees afire. By the time they rode out along the draw, Brownie trotting behind, the flames were dying down.

"Thank you for freeing my father's ghost," Silver Wing told Wade. "You have good heart."

Julia decided Silver Wing was right about Wade's heart. He'd helped the girl and was seeing to her welfare. Besides that, he was raising his brother's orphaned twins. And, of course, he *had* rescued her, backhanded though it had been. Good heart or not, though, it didn't excuse her for allowing him the liberties he'd taken at the cabin. Where had her wits gone? Why, she'd behaved like a loose woman!

He needn't expect her to forget herself again. Probably the strangeness of sleeping outdoors and her own foolish fears had contributed to the wanton way she'd behaved, but that was no excuse. Nor could anything excuse the fact she'd enjoyed every moment of being in his arms. If the major hadn't happened along ... No, she wouldn't dwell on that when she ought to be thanking her lucky stars he did.

"So you wounded Les Slocum," the major said to Wade as they rode alone. "Hope it's fatal. He's got two brothers as mean as he is, better watch out for 'em. Sam and the others got clean away, didn't so much as wing a one. I'm going to disband the outfit temporarily. No use to chase 'em when we ain't got a clue where they're headed."

"You can call on me any time," Wade told him.

I hope he sends Jack Crain the next time, Julia told herself. If he keeps haring off with the Rangers, I certainly don't care to stay on at the ranch.

Not that she meant to, anyway. At least not after she made sure Silver Wing could care for the twins properly. If Adelina left, as she'd hinted she wanted to, then the girl would have to learn to be housekeeper as well. Julia hoped it wouldn't take too long before she'd be able to return to Coventry.

Wade hadn't said one word in private to her since the major's arrival. Had she embarrassed him by her fervent response to his forwardness? Or was he disgusted with her wanton behavior?

Best to turn her mind to other things. "Do you like children?" she asked Silver Wing.

"Yes, little girls most."

"Good. Wade—Mr. Howland—has twin girls who need a nursemaid."

"I am happy to work for him," Silver Wing replied eagerly.

This was almost too easy. She'd be back in Coventry before she knew it, Julia thought. Why did it give her such a pang to realize this? There was no permanent place for her at the W Bar H, none at all. Unless—but, no, she'd already refused to marry him and he'd announced he had no intention of asking her to.

They arrived at the Rangers' night camp with Brownie bringing up the rear, his steps lagging. One of the men tied him to a stake apart from the camp, muttering, "Stinks like rotten fish, he does."

A hastily rigged blanket screened Silver Wing's and Julia's sleeping arrangement from the men's. Exhaustion swamped Julia almost before she got her boots off. She didn't rouse until the sounds of a waking camp woke her at sunrise.

By the time they were ready to ride, Silver Wing had fashioned a crude travois from a few branches tied together, helped by several of the Rangers. The hungry way they looked at the girl bothered Julia. She was reminded of what Great-aunt Polly had once told Widow Hayes about men.

"I decided quite early I was not a tasty morsel to be gobbled up by some voracious male, nor yet a workhorse for a man who expected a wife to cater to him as well as tend to all the chores. I've never regretted not marrying."

Julia had never quite understood what her great-aunt had meant until this moment. The men looked at Silver Wing exactly as though she was a tasty morsel. It made her uncomfortable even though their leers were not directed at her.

Silver Wing tied Brownie onto the travois she'd connected to the Indian pony she rode. "He's too old to keep up with us," she confided to Julia.

"That damn dog's sure riding in style," the man who'd taken over the job of leading old Hank's horse commented as they started off.

Watching how the travois bounced and lurched, Julia thought it might be practical but it looked anything but comfortable, even for a dog.

Some time later, the group split up, Wade and his hands who'd volunteered with him, continuing on with Julia and Silver Wing to the ranch, the others returning to wherever they were from.

They rode into the W Bar H as the sun was sliding down the sky toward evening. Inside the house, she found Adelina preparing food for Wade and the hands, to be eaten at the big kitchen table. Julia decided she and Silver Wing would be better off eating with the twins at the smaller table in a nook off the main room of the house. She was not going to have the girl gawked at by the hands, and the sooner they learned this the better.

Once she was satisfied that Julia had washed and changed clothes and had showed Silver Wing where she was to sleep—in the twin's bedroom where there was an extra cot—Adelina, clucking her tongue at the condition of Brownie, filled a wooden tub half-full of water outside. She handed Silver Wing a bar of brown soap and a brush and insisted the dog must be bathed pronto.

The twins watched Brownie's bath with fascination. Warm as it was, the dog shivered and cringed as he was soaped and rinsed. Once Silver Wing stepped back, he leaped from the tub and shook himself, sending water flying, showering his mistress, the twins, Julia, and Wade, just approaching.

"Damn dog," he muttered.

"Papa Wade said a bad word," Nancy told Julia.

Julia hid a smile as she wiped Nancy off. "Papas sometimes do that," she agreed. "But we don't."

Silver Wing, toweling Susan, apologized to Wade for Brownie's behavior.

"Dogs will be dogs," he said. "At least he'll smell better."

Later, not wishing to make extra work for Adelina, Julia set the table in the alcove and had Silver Wing carry in their food before the men came into the kitchen for the evening meal. The twins, excited to have company at their table, didn't want to settle down to eating.

"Listen to my story." Silver Wing said. "Small girl named Little Flower lived in her grandmother's lodge by stream." She went on to tell about the child, who would rather play than eat. First Crow swooped in and took a bite of food, then Fox crept in for his share, then clever old Coyote sneaked in and ate all the rest. Her grandmother thought the girl had gobbled it all up and refused to give her any more.

"And so Little Flower went to bed hungry," Silver Wing ended. She put her hand behind her ear as though listening. "I think I hear Brother Crow cawing on the roof," she added.

"*I* don't," Nancy said. But, as she watched Susan take a bite of the beef cut up for them, she followed suit.

Silver Wing knows more about nursemaiding than I do, Julia thought ruefully, wondering who would be teaching who.

After the men finished and filed out, Wade came into the main room. "So this is where you've got to," he said.

"I thought the twins needed company," Julia told him. "This way Adelina doesn't have to supervise them and they learn manners from us."

He glanced from her to Silver Wing and back, then nodded. "A good idea."

"Little Flower didn't eat her supper but me'n Susan did," Nancy told him.

"Nothing left for Brother Crow," Susan added.

Wade blinked, but all he said was, "That's good."

"Will you entertain the girls for a few minutes?" Julia asked Silver Wing. She then motioned to Wade to follow her onto the front porch.

"I hope you'll keep the hands away from Silver Wing," she said to him. "Especially Jack Crain."

"You've really got it in for him, haven't you? I wish I could convince you he's not as black as you paint him."

"That's as may be. But about Silver Wing—"

"I'm going to talk to them about her. As long as she lives at my ranch, she's under my protection. Never mind their opinion of breeds, she's out of bounds."

"Breeds?" she asked, frowning.

"What we call half-breeds around here."

"I hope not in their hearing!"

"Take it easy," he advised. "Silver Wing's safe enough here. I appreciate you eating with her apart from the men, though. No use tempting them."

"She does nothing to tempt any man!"

He sighed. "She doesn't have to. That's the way it is. It's different for you—you're a lady, and they know better than to get any ideas."

"But she's an innocent girl."

"Julia, I can't change the way my hands think."

She supposed he couldn't. That didn't make it right, though. "At the Ranger camp they looked at her like she—well, they leered."

He nodded. "That's why, in the long run, I think she'd be better off among her mother's people. As soon as I can, I hope to find a way to get her safely to them."

Julia shook her head. "I don't think she wants to go back there."

"There may be no choice."

Weren't they ever to agree on anything? His gaze caught hers, his gray eyes opaque, concealing his feelings. He held out his hand and she drew in her breath, but he didn't quite touch her. "About last night, there at the cabin—"

"I don't wish to talk about it," she cut in. "Ever. Rest assured it shan't happen again."

"You don't think so?" How soft his voice was . . . how warm.

She meant to tell him she was positive, but the words stuck in her suddenly dry throat. His eyes, no longer opaque, seemed to glow, holding her trapped within his gaze. Breathing grew difficult, she could feel the pulse in her neck throbbing.

His forefinger came up to stroke along her cheek to her lips, sending a delightful, if dangerous, tingling through her. "Once you start a fire, it sometimes keeps burning for longer than you want and can even burn out of control. Keep that in mind."

He turned on his heel, strode down the steps, and vanished around the side of the house. Julia stood, hand to her lips, his words echoing in her mind. *Out of control.* Was he talking about himself? Didn't he know the difficulty she was having controlling herself?

Walking slowly inside, she told herself she must leave the ranch as soon as possible. It was best for her and for Silver Wing as well. After she was gone, Wade would be forced to keep the girl here as the children's nursemaid—at least until he found a wife who suited him.

That thought wasn't at all soothing. Somehow it hurt to think of him marrying. What kind of woman would he choose? Perhaps Emma, if she hadn't been in love with another man, would have suited him quite well, her sister being of a more retiring nature, not prone to express her opinion unless driven to the wall. Emma would never have ridden off impulsively and been taken captive by Sam Bass. But her sister was married—happily, she hoped—and so was no longer a prospective bride.

Wade would have to look elsewhere.

She found Silver Wing in the kitchen helping Adelina clean up, with the twins underfoot. It occurred to her to wonder where and when Adelina ate and she asked, "Do you sit down at the table with the hands?"

Adelina frowned. "With them? Never. Me, I eat first or last, sometimes one, sometimes the other. By myself, when it is quiet."

"You could take your meals with Silver Wing and me and the twins."

"No, not possible. That is busy time, the men they need this, they need that."

"But, to eat alone . . ."

"I have time to myself then." Adelina's tone was dismissive, she was through discussing mealtimes. "You stay now, maybe?" she asked.

"I must go back to Coventry," Julia said.

Silver Wing stared at her. "You leave ranch?"

Susan, who'd been chasing her sister around the kitchen, stopped and tugged at Julia's hand. "Don't go away," she begged.

Nancy hurried over and grasped Julia's other hand. "Stay here," she said.

Since it was impossible to explain her reason to the twins, Julia crouched down, put an arm around each girl and changed the subject. "Why don't I help you two get ready for bed and then tell you a story?"

Both Susan and Nancy smiled. "We got a book," they confided in unison. "Papa Wade reads our book sometimes. Can you read?"

"Yes. I'll read a story from it this very night, if you like."

The twins jumped up and down, crying, "Now. Read now."

"Once you're ready for bed, I will."

After Julia saw to their washing up and getting into their nightgowns, Susan handed her a Mother Goose book. When Julia sat on Susan's cot, a twin to either side of her and opened the book of nursery rhymes, Silver Wing entered the room that was also to be hers and eased onto the cot, taking Nancy onto her lap.

The twins took turns requesting their favorite rhymes, which Julia read one after the other. Intent on what she was doing, she barely noticed how Silver Wing peered at each page as she chanted the words.

In the midst of *Black sheep, black sheep have you any wool*, Nancy said, "Papa Wade don't like sheep."

"Doesn't like sheep is what you mean," Julia corrected gently.

"Sheep 'n cows don't mix," Susan said. Frowning, she asked, "Doesn't mix?"

"Don't mix is right." Julia had never realized how difficult it might be to teach a child the proper way to speak. She certainly wasn't going to take on don't and doesn't tonight. Nor did she intend to get involved in asking why sheep and cows didn't mix.

In the pause that followed, Silver Wing asked, "What word says sheep?"

Julia pointed.

"I know cat," Susan announced, reaching over and turning pages until she came to the picture of a cat sitting in a cupboard.

Nancy leaned onto Julia's lap, saying, "I know cat, too." Almost simultaneously they stabbed their forefingers toward the page, settling on the word cat.

"Cat," Silver Wing said softly, her gaze intent on the page.

Julia finally realized what hadn't occurred to her before—that the girl didn't know how to read. If she left right away, who'd read to the twins at night? Apparently Wade was the only one who could read and she imagined he was often too busy. Maybe she ought to stay long enough to teach Silver Wing. The girl seemed bright enough and nursery rhymes would be easy to learn.

After she and Silver Wing finally settled the twins in their cots, Silver Wing said, "I go to sleep now."

Julia left her there and went back to the kitchen where she found Adelina setting the table for breakfast. "Silver

Wing, she has *mucho* to learn," Adelina said. "I stay until I teach her about meals. Very hard for her, a young girl alone here." She glanced reproachfully at Julia.

"I've decided I can't leave as soon as I hoped," Julia said. "I'll stay on awhile longer."

"*Bueno*. Good. I have heard from my daughter, she is no better. Pablo, her husband, he comes for me in fourteen days. I go back to Austin with him."

Though she'd known Adelina didn't intend to stay on at the ranch, Julia hadn't expected to be faced with a definite departure date. She chewed her lip. Silver Wing needed time to adjust to her new responsibilities, she couldn't very well be left alone until she'd been taught all she needed to know. Including reading.

"I'll ask Wade—uh, Mr. Howland—to find another woman to help out here," Julia said. "Maybe you know a woman in Austin who would like to work?"

Adelina shrugged. "Me, I ask when I get there. Hard to live on ranch so far away."

Later, as she readied herself for bed, Julia told herself another housekeeper/cook to replace Adelina was the best solution. Once that happened, Wade needn't be in a hurry to find a wife because by that time Silver Wing would be well trained as a nursemaid and would also know how to help the housekeeper if need be.

This meant she must remain at the ranch for a few more weeks. The idea wasn't altogether displeasing to her. Not because of Wade. No, because of the twins and Silver Wing. They needed her here at the moment.

She'd have to get a letter off to Emma, explaining why she was staying on. How far away her sister and Coventry seemed. What with being captured by bandits and all, she hadn't been at the W Bar H more than two days and yet, in some ways, it was almost beginning to feel like home.

How selfish she'd been to go dashing off to the train because she'd been left at the ranch with no man to protect her against Jack Crain. Adelina would certainly have tried to help—an iron frying pan could be a formidable weapon. She didn't have to like the man, but he could have been drunk the night he entered her bedroom. While that was no excuse, the likelihood of him bothering her while sober was probably nil.

He had, after all, been left in charge of the stock and all the ranch work when Wade and the other hands rode off with the Rangers—he would hardly have had time to pay unwelcome attentions to her. As usual, she hadn't thought the matter through and had acted on impulse. She was ashamed of deserting Susan and Nancy so abruptly, though they didn't seem to hold it against her.

Likely enough, she wouldn't see much of Wade during the day and, if she took care not to ever be alone with him, she'd be safe from her own impulsiveness where he was concerned. Julia nodded. Yes, her decision to stay on until Adelina had been replaced and Silver Wing was confident enough to be left alone here was the correct one. She could sleep nights, knowing she'd done the right thing.

In the morning, she caught Wade in the kitchen before he left after breakfast and told him her plans while Adelina was puttering about cleaning up.

"You'll stay on until I find another housekeeper?" he repeated.

"It's the least I can do." Her decision made her feel very noble. The conversation was going well, even though Adelina had somehow slipped away, leaving them alone.

"Yes, I agree it's the least you can do," he said. "After the inconvenience you caused by running off and getting mixed up with Sam Bass and Company, you do owe me a little consideration."

How quickly he could put her back up. "I admit the plan was ill-conceived," she said stiffly, "but I could hardly anticipate the consequences."

"No more could I." His half-smile made her belatedly understand there was more than one way to interpret her words and he'd taken her to mean the night under the cottonwoods by Hank's cabin.

"What I meant was . . ." she began, her cheeks flaming.

"No need to explain. Your staying on will give me a chance to look around without haste. Don't you agree haste is to be avoided?"

That depended on what or who he was looking around for. Or maybe not. Either a housekeeper/cook or a wife should be well chosen, not picked in a hurry. Still, if circumstances had been slightly different, Emma would have been suitable as his wife.

"It's too bad Emma chose someone else," she said without thinking.

"Because she's biddable? Is that what you believe I need in a wife?"

How did these conversations with Wade always get away from her? "Biddable?" she echoed.

"I was informed your sister was just that by the Coventry minister."

"She's certainly even-tempered." Julia shook her head. "Why are we discussing Emma?"

"I doubt the Reverend Miller would have described you in the same terms," Wade went on, ignoring her protest.

Julia sighed. "He doesn't like me. Or at least, he didn't care to have Ezra—that's his son—interested in me."

"Ah, I begin to understand why the Reverend Miller insisted you come in Emma's place. You obviously had no intention of marrying me by default, but apparently he hoped you would."

Julia couldn't even pretend to act shocked since she'd suspected something of the sort. She'd certainly been aware the minister wanted her gone from Coventry.

"Do you pine for Ezra?" Wade asked.

She blinked. "Ezra? Whatever for?"

He chuckled. "Your eagerness to return to Coventry had

me believing you must have someone waiting there. Not Ezra, evidently.''

"Or any man," she said indignantly. "I am quite capable of taking care of myself."

He raised his eyebrows, but didn't comment.

"Great-aunt Polly never married and she has managed quite well, even with the responsibility of raising Emma and me."

"I'm sure she's an estimable woman. Still, most young women tend to fall in love, don't they? Like your sister did."

"My great-aunt claims romantic love is greatly overrated. She may have a point. I love my sister, but I did wonder why she chose Floyd Biddescomb." Julia shook her head.

"I agree with Great-aunt Polly about romantic love. It can ruin lives." The grimness in his tone startled her. "You can be sure I'll never fall victim to such nonsense."

She'd never been romantically involved with any man, but she wouldn't go so far as to condemn it completely. Overrated, maybe, but that didn't mean nonsense. Why was he so against it? His tone had cautioned her not to ask.

In an effort to take control of the conversation once again, she said, "So you'll try your best to find a house-keeper/cook to replace Adelina?"

"Rather than look for a wife, you mean?"

Color rose to her cheeks again. "I really don't care. Either or both, it makes little difference. I shan't keep you from your work any longer."

She started to turn away, but he caught her hand, halting her. "Thank you for helping me when I need it the most," he said.

Disarmed by his evident sincerity and warmed by the touch of his hand, she smiled. "I can't leave those sweet little girls yet. Silver Wing isn't ready to assume all their care, she needs me to stay longer."

"I think we all do." His words seem to surprise him as

much as they did her. He released her hand and left the house hurriedly.

Julia stood where she was, one hand clasping the other, the hand he'd held. Here she was, standing in a daze because of him. And after she'd promised herself nothing of the sort would happen ever again.

Chapter 7

As the days passed, Julia established a routine for the twins, with Silver Wing helping. The girl also assisted Adelina with the kitchen and housekeeping duties, as did Julia.

"Soon I have no work to do," Adelina complained one morning after the first week. "You and Silver Wing do it all. That's what I tell Senor Wade."

"I don't understand how you did all this and looked after the twins, too," Julia said.

"Me, I never sit down before you come here," Adelina admitted. "It's good you teach the little ones to make their letters, that I could not do."

At the same time as she helped the twins to learn the ABCs, Julia was also teaching Silver Wing to read. The girl mastered the words so quickly that Julia believed she'd be through the complete nursery rhyme book soon, probably before it was time to return to Coventry. As far as could be discovered, the only other book in the house seemed to be the Bible. From nursery rhymes to the Bible would be quite a leap for a beginning reader.

Soon the twins would be ready to read. Wade must think

about acquiring appropriate books for them. She'd mention the matter when the chance came.

The twins bounded in the back door, followed by Silver Wing. "Brownie likes me," Susan cried. "He licked my face."

"Mine, too," Nancy put in. "I like him better 'n any dog in Texas. Even better 'n Mr. Tyson's puppies."

Brownie had fit in to ranch life without so much as a whine. Since his odor improved following his bath, the hands didn't mind him around. The twins adored him and insisted on visiting him often. They'd tried to sneak him inside the house once, but Brownie knew what his limits were and refused to cross the threshold, earning Adelina's approval. In her opinion, the house was no place for animals.

"Papa Wade said we could keep Brownie," Nancy said. "He wouldn't let us have one of Mr. Tyson's puppies."

"That's 'cause we're little, like the puppies," Susan added. "Papa Wade said we had to grow up to take care of a puppy."

"Then it's lucky Brownie's already grown up so he can take care of himself," Julia said.

" 'Cept Silver Wing had to give him a bath," Susan pointed out.

" 'N she feeds him," Nancy said.

"But he's old enough and smart enough not to get into trouble like puppies do," Julia said. "No one has to watch a dog like we'd have to do with a puppy."

"Dog begins with a D," Susan said triumphantly.

"I can make a D," Nancy added.

"You come and show me," Silver Wing told them. "I read about Old Mother Hubbard's dog after."

The twins needed no coaxing.

"She is good with them," Adelina said once she and Julia were alone in the kitchen again.

Yes, Julia thought. Soon Silver Wing could be trusted to assume unsupervised care of Susan and Nancy. But could she take care of them properly and do all of Adelina's work, too? Julia shook her head. She couldn't leave until Wade replaced Adelina.

"Silver Wing is good," Adelina repeated. "But those little girls, they need a mother."

Meaning her, Julia knew. The older woman still clung to the hope she'd change her mind, stay on and marry Wade. Since she refused to discuss the matter, Julia changed the subject. "Has Mr. Howland said anything to you about getting another housekeeper?" she asked.

As she spoke, the back door opened and Wade entered. "Did I hear my name taken in vain?" he asked.

"I was wondering if you'd found someone to take Adelina's place when she leaves," Julia said.

"Not yet. That'll take a trip into Austin. Be needing supplies soon. Maybe you'd like to make the trip, too, while Adelina's still here to take care of things. She tells me you're working too hard."

Julia glanced around, intending to frown at Adelina, but she'd left the kitchen, once again leaving them alone. Playing matchmaker, Julia thought crossly.

"I help, that's all," she said.

"Thought we could take a ride this evening," he said. "Show you around the spread when the sun's not so hot. You need to get out of the house."

She couldn't think of anything she'd rather do. Or anything that would be so ill-advised. "I'm not sure . . ." she began.

"I am. No harm in a ride, is there?"

"I guess not, but—"

"No buts. And you think about that trip to Austin."

"The girls do need some books. They're outgrowing their clothes, too. But you could take care of that."

He shook his head. "Nope. A woman's job, pure and simple."

She knew he was right. What man would take measure-

ments, chose the right material, and persuade a dressmaker to sew up two sets of the necessary garments quickly?

"How long a trip is it?" she asked.

He smiled and she tried not to allow the charm of his
smile to affect her. "We can thrash out the details on our
evening ride," he told her. "Right after dinner. Got to get
back to work."

With that he left, giving her no chance to say yes, no,
or maybe. Julia couldn't summon up annoyance, though,
she was too excited about riding with Wade.

He's right, she told herself. If I can get this worked up
about a simple outing, I've been housebound too long.

In his bedroom after the evening meal, Wade ran a hand
over his hair. Too long, he knew, in need of a trim that it
wouldn't get until Austin. He wasn't so foolish as to be
getting slicked up to take this ride with Julia, but a man
liked to look his best. Monette never had any complaints
about his appearance—or his performance.

He hadn't thought much about her lately. Somehow he
was looking forward more to Julia going to Austin with
him than he was to seeing Monette once he got there.
There was something about Julia that continued to draw
him to her. He kept finding excuses to touch her, even
though the contact fired him up and then left him to burn.

If only she was a more accommodating women. Not in
the same way Monette was, just more, well, biddable—the
Reverend Miller's word was a good as any. She had a mind
of her own, forcing him to struggle for every gain. Make
a difficult wife, she surely would. If she could bring herself
to accept him, that is. He was by no means certain she
ever would, even if he meant to ask her, which he didn't.

On the other hand, how well she fit into his arms, how
soft her skin was, how her scent drove him mad with need
. . . Enough of that, if he kept on imagining holding her,
he'd be in no shape to mount Thor.

He wanted her, true enough, unwise though it was, she being an innocent and all. Wanting a woman wasn't falling in love, though. That was something he never would do. Look what love had done to his brother. Made a man crazy, that's what, made him take leave of his senses and act like a born idiot. Grant hadn't been a fool by any means—not till he met Teresa Sue.

Wade shook his head. Enough of that, too. What was done was done. They were both dead and buried.

He left his room and saw Julia coming down the hall toward him. She wore the divided skirt of her riding dress but not the jacket. Instead, a white shirtwaist set off her blond hair and blue eyes. The Texas sun had given her fair skin a golden sheen.

"I fear I don't have an appropriate riding hat," she said as she neared him. "As you may recall, I lost mine when trying to escape from Les Slocum. Actually it blew off because I took out the hatpin to use as a weapon."

He grinned. Never at a loss, that was Julia.

"While I appreciate you lending me your hat to get back here," she went on, "it was a trifle large, though it did keep me from being burned to a crisp."

"I anticipated the problem," he told her. "Some of my brother's wife's things are stored in a trunk in the barn. I found a riding hat among them. One of the twins is wearing it over her ears at the moment."

When they reached the main room, he plucked the white hat from Nancy's—or was it Susan's—head, he was never sure unless they spoke, and handed it to Julia.

"Thank you," she said as much to the child as to him.

"We get our ponies soon, Papa Wade?" Nancy asked him. The twins' voices were slightly different, thank the Lord, or he'd never be able to tell them apart.

"When I come back from my next trip to Austin," he promised.

"Then we ride with you?" Susan asked.

"Once you learn how to." He ruffled her dark hair, then did the same to Nancy so she wouldn't feel left out.

Strange how traits were passed along from one generation to another. Teresa Sue had been as blond as Julia and his brother's hair was a sort of medium brown. Neither of them had gray eyes. Look at the twins—spitting images of him. Grant had remarked on it more than once, joking that everyone took him for their father.

Only not quite joking. There'd been an undertone of the same jealousy that finally drove Grant to his death, even though Wade had been nowhere near Teresa Sue at the time she'd gotten pregnant. He'd been riding with the Rangers across the border in Mexico. Been gone two months in all. In any case, he wouldn't have touched her with a ten-foot pole, not his brother's wife.

Julia brushed her fingers across the white hat. "Much more attractive than mine was," she said and set it on her head. "It really fits quite well, don't you think?"

She could have no idea of how lovely she looked. Grant's wife had been pretty, but Julia was beautiful, no matter what she had on.

"I'll take good care of the hat," she assured the twins as he ushered her from the room.

Julia shot him a sidelong glance as they neared the horses. "I see you've given me the chestnut mare," she said.

"Dodie? Didn't you choose her to begin with?"

"Is that her name? I guess you might say I'm used to Dodie by now. I picked the most docile horse I could find. Not all horses will accept a sidesaddle. She did. I'm sorry I lost it. Les Slocum hid the saddle somewhere at the cabin but then didn't know how to put it on her when he lured me away."

"It happened to be the only sidesaddle on the ranch. I hope you don't mind riding astride. I noticed you did very well when we rode back here."

"I suppose I shouldn't admit to being unladylike, but I prefer riding astride."

"You're always a lady."

She eyed him as if assessing whether or not he was really speaking his mind but didn't comment.

He boosted her onto Dodie. "Here we go again, " she told the horse. "I do hope you remember that I can be as stubborn as you."

He smiled. She had the mare down perfectly.

"Do you know this makes me feel rather strange," she said as they started off. "I can't help but look back on the first time I rode away on Dodie. Such a foolish thing to do. I tend to be impulsive, it's one of my worst traits. I wouldn't even be here at the W Bar H otherwise."

"You came on impulse?"

"I'm afraid so. It seemed like such an adventure to someone from Coventry—all the way to Texas! It never occurred to me to wonder how you'd feel to be confronted with the wrong girl. Of course, I didn't anticipate the marriage would be planned for the same day Emma would arrive."

"I might have been a tad hasty," he admitted. "It seemed like a good idea at the time."

"I don't believe any advice about women you might get from Jack Crain should be acted on. Whatever you may think, he doesn't understand women, not one little bit."

"Jack's all right." He let it go at that, aware that she had such a down on poor old Jack that nothing he said would change her mind.

"I thought we'd ride down by the creek," he said. "It's one of the prettiest spots on the ranch with the trees and all."

"Did you start the W Bar H?" she asked.

"Our father, Grant's and mine, did. His name was William, that's why our brand is W Bar H. Unlike most people in the South he believed in the United States. By 1859 he got fed up with the politics in South Carolina, sold the

family plantation, and came west. He became good friends
with Sam Houston and it about killed him when old Sam
got kicked out of the governor's office in '61 because Texas
seceded. But by then he had the land here and was just
getting a good start with the cattle, so we stayed."

"The Civil War never did affect the West much, I've
heard."

"It affected Pop. Against his wishes, my brother Grant
enlisted in the Confederate Army. Mom died about then.
What with the war between the states, losing her, and Grant
defying him, Pop sort of lost heart. It's too bad he didn't
last long enough to see the war end and Texas get readmit-
ted to the Union."

"Your brother must have survived the war," Julia said,
"because the twins are only four."

Wade nodded. "Never got out of Texas. Came home
when the war ended, by then he'd met and married Teresa
Sue and so he brought her to the ranch with him."

Julia thought he'd go on to tell her what happened
to them. When he didn't, she asked, "Were they in an
accident?"

"You could call it that." The tone of his voice warned
her that was all he intended to say about the matter.

"Now you're running the ranch by yourself," she said
finally.

"Got me some good hands and Jack keeps 'em busy."

She supposed Jack Crain might be a good overseer, or
whatever Texans called them. If so, it well might be his
only good quality. The sight of him made her skin crawl.
Luckily she rarely did see him, and never face to face,
because she took care not to enter the kitchen when the
hands were eating.

They crested a rise and paused. Below lay a wavering
line of trees—cottonwoods—that must follow the wandering path of the creek he'd mentioned. How welcome the
green of their leaves was to her eyes, still accustomed to

the greenery of the East rather than the brown and gold
of Texas.

"Does the creek have a name?" she asked.

"Pop named it after my mother—Rose Creek."

"I think I would have liked your father. I never got to
know mine."

"You mentioned a great-aunt raised you and your sister."

"Our mother died in childbirth and the baby, a boy,
died, too. Our father couldn't cope with two little girls so
he brought us to Great-aunt Polly and set off for California.
He sickened and died on the way but we didn't hear until
a year later. They thought it was cholera."

Dodie had behaved remarkably well so far but now she
decided she didn't want to start down the hill toward the
creek. Instead, her idea seemed to be to return to the
corral.

Julia's attention had wandered while she spoke of her
parents and she had to fight to bring Dodie's head around
and insist she obey her rider. Once the mare saw that she
wasn't going to get her way, she gave in with a frustrated
snort and followed Thor down the rise.

"I hear you chuckling," Julia complained when she
caught up with Wade near the bottom of the hill. "You
knew what would happen when you saddled me with this—
this recalcitrant beast."

"Now there's a ten-dollar word if I ever heard one," he
commented. "You train for a teacher?"

Julia shook her head. "I didn't think I'd have the
patience. Besides, the millworkers in Coventry make more
money than the local teacher. My vocabulary is due to my
great-aunt, who made Emma and me learn a new word
from the dictionary every Monday, then we had to use the
word in a sentence at least once every day that week."

"Could be Polly and I wouldn't get along as well as I
thought," he commented. "I don't even own a dictionary."

"You soon will. That's one of the books we need to buy
in Austin."

"So you've made up your mind to come with me. Good."

Had she? Apparently, since she'd said, "we."

"You haven't answered my questions about the trip," she told him as they approached the creek, riding under the trees on this side of the water.

He halted Thor. Dodie needed no persuasion to stop and they both dismounted. Wade's behavior was exemplary, he took no liberties while helping her down, nor did he hold her a second longer than necessary. She wasn't sure whether she was pleased or disappointed.

The ruins of what looked to have been a small gazebo nestled under the thick branches of one of the cottonwoods. The sight distracted her from her quest for information about Austin. "What a shame to let this fall down," she said, picking up an intricately carved railing. "It must have been a charming little building."

"The weather here is tough on wood," he said.

"But why would you let it fall into rack and ruin? Can it be repaired? What a delightful place it would be to bring the twins for a picnic."

"They've never been to this spot." His tone was final, meaning he'd said enough.

Julia, though, wasn't to be silenced so easily. "I don't see why not. With someone watching them, the creek wouldn't be dangerous." Actually the water was so low right now that Susan and Nancy could have gone wading in it with no danger at all.

He didn't reply.

She shot him an exasperated look. "What's so awful about this spot anyway?"

"Their parents died here." The words came grudgingly, as if pulled from him.

Julia was silenced only for a moment. "If being here troubles you so much, why did you bring me to this particular place?" she asked.

"I wish I hadn't." He made a move toward the horses. She put a hand on his arm, stopping him.

"You may as well tell me the whole story. Bottling things up makes them harder to get over."

"Great-aunt Polly's advice again, I suppose."

"Why not take it? As Emma and I came to realize when we grew older, she was more often right than wrong."

"It's no secret—people hereabouts knew what Grant was like, so they pretty much figured out what must have happened. Officially it was an accident."

"But not really?"

"Once Grant married Teresa Sue he was an accident waiting to happen. The gazebo was my mother's and Teresa Sue liked to come down here, so she was always after him to paint it and fix it up. I was active in the Rangers then, could afford to be away since Grant was here running the ranch. Anyway, I was gone a lot so I never did much around the place."

She waited for him to go on. What he did, instead, was to walk to Thor and remove a blanket from the saddlebag. Motioning to her, he headed from the stream bank and spread the blanket onto the ground.

"Thought we might set for a while," he said. "Join me?"

Julia did as he asked and they sat side by side on the blanket rather carefully not touching. The sun was low enough so the heat of the day was fading and a slight breeze ruffled the leaves above their heads. Water gurgled and burbled at their feet and somewhere near by a bird was trilling—probably a mockingbird from the many different sounds he made. She found it hard to imagine a more peaceful spot.

"I can see why your mother had her gazebo built here," she said finally when he didn't speak. "It's so restful by Rose Creek."

"Grant was jealous." Wade threw out the words as if anxious to be rid of them. "With no reason to be, either. Teresa Sue was a pretty girl but she wasn't a flirt. Somehow Grant got it into his head she was seeing other men behind his back. I didn't know it at the time, figured it out after-

ward, what he did was set up a trap to catch her. Said he
was riding to Austin, be gone for a week. Came back in
two days, riding in at dusk.''

Again he fell silent. At last he sighed and went on. ''Never
told anyone this before, it's hard. Teresa Sue wasn't in the
house so he crept down here to the gazebo and, sure
enough, she was talking with a man. So he drew his gun
and shot at the man. But Teresa Sue moved as he shot.
The bullet went through her neck and hit the man in the
chest. She bled to death. Her Cousin Ken, paying her a
surprise visit from Louisiana, died the next day.''

''What a tragedy,'' Julia said, feeling the words were
inadequate to express her horror at this heart-shattering
story.

''Worse to come. Once Grant found out who Ken was,
he came back down here and shot himself. I rode in from
the Panhandle—been there with the Rangers—just in time
to hear the shot and find him dead. Ken lived long enough
to tell me what had happened. Three people dead, just
because my brother was so insanely in love with his wife
that he couldn't think straight.''

Julia was taken aback by his last few words. ''Don't you
mean his insane jealousy affected his judgment?'' she
asked.

He scowled at her. ''I meant what I said. If that's what
love brings a man to, I want no part of it.''

There was a difference between love and jealousy, but
she saw reasoning with him would be futile. ''I also meant
what I said when I called it a tragedy,'' she told him. ''For
the twins, and you as well.''

''We've survived. God willing, Nancy and Susan will
always believe it was an accident.''

''Of course they must never be told the truth.'' She
tipped her head to one side, regarding him. ''I wondered
about the somewhat cold-blooded way you sought a wife,''
she said. ''Now I think I understand. You're afraid of falling

in love so you believed you weren't likely to commit that error with some stranger."

Wade eyed her with suspicion but at least his scowl had vanished. "I wouldn't put it quite that way."

"Oh? How would you put it?"

"The girls needed a mother. People you hire come and go but, once you marry her, a wife stays."

"Well, I hope you would have come to at least *like* Emma. She's quite loveable, you know."

"Since she married another man, whether I would have come to like your sister is beside the point."

"I do believe she's far better off with Floyd Biddescomb, even if he is a mother's boy. At least he loves her."

"You sound peeved with me. Because of what I said about love?"

"There's nothing wrong with love! I hope I fall in love someday. Anyone who doesn't misses a wonderful and essential part of life we're all meant to experience."

"You said yourself your Great-aunt Polly refused to fall in love."

"I did not. I said she refused to marry. There's a difference."

He smiled wryly. "As I mentioned once before, you must take after her then—refusing to marry me."

"You don't love me. Why should I marry you?" Once the words were out, she regretted them. But there it was, in a nutshell. If and when she married, she wanted to be loved. "Anyway," she added, "you told me you had no intention of asking me."

"After thinking it over, I can see certain advantages," he told her. "For one thing, it'd save me searching for a new housekeeper."

Before she rose to the bait, she caught the teasing glint in his eyes and smiled. "You're wrong. I'd insist on a housekeeper. As well as requiring a complete trousseau. A girl only gets married once."

He held up a hand. "Truce. We may never agree on

anything, but that's no reason we can't be friends. After all, you were almost my sister-in-law."

"So I was."

He held out his hand. "Shake?"

Up until then she'd been perfectly fine, if upset by his terrible tale. When he clasped her hand in his, though, everything went downhill. Gone, her determination not to succumb, gone her cool assessment of her feelings, and fading fast, her ability to pull away from him.

"Julia?" She heard what she'd begun to recognize as the tell-tale hoarseness in his voice that meant he was as badly afflicted as she was.

She made the mistake of meeting his gaze. What she saw in his eyes made whatever remained of her resistance collapse like the ruin of the gazebo behind her.

As she leaned toward him, with one final burst of will, she whispered, "Don't kiss me."

He paid absolutely no attention to her plea. She didn't mind, since she hadn't really meant it anyway.

Chapter 8

Wade groaned as he felt Julia respond to his kiss. Far better if she pushed him away. Instead she snuggled close, closer, until the softness of her breasts pressed against him. How could any man be expected to resist the temptation to deepen the kiss, to crush her to him?

He hadn't meant to touch her—that wasn't why he'd brought the blanket along. Or was it? With his need for her like a chronic ache, maybe he'd hoped the blanket would come in handy.

Yet this wasn't the right place to make love with any woman—he shouldn't have brought her to this tragic spot. He'd stop, they'd ride back. In just a minute or two. He needed to savor her lips a little longer, to breathe in her scent, to feel the curve of her breast under his hand.

Holding her in his arms was like nothing else. As well as arousing him almost past bearing, it satisfied something deep within him, something he couldn't define, almost as though she belonged where she was.

Her fingers tangled in his hair as she urged him closer. Didn't she know he wanted to be closer still, wanted nothing between them, wanted to lie with her, skin to skin, with nothing covering them but the warm Texas air?

Julia, so contrary and stubborn. And so soft and sweet-smelling, so desirable. Her unpracticed responses were all the more exciting for being innocent. He wanted, he needed to be the man who taught her how to make love, to enjoy the most intimate of caresses.

"Wade," she breathed against his lips. "I don't know what's happening to me—I feel like I'm melting inside."

"You want me," he murmured, trying to control the wild surge of passion her words evoked in him.

She would be warm and welcoming, as eager as he to find completion with each other.

"What do I want?" she whispered.

Show her, his throbbing body insisted. She's ready, show her what she wants.

Not here, what was left of his mind warned. *Not in this cursed spot.*

In Austin, he promised himself. Wait for Austin. Not now, not here.

Exerting all his will, he pulled back, releasing her. "I shouldn't have touched you," he said hoarsely. "It's like setting a spark to tinder."

Deprived of Wade's embrace, Julia had never felt so bereft. She tried to make sense of his words. Spark? Tinder? That combination created flames like the ones licking through her only moments ago.

"Which am I?" she asked, hearing the same throaty rasp in her voice that he had in his. She cleared her throat. "The spark or the tinder?"

He smiled and touched the tip of her nose with his forefinger. "There's no one like you, Julia. You're the spark, I'm the tinder, and together we're going to get burned."

She nodded. "I feel rather singed as it is." Her hands went to her hair, smoothing and rearranging. She picked up the hat she'd set aside and put it on. Rising, she readjusted her clothes. Her cheeks felt hot, she supposed they were quite pink. Her mouth still felt the pressure of his and she touched her lips with her fingertips.

He caught her wrist and brought her fingers to his own lips. The warmth of his mouth radiated through her.

"We'd better git," he told her as he let her go.

"While the gitting's good, you mean?" she asked, deliberately using the Texas variation of get.

"You got it." He grinned at her.

None of this should have happened, she knew, and yet she wasn't upset. Instead of being ashamed, she reveled in the knowledge that Wade desired her, for his caresses made it evident he did. Love wasn't mentioned, wouldn't be mentioned by either of them. This didn't necessarily have anything to do with love, did it? She couldn't answer that question.

Perhaps her attitude was wrong. Unladylike. Maybe she was the wanton she'd accused herself of being—but she didn't care.

He helped her remount Dodie and then swung onto Thor. Dodie immediately responded, apparently eager to return to the corral.

"You have to repair the gazebo, you know," she said as they climbed the rise. "Leaving it in ruins doesn't help."

"Rebuild is more like it."

She shrugged. "I'm no carpenter. Rebuild, then."

"We'll see."

It was enough for now that she'd put the idea in his head, Julia told herself. He couldn't go on blaming himself for his brother's death forever. Or maybe it wasn't blame so much as anger at his brother. Great-aunt Polly would say, "The dead no longer deserve your anger," but she didn't think it was the right time to repeat this advice, sage though it might be.

"Austin's a long day of riding," he said. "Get up early, get there late."

"Must I ride Dodie?"

"One thing about that mare, she's a stayer. Gets you where you want to go."

Julia sighed. "I assume that means yes. But I'd change what you said to she gets you where you want to go as long as you keep reminding her you want to go there."

Wade chuckled. "Dodie's a good woman's horse."

"Probably because if a man had to ride her he'd have sold her long ago."

Dodie turned to look at her, exactly as if she'd understood every word. "Never mind listening," Julia told her. "Don't you know eavesdroppers never hear good of themselves?"

"We can get in some target practice on the way," Wade said. "I made up my mind back there at old Hank's cabin that you need to learn how to handle a gun. Once you learn, you can teach Silver Wing. Texas women should be able to shoot."

Julia stared at him. "I've never handled a gun in my life."

"Then you won't have anything to unlearn."

It had never occurred to her she'd need to know how to shoot. She grimaced. Would she ever be able to point at something alive and be able to pull the trigger? Still, Wade had a point. Texas did have bandits and, according to Adelina, dangerous Comanche Indians.

"I don't want to target shoot at any animals," she said.

"Stationary targets only," he assured her.

"Where will we stay in Austin?"

"Hotel." He glanced at her. "Separate rooms, of course."

She hadn't expected anything less. Share a man's room? Never! Kissing was one thing, that quite another.

"We will be traveling alone, the two of us?" she asked.

He shook his head. "One of the hands will come along. He can drive the twins' ponies home. Not a good plan to ride alone, anyway."

"I suppose you'll never let me forget my doing so. But,

really, how could I know I'd ride right into a train robbery?''

"Texas is a big state and one you can't take for granted. Remember that. It's one of the reasons we need the Rangers.''

They were close enough to the house so that Brownie came running to meet them. Just as at the cabin, he didn't bark at people he knew.

"Since his bath, I'd say he might only be the second ugliest dog in the state," Wade commented.

"He likes it at the ranch.''

"Yeah. He fits in better than I figured he would. Silver Wing, though . . .'' He paused and didn't go on.

"She's doing very well with the twins and is a big help to Adelina. I'm teaching her to read—she's a very quick student.''

"Don't get your back up. She makes the hands restless, is all. I'm not for shipping her off to the Apache tomorrow, but she can't stay indefinitely.''

Julia had thought about bringing Silver Wing back to Coventry with her, but how could she? There was hardly room for her at Great-aunt Polly's anymore, much less another person. And Coventry would be like an alien country to Silver Wing. It was beginning to seem that way to Julia as well. Whoever would have imagined she could grow accustomed to Texas so rapidly? The ranch even seemed like home.

It hurt to think of leaving Nancy and Susan, so she tried not to. As for Wade . . . She took a deep breath and let it out slowly.

"When do we leave for Austin?" she asked.

"Tomorrow.''

Julia raised her eyebrows. "You believe in short notice.''

"Be ready by six.''

She glanced at her brown riding skirt and fingered the material, somewhat the worse for wear. It hadn't been new when she came. In fact, she hadn't brought an extensive wardrobe along. Not that she owned one, but she had packed only what she thought she'd need for the trip.

Evidently Wade noticed what she was doing because he said, "If you have no objection to looking through Teresa Sue's trunk, you might find another riding habit."

She supposed he thought she might not wish to wear a dead woman's clothes, but she didn't mind, having been brought up with Great-aunt Polly remodeling clothes from the attic trunks for her and Emma. "Waste not, want not," was the household motto.

"Thank you," she said.

When they pulled up by the corral, one of the hands was waiting, the dark one they called Jamie. Adelina had told her the man's name was really Jaime, pronouncing the J as H in the Mexican fashion.

Jamie ducked his head to her, then said, "Boss, gotta talk to you."

Wade dismounted, helped her off Dodie, said he'd see to the horses and turned to Jamie. Julia started for the house, changed her mind, and walked over to the barn instead. She'd seen the leather trunk that must be Teresa Sue's when she'd toured the grounds.

If she were to leave early in the morning, she'd have no time to wash any of her things and she badly needed clean clothes. Sure enough, when she lifted the lid of the unlocked trunk in the barn, she saw it contained women's belongings. Deciding she'd examine the things carefully when she had more time, she settled for lifting out a dark blue riding habit with white trim and, thankfully, a divided skirt. It seemed to her the fit would be reasonable. After choosing some underwear, she shut the lid. With the clothes laid over her arm, she started out of the barn only to find someone blocking her way.

"If it ain't Miss Sommers," Jack Crain said. "Miss Julia Sommers."

"I'm in rather a hurry, Mr. Crain," she said sharply.

"Going into Austin with the boss, I hear." He nodded

at the clothes she carried. "Find a pretty nightdress in that trunk, did you?"

She wouldn't stoop to reply to such a remark. "Mr. Crain, please be kind enough to allow me to pass."

" 'Course, could be you won't need nothing like that. The boss has him a redhead lady friend in Austin, you know—name of Monette."

"Mr. Crain!" Julia's voice rose.

Brownie appeared in the doorway behind Jack Crain. He walked stiff-legged toward her, growling at the man. Jack, who was smirking at her, turned and glared at the dog. "Get the hell away from me," he ordered.

Seeing her chance, she skirted Jack and, with Brownie as escort, stalked from the barn. The dog stayed by her side until she reached the back door. Entering the house, she found a leftover piece of meat and tossed it outside to Brownie who caught it in midair.

"Good dog," she said to him before turning away. Brownie could pick out the bad ones—he'd growled at Les Slocum, too, she recalled.

It would do no good to tell Wade what had happened, she knew. He'd probably just say Jack Crain was teasing her. Which he was, but in a suggestive, leering way that turned her stomach. Before she left tomorrow morning, she'd be sure to remind Silver Wing to be careful of him.

Wishing what he'd said wasn't burned into her mind, she told herself not to pay any attention to his insinuations. Unfortunately, she continued to wonder who Monette was. If she truly was a lady friend of Wade's, why hadn't he asked her to marry him instead of sending East for a woman he'd never seen?

Which reminded her—she really did need to write to Emma and Great-aunt Polly and explain things. As soon as we return from Austin, she promised herself.

Later, when she climbed into bed, for the first time since her arrival she pictured Wade, in his bed, just down the hall from her. She couldn't imagine him in a nightshirt but what else did a man sleep in? Maybe she'd ask Emma in the letter. But, no, she couldn't do that because their great-aunt would also read the letter and wonder exactly what was going on in Texas.

What *was* going on? Julia sighed. More than ought to be, certainly.

Early the next morning, Julia dressed in the blue and white riding habit, which was, as she'd suspected, quite a good fit. With the white hat and a pair of dark blue gloves of her own, she felt more stylish than she had since she'd arrived here. Carrying her carpet bag, she stopped in the kitchen for a cup of hot Mexican chocolate, aware she was growing overfond of Adelina's deliciously sweet concoction.

Adelina, packing food for the trip, handed her a tortilla, which she ate quickly. Bidding Adelina *adios,* she picked up the leather bag of food along with her own bag and hurried outside.

The horses were saddled, with Wade and Jamie waiting. Wade attached her bag to the mare's gear, added the bag of food to Thor's and helped her mount. He swung onto Thor and the three of them set off. Brownie escorted them to the invisible line that he'd set for how far he intended to go away from the ranch house, then turned back.

"Knows where home is, that one," Jamie said. "Good dog."

"If ugly," Wade added.

Jamie shrugged. "Looks don't count in dogs." He touched his wide-brimmed hat. "Brownie, he knows who his friends are."

Looks counted in women, though, Julia thought. Pretty girls were always chosen first. She was aware she wasn't unattractive, but she didn't consider herself really pretty, like Emma. What did Monette look like? Red hair, Jack Crain, had said. Carroty or a beautiful auburn?

"It's a lucky man who knows who *his* friends are," Wade said.

Jamie shot him a quick glance. "Dogs, they are never wrong. A man, he can be wrong."

Julia eyed Jamie sideways, wondering what or who he was referring to. Wade, though, didn't seem to think by "a man" Jamie meant him. Perhaps he didn't.

"Before it gets too hot," Wade said, "we'll stop for a few rounds of target practice." He jerked his head toward Julia. "She'll be doing the shooting."

"Senorita Sommers shoots?"

"Not yet, Jamie," she said. "Mr. Howland thinks I should learn."

Jamie nodded. "In Texas, is good for all to know."

Sometime later, Wade drew up Thor near a draw. From the looks of it, no water had flowed along there for years. Apparently at one time there had been water, as a half-dozen dead trees along the draw attested.

They all dismounted. Wade opened his saddle bag, lifted out a small wooden box, opened it, and showed the contents to Julia.

"Why—why it's beautiful," she said, staring at the small revolver inlaid with gold. "I've never seen such a pretty one before. Is it a Colt?"

He shook his head. "Beaumont-Adams, made in London. A .32, not a .45. Not so heavy, easier for a lady to shoot. They call this a pocket revolver. Won it in a game a couple years back."

Wade gambled? Julia told herself she shouldn't be surprised, no doubt most Texan men did.

"Take it out and hold it," he added.

Julia took off her gloves, tucked them away and removed the revolver, holding it awkwardly in her right hand while Wade eased out the five bullets from their individual holders within the box.

"The cylinder holds five, not six like the Colt," he said. "You have to remember to reload after five shots."

He showed her how to snap the cylinder to one side and supervised how she loaded a bullet into each chamber. "You never point a gun or revolver, loaded or unloaded, at anyone unless you mean to shoot him. And you never, ever draw any gun toward you by the barrel."

She nodded, uncertain she'd ever be able to point it at any living thing.

"With this Adams," he went on, "you can fire by a simple pull of the trigger or by cocking the hammer ahead of time. So don't touch the trigger until you're ready to go—and that's after you take aim." Taking the revolver from her, he demonstrated how to aim it. "You try now. Aim at the nearest dead tree." He pointed.

Julia sighted as best she could and pulled the trigger. The sharp crack made her blink and she felt the barrel of the gun jerk upward.

"Got to be prepared for the recoil," he said. "Not much with a revolver, but it's there."

"Did I hit the tree?"

"No, senorita," Jamie said.

"That comes with practice," Wade added.

On her fifth try she saw a chip of dead bark fly as the bullet smacked into the tree trunk. "I hit it!" she cried. "I really did hit it!"

It had never occurred to her she might actually enjoy shooting a gun—no, a revolver. Wade had already taught her that rifles and carbines were guns.

"You're a natural." Wade's praise elated her. If they'd been alone she might even have flung her arms around him.

"On the way home from Austin you'll learn to shoot a Winchester," he went on. "I'm telling you now, a carbine has a lot more recoil than that Adams of yours."

"Of mine?" She ran a caressing finger over the barrel and quickly removed it. "Hot!"

Wade grinned. "You learn fast. The revolver is yours. We'll pick up more .32 calibre bullets in Austin and you'll be all set. Need some more practice, though. We'll get to cleaning revolvers later.''

After thanking him, she stowed her gift back in its protective box and slid it into her saddle bag. Even Great-aunt Polly could hardly think it improper or compromising to accept the gift of a revolver from a man—at least in Texas.

They remounted and rode on. And on. And on.

By the time the buildings and trees of Austin came into view, the sun was low and Julia was about ready to fall off the mare. Wade had said it was a long day's ride and he hadn't been exaggerating.

Jamie left them at the town's first intersection. He'd be visiting and staying with friends while she and Wade transacted whatever business had brought them here.

"I can't wait to get to the hotel," she told Wade as they continued along Pecan Street. "I hope I'm able to walk once I dismount."

He smiled. "I wouldn't mind carrying you in but I admit it might cause talk."

She shot him what she hoped was a quelling glance, though secretly thrilled at the idea of being carried anywhere in Wade's arms. They neared a three-story frame building with a neatly lettered sign announcing it was the DYNASTY HOTEL.

"Is that where we're staying?" she asked.

His "no" was so curt she raised her eyebrows. Evidently noticing, he added, "There's a gambling hall connected with the hotel. Noisy."

As they drew closer she saw the extension to the right of the hotel with a much gaudier sign—FRENCHIE'S. FARO. VINGT-ET-UN.

"Twenty and one," she muttered. "A gambling game?"

"Sometimes called blackjack. Didn't anyone in Coventry gamble?"

She shook her head. 'The Reverend Miller and the other clergymen would never stand for such a thing."

"Something tells me I wouldn't take kindly to your home town."

She could believe that.

They turned at the next corner onto Trinity Street and soon came to a rambling two-story structure called The Lone Star Inn. "This is it," he announced.

They dismounted in front. A boy led the horses toward the back stables, promising to bring their belongings to their rooms.

Wade ushered her into a small lobby containing a horse-hair settee and two chairs. The clerk at the desk, after an appraising glance at her, allowed as he had two rooms available for Mr. Howland and his guest.

"Not overlooking the stable," Wade told him, as he scribbled their names into the register.

The clerk, protesting he had no such thing in mind, handed over two keys. With his arm under her elbow, Wade directed Julia to the stairs. Though her legs felt as though they scarcely belonged to her, she managed to climb to the second story. He unlocked her door and handed her the key. As she entered, the hostler boy appeared at the far end of the corridor with her carpet bag and Wade's.

"Locked your saddlebags in with the gear," the boy told Wade, who handed him a coin.

Wade set her bag inside her open door. "After you rest, we'll see about some food," he said.

She nodded, feeling far more tired than hungry. She entered her room, locked the door behind her, crossed to the bed, and, after removing her hat and boots, sprawled onto her back with a sigh. Her eyes closed.

A repeated tapping on her door woke her from a deep sleep. She glanced about the darkened room groggily, for a moment not understanding where she was. Sitting up, she called, "Who is it?"

"Wade. Time to eat."

Her stomach rumbled, reminding her the last meal she'd had was on the trip, at noon. "I'll be a few minutes," she told him.

She found matches and lit the lamp. Opening her satchel, she hung tomorrow's dress on a wooden peg and removed the other contents into the top drawer of an oak dresser. A wash basin and pitcher stood atop the dresser under a gilt-framed oval mirror. After washing her face and hands, she ran a brush through her disordered hair before twisting it into a coil in back and pinning it there. She smoothed what wrinkles she could from her riding habit and pulled on her boots.

She'd been too tired to take much note of her room, now she saw it was quite pleasant, besides being clean. Two windows framed with white curtains looked out into the gathering darkness. Besides the bed, dresser, and commode stand, there was one chair next to a small table. And two doors. She frowned. One led to the hall. What was on the other side of the second door? She walked over and found it locked though there was no key in sight.

She unlocked and opened the door to the hall. Wade was lounging against the wall next to a lamp in a sconce. "Ready?" he asked.

She hesitated, then decided the extra door could wait until after they'd eaten. After all, it was locked.

The hotel's small dining room was empty except for an old man at a rear table. Wade seated her, crossed to a swinging door which he opened, and called, "We're here."

He returned to the table and seated himself. Almost immediately a middle-aged woman pushed through the door with a tray. Tonight's entrée was evidently stew because that's what they were served. Julia found it palatable and ate most of her serving. Coffee and bread came with the meal.

When they finished, Wade said, "I guess you're too tired to take in any of the sights tonight."

"Correct. But thanks for waking me to eat. I was hungry."

"I'll see you to your room, then."

She wanted to ask him if he were going out, but it was none of her affair so she didn't. At her door, she produced her key and unlocked it. Leaving the door wide open she pointed at the second door inside the room. "I don't know where that leads," she said. "It's locked but there's no key on this side. I don't like that."

"Don't worry about that door," he said. "I know where it leads."

"Where, for heaven's sake?"

"I have the room next door to you. That's a connecting door between the rooms. So you see, nothing to be upset about."

She stared at him. "Is the key on your side?"

"I didn't pay any attention. Want me to look? Better yet, we'll both look."

Julia followed him to his door and watched him unlock it. Don't worry about a door connecting her room with his? How could she not?

He ushered her in and she immediately crossed to the door in question. No key was in the lock. She slanted a look at him.

"That's a mistrustful stare if ever I saw one," he said. "I swear I didn't pocket any key."

She wanted to believe him, but, as things stood, she knew she'd not sleep a wink.

"Maybe . . . ," he added, inserting his room key into the lock. Nothing happened. "Let's try yours." Hers didn't work either.

"Got the answer," he said, indicating she should precede him from the room. He shut and locked his door, then stepped to her still open door and entered. She trailed him inside. Lifting the chair beside her table, he carried it to the connecting door, put the top of its back under the doorknob and edged the chair along the floor until it fit solidly under the knob. "Solved?"

She felt embarrassed to meet his gaze after having mutely accused him of—what? Planning to creep into her room at midnight through that door and molest her? Wade would never do that, and she knew it.

She bit her lip. "I've never stayed in a hotel room alone," she admitted. "On the trip, I always shared a room with another woman. I guess I'm a little edgy."

"If you'll stay up for a few minutes, I'll go down to the desk and see if they have a skeleton key that fits the connecting doors. You'll feel more secure if you have a key on your side."

"The chair will suffice."

"Wait, I'll be right back." He turned on his heel and left the room, closing her door behind her.

She felt like a fool for causing such a fuss. Once she knew he was in the room beyond the locked door she should have dropped the matter. He was probably insulted because she'd more than implied she didn't trust him.

By the time Wade returned she was on the verge of tears. Here he'd been so nice, so patient, giving her that beautiful revolver and teaching her to use it. What had he ever done to make her mistrust him? Nothing. What was wrong with her?

He held up a key with a blank tag on it, instead of a room number like theirs had. Setting the chair aside, he inserted the new key in the connecting door lock, turned it and opened the door. Closing it, he relocked the door and left the key in the lock.

"All fixed," he told her.

"Oh, Wade, I'm sorry. I didn't mean . . ." Her voice broke, and she desperately blinked back tears.

"You're tired," he said brusquely. "Get some sleep. Good night."

He turned away and left her room. She stared blankly

at the closed door for long moments before stirring herself to walk over and lock it behind him.

Eyes swimming with tears, she stumbled to the chair and sat down. She'd insulted him. Where was he headed now? Not to his room, she was sure. Where, then? To see red-haired Monette?

Chapter 9

Wade strode out of the Lone Star, heading for Pecan Street. Frenchie's wasn't far, he could be there within a matter of minutes. Monette would be delighted to see him; a warm welcome awaited him in her arms. He nodded. Right.

He knew where he stood with Monette. She was as unlike Julia as a woman could be.

That damn connecting door. Still, he'd understood Julia's concern about it—up till the point where he'd told her his room was on the other side. She should have realized then she was perfectly safe.

What it amounted to was—she didn't trust him. True, he'd held her in his arms and started to make love to her—what, twice? But he hadn't forced himself on her, she'd welcomed his advances. He'd done nothing underhanded, she had no reason to suspect he might.

Hell, the damn door had been locked. She must have figured he'd concealed the key and intended to use it after she was in bed, asleep. As if he'd do such a thing! Even if it hadn't been against his code, there were enough available women in the world so he didn't need to sneak up on her.

That spinster great-aunt of hers must have filled her head full of nonsense about men. Come to think of it, hadn't she imagined a man had crept into her room that first night she'd spent at the ranch? He shook his head. Lord save him from man-hating spinsters—and the women who listened to them.

Frenchie's was just ahead. He'd surprise Monette. Imagining her delighted squeal when she saw him made him smile. They'd known one another for going on three years now. He didn't suppose she was entirely true to him but he knew he was her favorite. Not that she was a paid whore, no, not Monette. If she honored a man with her favors it was because she wanted him.

An honest woman in her way. Maybe not when it came to the vingt-et-un table, gamblers could never quite be trusted when they plied their trade. But honest enough not to lie with a man she hadn't taken a shine to. She flirted with them all, but she favored few. Quite a gal, Monette.

Outside the door to Frenchie's he hesitated. Asking himself what the hell was the matter with him, he started inside, only to be forced to dodge aside when a man came flying through the open door to fetch up on his face in the dust of the road.

"And stay out!" an unseen voice called after him. Fred, the bouncer, no doubt—black as sin, six feet five, and all muscle. Fred was one of the reasons Monette had few problems in running Frenchie's.

Wade eyed the man sprawled in the dirt. Skunk drunk, he was levering himself onto his hands and knees to crawl out of the middle of the road. Wade shrugged and turned to face Frenchie's again. A moment later he found himself retracing his steps toward the Lone Star. Just as well. He was bone tired, best to put off seeing Monette till tomorrow night.

Being tired had never made him turn back before. Why was he doing it now? Couldn't be the drunk—Fred threw troublesome drunks out with regularity. Not till he reached the hotel did he admit the truth. It wasn't Monette he wanted to make love to. No, it was stubborn, wrong-minded Julia.

Julia lay on her back in bed staring up at the ceiling, which was faintly illuminated by the light from the hall sconce creeping in under the door. Overhead was a discoloration where water must have leaked through the roof at one time. The stained blotch was roughly the shape of the state of Texas.

Texas. Where she was at the moment. Where Wade lived. And Monette as well.

She turned onto her side but the change in position didn't dislodge her thoughts. She'd more or less driven him to another woman with her unreasonable behavior, hadn't she? Deep down, she trusted Wade—so why had she acted as though she suspected he might act nefariously? Might sneak into her room uninvited through that blasted connecting door?

A scraping sound made her sit bolt upright. Was that slight noise coming from the room next to hers? From Wade's room? She bounced from the bed, padded over to the connecting door and put her ear to it.

Yes, he was inside. By what she could make out through the wood of the door, he was undressing and climbing into bed. If he'd gone to see Monette, he hadn't stayed very long. She pictured him stretched out in a bed similar to hers, wearing—what? Maybe nothing at all? Heat began to collect inside her, as she contemplated a Wade with no clothes on, despite the fact she'd never seen a naked man.

Boy babies, yes. Did those odd parts grow as the baby grew into a man? They must. But she couldn't picture it in her mind. Thinking about the possibility made her pulses pound.

Go to bed, she advised herself. This is getting you nowhere.

She did, lying on her back again with no cover over her because she was much too warm. Even the thin cotton of her nightgown seemed too much, but she'd never gone to bed naked in her life. Did Wade ever wonder how she looked with no clothes on? If so, did it make him feel like he was burning up inside and out? She certainly was. Why had the thought of him naked never occurred to her? For all she knew he wore a nightshirt. Didn't most men?

Had he fallen asleep already? She was never going to get any sleep tonight if she didn't banish him and those parts she couldn't quite imagine from her mind.

Covered by a nightshirt, she told herself firmly. He was *not* lying naked without any covers. In any case, he was probably sound asleep. Unlike her.

She eased from the bed and crossed to the connecting door again, pressing her ear to the wood. No sound from his room came through. Her hand accidentally brushed against the key and immediately a wild thought burst free. *She could go and look.*

Never!

Yet the key was on her side. If he was sleeping, he wouldn't even know she'd crept in and out out of his room. And her curiosity would be satisfied, one way or another. If he wore a nightshirt, then she could rid herself of picturing him sleeping naked. If he *was* naked, she'd complete her unfinished image.

But what if he woke?

I can be very, very quiet, she assured herself. Emma had often complained about the way she crept up without warning, like a stalking cat.

Yes, but what if he's not actually sleeping?

She could open the door and listen before actually going

in. Sleep made people breathe differently. Having shared a room with her sister all her life, she knew how it sounded.

Not much harm in just opening the door, was there? She'd probably lose her nerve at that point anyway and change her mind.

Excitement tingled through her as she closed her fingers around the key and cautiously turned it until the door unlocked. Holding her breath, she eased the door open slightly and listened.

His breathing came to her—slow and deep, in and out. He slept. She hesitated. What now? She couldn't just turn back unsatisfied. Since he'd never suspect she'd be sneaking into his room, he'd undoubtedly sleep straight through her quick peek if she were quiet enough.

This is a mad impulse, some cautionary part of her mind warned. *Go back to bed.*

But she'd come this far. It wouldn't take any time at all to tiptoe across the room. And there was enough hall light leaking under his door to tell whether he slept naked or not. She wouldn't be like Psyche holding up a candle to see Cupid asleep, no hot wax to drip on him.

Wondering for the first time exactly where that hot wax had fallen on Cupid, Julia stifled the impulse to giggle. She was so keyed up now she'd never fall asleep unless she went ahead.

On her toes, she inched cautiously across the room toward the bed. No boards creaked underfoot, she made no noise at all. She halted once, uncertain about his breathing—had it changed? Poised to retreat, she listened until she was satisfied he still slept.

Madness, the voice in her head repeated. *Sheer madness.*

She paid no attention, focused on reaching her goal undetected. One quick look, that's all she'd need before hurrying back to her own room. She wanted to know, she needed to know. A few more steps and her curiosity would be satisfied.

Without warning something ran over her foot. Julia caught back her startled gasp too late.

Wade shot straight up in bed, reached under his pillow for his Colt and snarled, "Hold it, I got you covered."

"Oh!" The squeak was very definitely feminine.

"Who the hell . . . ?" he began, peering into the darkness at the white-garbed figure by his bed.

"It's me. Julia. Don't shoot."

Wade put aside his gun, yanked the sheet over his nakedness and reached for her, grasping her arm. He pulled her closer despite her resistance. "Coming to keep me company?" he asked.

"No! What I think was a mouse ran over my foot, otherwise I . . ." her voice trailed off.

"You came into my room because you're afraid of a mouse?" Disbelief coated his words.

"You don't understand. I don't even know if it was a mouse. It might have been one of those horrid scorpions and it's right here in your room."

He let her go. "In that case, you'd better sit on the bed and put your feet up, while you explain."

She sat at the foot of his bed, out of his reach, drawing up her feet. "I can't explain," she wailed.

"You can't explain why you're in my room?"

"No, I can't," she said defiantly. "I won't. But it wasn't what you said—to keep you company."

"Sleepwalking?" he suggested, not believing it for an instant.

"I don't sleepwalk. I—I just wondered if you'd come back."

"Come back from where?"

"From wherever you went after we ate."

"Julia, you're not making sense."

"How can I, when it was senseless to begin with? I should have known you wouldn't wear a nightshirt." Her tiny gasp clued him to the fact she blurted out something she regretted. Part of the truth?

"Why don't you tell me what a nightshirt has to do with all this."

"I can't."

He eased down toward the end of the bed and touched her shoulder.

"Don't!" she cried. "You haven't any clothes on."

"I sleep naked," he said shortly, his patience ebbing.

"I know that—now," she whispered.

A thought occurred to him. He rejected it as ridiculous at first, then examined it again. Julia was an impulsive girl, but even so, it seemed impossible that she would have risked . . .

"Oh, all right," she muttered. "I can see you'll keep at me until I confess. I got to wondering—" she broke off. "I just can't tell you—it's too embarrassing."

"You wondered whether I wore a nightshirt or slept in the buff?"

He could hardly hear her "Yes."

Wade broke up, uncontrollable laughter spilling from him. Hearing her indignant huff, he reached for her, pulled her close and wrapped his arms around her, still chuckling. "You're priceless," he said. "I wouldn't trade you for a hundred—"

"I'm not yours to trade," she sputtered angrily, trying to free herself. "And I don't find it amusing."

"Don't go away mad," he said. "At least wait until I light the lamp so we can make sure what crawled over your foot wasn't a scorpion."

Forgetting for the moment he wasn't dressed, he rose and lit the lamp on his dresser. Julia's sudden intake of breath made him grab for a towel, the cloth barely adequate to wrap around his hips and tuck in. She was seeing more than she'd bargained for, he told himself, trying not to grin.

Noticing her confusion as she tried not to look at him,

he saw that her nightgown, though modest as far as covering her from neck to toe went, was made of a thin cotton close enough to transparent to suggest what lay concealed beneath the cloth. As he stared at the outline of her soft curves, his amusement fled, replaced by rampant desire.

"Julia?" he said softly, his gaze fixed on her.

Her breath caught as she looked into Wade's eyes. The glow in their depths was more than a reflection from the lamp, it matched the heat beginning to consume her. He took a step toward her and, in anticipation, her heart tripled its beat. He was going to kiss her, she knew, and, whether she should let him or not, driven by her need to feel his lips on hers, she was helpless to resist.

As he gathered her into his arms, the delicious shock of feeling the warmth of his skin through her nightgown made her knees weak. His mouth sought hers, his tongue plunging between her parted lips to caress inside. She twined her arms around his neck, eagerly savoring their kiss as his hands stroked the curve of her hips, urging her closer.

Each caress added to the heat inside her until she felt she was melting. His skin, smooth under her hands, barely concealed the hardness of his muscles. How strong, yet how gentle with her. His mouth left hers to trail down to her breast. His lips were hot through her gown as they teased her nipple, making her moan in half-anguished pleasure.

Just when she thought she could no longer bear the intensity of the sensations flickering through her, he lifted her in his arms and carried her to the bed, easing her down and lying beside her. Before she realized what he meant to do, he'd pulled her gown up over her head and off. With a groan he held her close, her breasts against his chest, his bare skin like a soul-consuming fire where it touched hers.

Her will had departed even before the first kiss, and she didn't even want to try to find it. What she wanted was more of Wade's lovemaking. More and more and more. His hand slid over her hip and between their bodies, seeking and finding the secret part of her that ached with need.

Thrills rocketed through her, a throbbing began deep inside her. "Please," she whispered, unaware of what she asked for, but knowing he could provide it.

As she quivered under his touch, he gently eased her legs apart and rose above her. Something hard probed at where she throbbed and she instinctively opened to it. Slowly the hardness slipped inside her, a strange, wonderful invasion that she encouraged by raising her hips. The throbbing inside increased, reaching a crescendo that took her away from herself.

She was vaguely aware of him crying her name as he plunged deep within her, dimly conscious of a flash of pain gone as quickly as it came, overwhelmed by the wonder of what was happening.

Gradually, the intensity abated and faded until all that was left was the lazy enjoyment of being held in his arms. Still holding her, he turned so they were lying on their sides, her head on his shoulder.

"So that's what it's for," she murmured.

His throaty chuckle told her he knew what she meant. "Julia," he said. "You're a prize. A beautiful, desirable, impulsive woman."

His words pleased her but wasn't there something more he should be saying? What about love? Wasn't this a part of loving someone? She waited but he didn't add to what he'd said.

Did she love him? Would she have allowed this to happen if she didn't? She didn't seem to have had any choice, though. Was it love that urged her on? He hadn't mentioned it so maybe it wasn't. She wished she could ask him but knew he was the last person she'd ever question about exactly what love was.

His hand cupped her breast, his thumb sliding back and

forth across her nipple, teasing it to fullness and starting a slow surge of heat within her again. The kisses and caresses began again, sweet and hot, until she felt the pleasurable ache of need. She explored his body, her hand closing around his strange male part.

He lay back, letting her satisfy her curiosity, finally groaning and removing her hand. He pulled her on top of him, showing her without words how to fit herself over him until he was buried within her. He began moving slowly, enticing her into wriggling against him, deep thrilling waves coursing through her.

When the intense throbbing began she moved with him in a wild rhythm she gave no conscious thought to and again reached someplace that seemed to be a part of another world.

This time, as the time the glow faded, sleep claimed her.

Through a haze of drowsiness, Wade gazed at Julia, curled close to him, sound asleep. He smiled, eased from the bed, snuffed out the lamp and crawled back in next to her, put an arm over her, and closed his eyes. Right now it was impossible to believe this had been a mistake. How could he, when making love with her had exceeded anything he'd ever imagined? She'd been an innocent, true, but her natural, unpracticed passion had entranced him. He was damned if he intended to lie awake worrying about tomorrow.

When he woke, the sun was shining in through the curtained windows. Another great Texas morning. As he stretched, he realized something was missing. Someone. Julia. She must have roused earlier. He sat up and saw the connecting door was closed. He smiled wryly. Locked, too, he'd bet. But she'd left something behind. On the floor, half-under the bed, was her white nightgown. He picked it up.

She'd left more than that, he discovered as the feel of

the soft cotton under his hands made the heat rise in him. Damned if he didn't want her all over again.

Enough, man, he told himself. You came to Austin on business and your time here is limited. Even if she'd agree, you can't spend all day in bed. He thrust the nightgown into a dresser drawer.

After washing and dressing, he started to knock on the connecting door, changed his mind and headed for the door to the hall instead. On his way, he noticed a tiny hole where the molding met the floor. Mouse hole? He grinned, unlocked the door and went out, whistling. He tapped on Julia's hall door.

"Who is it?" she called.

"Wade."

"Just a moment."

The door opened sooner than he expected—she must have been ready and waiting for him.

"Good morning," she said brightly.

Too brightly. Damned if he was going to let her get away with pretending nothing had happened. "I found the mouse hole," he said.

Her cheeks turned a bright pink, charming with the flowered blue dress she wore. She refused to look directly at him, so he tipped her chin up with his forefinger. "It's a fine morning, Julia," he said softly. "The sun's shining and we're here together."

Her blush slowly receded and she smiled slightly. "Yes. Wade, we are."

Breakfast over, they set out on their various errands. A dry goods shop near the corner of Congress Avenue and Pecan gave Julia the name of the dressmaker living above the store. She proved eager to help and so Wade left Julia with her, the two of them discussing the suitability of the various bolts of material for four-year-old twins.

"There's a stationers up the street that sells books," he told her. "I'll meet you there in two hours."

He hurried off to buy the supplies he needed, encountered no problems, and was strolling back toward the bookstore when a woman called his name.

"Why, Wade Howland, when did you get into town?"

Monette, decked out in bright green decorated with gold braid and flourishing a green parasol to match, crossed the street toward him.

She was a sight to behold, as usual, but, though it had never occurred to him before, maybe a trifle overdone. Monette tipped the parasol back to pout up at him. "How could you come to Austin and not drop in to see me?"

"I—uh—I haven't had time," he said. "Got in last night but was just too tired to do anything but go to bed."

She tapped his chest with her forefinger. "A poor excuse, sir. I'll expect you tonight without fail."

Standing in the stationers with a book in her hand, Julia looked through the glass window at the front of the store and saw Wade talking with a woman wearing emerald green. A pretty red-haired woman. She couldn't hear what they were saying but the woman was certainly flirting with him. Monette, beyond a doubt.

Ashamed of what she was doing, but unable to stop herself, she edged toward the door and set it ajar, listening.

"I'll see you at Frenchie's tonight," Monette was saying. "No silly excuses." She slanted him a coquettish smile and sashayed off, her bustle swishing back and forth in a way that Julia supposed was attractive to men. Wade certainly seemed transfixed.

She eased the door shut and retreated toward the back of the store, confused and disturbed. It's not as though you didn't know about Monette, she chided herself. She hadn't, though, expected the woman to be employed in a gambling hall. Still, it might explain why Wade hadn't chosen her when he searched for a wife. Judging from what she'd just watched, Monette didn't act like a woman who'd take kindly to raising two active four-year-olds.

What had Wade intended? To leave Emma at the ranch with the twins while he rode in to Austin to see Monette?

Julia tamped down her rising anger. She had no claim on Wade, and, besides, she didn't want him to guess she'd seen him with Monette. Here he came now.

"Find a dictionary?" he asked.

"Yes." She proffered the book she held. "It's rather dear, though."

"We'll take it."

"I selected a few others for the twins." She gestured toward several books piled on the counter. "And one for myself. Naturally I'll pay—"

"You'll do nothing of the sort." Brushing aside her protests, Wade paid for them all and the proprietor agreed to have the books delivered to the Lone Star.

"Want to come with me to look at ponies?" Wade asked her.

If she didn't agree, he'd wonder why. And she wanted to go anyway. The last thing she needed was to be alone with her thoughts.

As they left the stationers, she said, "The dressmaker promised me she'll have everything ready by tonight. Her two daughters also sew and will help her. It will cost a bit extra, though."

He waved away the extra cost. "Sorry you came to Austin?" he asked.

"No," she answered honestly, then added, "after all, I learned to fire a revolver on the way."

"Among other things." His smile was so intimate her knees all but buckled. Blast the man. Why was he acting this way when tonight he'd be off to see Monette. She wondered what excuse he'd use.

Unable not to prod, she said, "You mentioned that you'd

won the revolver you gave me in a game. Was it vingt-et-un?''

"As a matter of fact it was. Why?"

She kept her tone as bland as she could. "Well, we did pass a gambling hall on the way to the Lone Star. It occurred to me you might find occasion to gamble when you visited Austin."

He shrugged. "Sometimes. Not unless I have money to burn. Gambling's a dead end."

"I've never gambled," she persisted.

"Ladies usually don't. At least not in Texas."

Ladies? Didn't he consider Monette a lady? If she wasn't involved in the gambling, why was she inviting him to meet her at a gambling hall? At Frenchie's. Belatedly she made the connection. Monette sounded like a French name. Was it possible Frenchie's belonged to her? She'd never heard of a woman running that kind of establishment, but then there weren't any such places in Coventry. Texas was so very different that anything could be possible.

"If you're interested in learning vingt-et-un," he said, "I'll teach you once we get back to the ranch. All it takes is a deck of cards and the ability to count to twenty-one."

"We'll see," she told him, using his phrase. "Maybe after you rebuild the gazebo."

He frowned at her. "What does that have to do with it?"

She smiled, not answering.

He shook his head, muttering, "Women."

The ponies were in a large corral that contained a number of horses for sale. Jamie met them there. Wade asked her opinion, but when she told him she knew absolutely nothing about ponies, he consulted with Jamie instead. Between them they picked a dappled gray and a bay with a white star and two white stockings, both geldings.

Wade paid for the ponies and Jamie led them off after they agreed on a time and place to meet on the day after tomorrow—early—for the journey back to the ranch.

"We still haven't seen the sights," Wade said to her as they walked toward the hotel.

"Perhaps tomorrow? I plan to nap for a while after the noon meal." Which was the truth. She needed the sleep she hadn't gotten last night.

"That sounds appealing. I may join you." His smile warned her in what direction his thoughts lay.

Despite the thrill that flashed through her at the idea of lying in his arms again, she shook her head. "I meant alone, and you know it."

Last night had been a fluke, a once in a lifetime happening she'd never forget. But she didn't intend to repeat it. Especially with Monette in the offing.

Later, as she lay alone in her bedroom, stripped down to her shift against the heat, she stared at the Texas blotch on the ceiling and thought about Monette. Maybe she was taking the wrong tack by saying never again. Tonight, for instance, Wade could hardly go off to Monette if she arranged it so he spent the night with her instead.

How coldly calculating! She wasn't that kind of person. On the other hand, there was nothing cold or calculating about what would happen between Wade and her if she tempted him. The problem was, she'd never deliberately tempted a man in her life. Exactly how would she go about it?

Chapter 10

After the evening meal, Julia was still casting about for some method of keeping Wade at her side. She'd given up on dressing to attract him. The blue figured cotton she wore was a nice enough gown, even if she hadn't brought along the proper petticoat with bustle attachment, thinking she might, in the heat, be more comfortable with less heavy undergarments. Nor was she wearing any corset, since she'd found it almost unbearable in the Texas summer weather.

Nothing about the blue dress suggested the coquette, not by any stretch of the imagination. What it suggested, if anything, was respectability. Modesty. And, perhaps, the need for the wearer to be a bit more stylish.

Thinking back over her clothes, Julia decided that even if she had everything she owned at her fingertips, not one garment could be counted on to lure a man.

She sighed as Wade pulled back her chair from the table. "Something the matter?" he asked.

Rising, she essayed a smile. "I was hoping you'd like to take a walk," she said. Anything to kill time. "Maybe by the river. I find the river fascinating. The man in the stationers told me there are two rivers named Colorado. Austin's is a Texas river that empties into the Gulf of Mexico. While big, it's not nearly as large and long as the Colorado River that arises in the Rocky Mountains and flows all the way into the Pacific Ocean.''

Wade nodded. ''Anywhere near the river, though, we're fair game for mosquitoes this time of day.''

Mosquito bites were annoying rather than romantic. ''Just a walk around the town, then.''

As he escorted her from the dining room and out of the hotel, she found herself thinking of the mouse hole he'd discovered in his room. Could she ask him to come into her room and check for mice? That was plausible enough, but then what? She couldn't imagine flinging herself into his arms, even though she might want to. When she'd practiced flirtatious glances in front of her mirror earlier, she decided coquettes must be born that way, because she didn't seem able to get the hang of the languorous look. All she'd managed to do was to simper into the mirror.

Back in Coventry, she'd been rather flattered when Ezra Miller had told her what he liked best about her was that she wasn't a flirt. At the moment, though, she couldn't view that as a compliment.

Even Emma had a knack for come-hither glances—she'd cast more than a few at Floyd and look what had come of it. Of course, Emma had had marriage in mind, while she certainly did not. All she wanted was a way to keep Wade with her for the entire evening.

How about the entire night? Gambling halls probably never closed. Julia bit her lip.

''What's troubling you?'' Wade asked. ''You haven't said a word since we began this walk and now you're frowning.''

''I'm perfectly fine,'' she said, doing her best to sound convincing. If she weren't careful, the next she knew he'd be asking if he could help. Actually, the only person she could think of that might be able to come up with useful advice was the very person she was trying to keep him away from. Monette.

"I was just thinking," she said, choosing a subject at random, "how very different the capital of Texas is from those in the east."

"Why? We have a fine capitol building at the end of Congress Avenue—I'll take you to see it."

"We've already turned back," she said. "Another time, maybe. I really wasn't referring to your capitol building anyway. What I meant was Austin is more of a frontier town than a city."

"That'll come in time. Texas was on the wrong end of the War between the States, and that cost us. As Pop said, if they'd listened to old Sam Houston, we'd never have left the Union in the first place."

He went on discussing state politics and she listened with half an ear, intent on her own inner politics. Why was she so set on keeping Wade from Monette tonight? Was it merely because she wanted his company or did she have a different reason, one she wasn't facing up to?

Could the reason be that she couldn't bear to think he might hold Monette in his arms and kiss her? Make love to Monette as he had last night with her?

"No!" she cried.

"No?" he echoed. "You don't believe that one day Texas will be the wealthiest state in the Union?"

"Um, well, I could be wrong," she hedged.

"Kind of surprised you admit to it."

"I don't always insist I'm right," she countered.

He raised his eyebrows but kept silent.

A man riding by flicked his fingers toward his hat, calling, "Howdy, Wade. That the new missus?"

"Howdy, Reb," Wade said. " 'Fraid she's not."

"Knew she was too purty for the likes of you." Looking back over his shoulder, the man smiled at her.

"Have to watch out or he'll be calling on you," Wade said. "Reb Jackson's looking for a wife."

Hearing a note in his voice she couldn't identify, she asked, "Don't you like Mr. Jackson?"

He shrugged. "Friend of mine. Nothing wrong with him."

The man's last name had triggered an idea. "Instead of waiting until we return to the ranch, maybe when we get back to the Lone Star you'll make good on your offer to teach me to play blackjack."

"Could do that, if you like."

"I'm sure it's a game I'll enjoy."

He eyed her sideways. "Planning to turn into a gambler, are you?"

"One never knows," she told him, holding onto her hat as the rising wind caught at it. Dust swirled around her. "It surely does blow in this country, doesn't it?"

"Have to admit to that. Get used to it, though. Probably a good idea to go back to the hotel before you lose that pretty little hat of yours. Don't see many of them hereabouts. Most women wear bonnets."

"I would, too, if I were a Texan. The sun in your state is something fierce. Of course, I could carry a parasol—if I'd thought to bring one." She shot a quick glance at him to see if he'd find the mention of a parasol significant because of the elaborate one Monette had been carrying.

His expression didn't change; her shot had missed the target.

"Back East they call my hat a Dolly Varden," she added. "It's all the rage."

"See you're not wearing a bustle, though." He lifted a hand as though about to pat her familiarly on the place where a bustle normally sat. Evidently changing his mind, he dropped his hand without touching her.

Julia couldn't help but recall what he'd said about touching her: *You're the spark and I'm the tinder.* A frisson wriggled along her spine. How right he'd been!

"We could postpone the card game, if you like," she said, testing him. "I didn't think to ask if you had other matters to attend to. It was remiss of me."

"Nothing more important than teaching you blackjack."

Had she won a round or was he planning to visit Monette later, as she suspected he might? There was no way to tell at the moment.

At the hotel, they found the dressmaker waiting in the lobby with the finished clothes for the twins. Julia thanked her while Wade paid her. After she left, he asked the clerk for a deck of cards.

Carrying the package of clothes and the cards, Wade escorted Julia up the stairs.

"I have a table in my room," she said as they climbed, unable for the life of her to recall if his room had a similar table.

"I'll bring an extra chair from my room. As soon as you're ready, unlock the connecting door."

As she shut herself into her room she reflected Wade was most considerate, giving her time alone to refresh herself. After she'd washed the dust from her face and hands and tidied her hair, with great daring, she unlaced and took off her walking boots. After all, it wouldn't be the first time Wade had seen her in stocking feet.

Shortly after she unlocked the connecting door and set it ajar, Wade pushed the door open and carried his straight-backed chair in, placing it at the table at a right angle to hers. He seated her, then sat down himself and spread the cards on the table, face up.

"I take it you've seen a deck of cards before."

Julia nodded. "Great-aunt Polly was fond of whist and played weekly with several friends. Emma and I were expected to substitute if one or more of them couldn't come. But I remain an indifferent whist player."

He nodded, pushed the cards together and shuffled them. "First of all, there are the stakes," he said.

She blinked in confusion. "Stakes?"

"You can't learn a gambling game without playing for some reward. In this case, we won't use money. We can substitute matches, since we both have a box of them in our rooms. I brought mine along."

"So the matches become the stakes?"

He shook his head. "Some gambling halls have flat rounds of different colors they call chips. The chips represent money, each color is worth so much. The matches will represent whatever we decide our stakes will be."

"If not money, what?"

He smiled at her, one of those smiles that warmed her in forbidden places. "The winner gets to choose."

"I don't know . . ."

"Where's your gambling spirit? After all, you may win."

True. And then she could choose. She knew exactly what her reward would be. No Monette tonight, though of course she wouldn't mention the name.

"I guess that's fair enough," she said.

"Good. Now we draw for high card and the one who turns over the highest deals first." They did and he won the deal. "We'll play a few practice hands to begin with." As he dealt the cards, he went on explaining what the point of the game was and how to decide whether to hold onto the two cards you already had or ask to be dealt an additional one or more. "Remember," he finished, "if your cards add up to over twenty-one, it's a bust. You lose."

"This isn't nearly as complicated as whist," she said after a time. "It's really quite simple."

"There are various extras you can learn later, if you wish. Tonight we'll stick to the basic game, making twenty-one with your cards or beating the dealer's hand under twenty-one."

She supposed the Reverend Miller would be shocked at her learning a gambling game, but she found it fun. And they weren't playing for money, so it really wasn't gambling. Some things didn't seem as sinful in Texas as they had in Coventry.

After they began to play in earnest, sometimes she had more matches than he, sometimes he had more. The game seesawed back and forth until she hit what Wade called "a losing streak." Eventually every last match she'd had in front of her was piled with Wade's.

"I lost," she said mournfully.

"That's about the size of it. Sometimes you win, sometimes you lose."

She eyed him. "So that means you get the reward. Your reward."

"Yeah." He gathered up the cards and formed them into a neat deck, setting it at the center of the table. He then divided the matches and began putting them into their individual containers.

Julia had been determined to wait him out, but couldn't control her curiosity. "If I lose, you win," she said. "What is it you win?"

"I'll tell you as soon as I put everything away." Back went her matches onto the dresser near the lamp. Carrying his matches and chair, he vanished through the open connecting door.

When he returned, he had his hands behind his back, obviously hiding something.

"Well?" she urged.

"Keep in mind that you may decline, but, if you do, it's the same as owing me money. Sooner or later, you'll have to pay off the debt."

"Tell me!" she cried impatiently.

"As the loser, your penalty is to put on this nightgown." He whipped one hand around to the front to reveal her crumpled white nightgown.

She blushed, realizing she'd left it in his room. "That's not so difficult," she managed to say.

"Wait, I'm not through. To don the nightgown, you must disrobe first. You'll do all of this in front of me, with the lamp staying lit."

Julia drew in a shocked breath. "Undress in front of you? I couldn't possibly!"

"You have one other choice.' "

"What is it?" she demanded.

"To let *me* take your clothes off."

"Good heavens!"

Wade watched Julia's rapidly changing expressions with amusement. From the moment he'd caught a glimpse of her at the stationer's window after Monette had accosted him, he'd surreptitiously watched while she opened the door a tad to eavesdrop, then scuttled to the back of the store before he came in.

She had, of course, heard Monette invite him to French-ie's tonight. In view of her attempts to keep him occupied this evening, Julia obviously didn't realize that he'd had no intention of going. When he'd caught on to what she was doing, he made up his mind to find a way to turn the tables. He'd meant it to be a joke but then, with her request to learn blackjack, she'd handed him the chance to take things a step further.

Without warning, she snatched her nightgown from his hands. "You're no gentleman!" she cried.

"Then you shouldn't have gambled on me being one. Care to tell me what you would have demanded of me if I'd lost?"

"It certainly wouldn't have been to take your clothes off in front of me."

He grinned. "But I'm perfectly willing to. Sitting down on her chair, he eased one boot off, then the other.

"Don't you dare go any further."

"Not even my socks?" he asked, sliding them off.

"Stop it!"

"I might consider it, if you start paying off your loss." As he spoke, he began to unbutton his shirt.

"Don't—I mean I can't . . ." Her words trailed away as he yanked off his shirt.

"I promise I won't touch you." He unbuckled his belt.

"Wait, stop! I—I'll try."

He watched while, her color high, she fumbled with the tiny buttons at the front of her dress. There seemed to be a hundred of them, he thought, desire beginning to take precedence over amusement.

The top of the gown, separate from the skirt, opened at last to reveal a lace-trimmed undergarment he didn't know the name of. The sight of it, though, fueled his increasing need. He tried to catch Julia's eye but she was gazing determinedly over his head as she shrugged off the waist.

After releasing the fastenings of her skirt, she slid it down and stepped out of it. Her white petticoat, ruffled at the bottom, was tied at the waist. She took a deep breath before removing it, standing there in lace-edged white drawers that ended just below her knees and the frilly top—what did they call them, camisoles?—that concealed her breasts.

When she bent to remove her white stockings, his breath caught. In this position, her breasts were partly, teasingly revealed. Stockings tossed aside, she straightened and looked directly and challengingly at him.

He swallowed, gazing back with open desire. He was so consumed with wanting her, it was all he could do not reach for her and pull her into his arms. Since he'd promised he wouldn't touch her, he forced himself not to move.

Her gaze slid from his face down his body and her expression changed. Smiling slightly, she reached for the ties at the top of the camisole and ever so slowly undid them, deliberately teasing him now, he realized, which did nothing to cool him off. First one breast eased free of the garment, then the other—round and white with the pink-tipped nipples standing erect. He licked his lips.

Now nothing remained but the drawers. Would she never get them off? He was so aroused he could hardly breathe. When her drawers finally dropped to the floor and she stepped out of them, he took a step toward her.

Her eyes widened. "You promised not to touch," she said and he understood she meant to make him pay for what he'd made her do. He stood still.

She minced toward him and circled him, within arms' reach, infinitely desirable. By gritting his teeth, he managed to keep his hands at his sides. Stepping behind him, she moved closer, so close her nipples grazed his bare back. Easing around to face him, she smiled up at him.

"Now it's time for me to don my nightgown," she said throatily.

"Is it?" he rasped.

"I thought that was what you wanted."

"Changed my mind."

"Did you?" All wide-eyed innocence, the little tease.

Gazing into her blue eyes, lost to everything but her nearness, her scent enchanting him, he shucked his Levi's as fast as he could without doing himself an injury.

Her glance flicked down, then back up to meet his again.

"Don't you agree a nightgown might get in the way?" he murmured.

She replied by reaching out and touching his lips with her forefinger. "You did this to me once," she whispered.

He licked her finger and she drew in her breath. Grasping her hand, he kissed each finger in turn. "Wade," she breathed. "Oh, Wade."

His arms slid around her and he pulled her to him. His lips met hers in a deep, heated kiss, his need for her mounting with her eager response. Rather than diminishing his desire for her, what had happened last night had made him want her even more.

No man could ever tire of making love with beautiful Julia. Not that he ever meant to let another man near her.

Drunk with passion, he scooped her into his arms and strode to her bed, eased her down and lay next to her. He tasted each breast, her tiny, gasping moans heating him almost to the point of no return. He trailed kisses down to her thighs, easing her legs apart to reach his goal.

She gasped when his tongue touched her and arched to meet him. Overwhelmed, he rose above her and eased inside her welcoming moist warmth. All thought vanished, only feeling remained and the delight that her passion matched his.

Afterward he held her, reluctant to ever let her go. But then, he didn't have to—they had all night.

Julia lay contentedly in Wade's loose embrace. She was sure he'd thought he'd tricked her into making love, having no notion that was what she intended to have happen, if she could ever have figured out a way to begin.

She wondered if she would have felt the same if there'd been no Monette involved and smiled to herself. Maybe she wouldn't have faced what she wanted, but she certainly would have wished for last night to happen all over again.

Though undressing in front of him had been an ordeal, once she got started and saw how her disrobing affected him, she'd begun to enjoy tantalizing him. Being wanton could be quite a delightful pastime.

Not that she'd act in such a fashion with any man but Wade. Impossible! No other man could ever make her feel the way he did.

Had she suspected what would occur between them once they arrived in Austin? No, how could she, when she hadn't yet understood the magic between men and women? She did now and it made her wonder if this meant he was the only man in the world for her. She thrust the thought away for the present. As Great-aunt Polly would say, "Don't fret over the day that hasn't come."

She snuggled closer to Wade, happily aware the night wasn't yet over.

* * *

At daybreak, Jamie was waiting at the appointed meeting place, the two ponies in tow. They rode out of Austin, heading for the W Bar H. Heading for home.

On the way, Wade, true to his word, instructed her in the art of firing his carbine. He seemed to think she did pretty well, even though she hadn't hit anything she'd aimed at and had a sore shoulder to boot. At least she'd learned how to handle the gun.

Though the journey took just as long, somehow it seemed shorter to Julia, as she indulged herself with pleasurable remembrances. Every time she glanced at Wade she felt a tiny frisson and, if she happened to catch his eye and he smiled, a tinge of excitement as well.

By the time they neared the ranch, she was riding in a glowing haze, tired but happy. "Maybe we'll find Brownie waiting to greet us," she said.

"That don't look like Brownie," Jamie muttered, pointing at the approaching rider. "Trouble comes, boss."

Even from a distance she recognized Jack Crain and wondered at Jamie's words.

Jack turned his mount as he neared so that he rode next to Wade. "Sam Bass turned up again," he said. "The major sent a message. Rangers'll be by in the morning to pick you up."

Wade nodded. "Everything going okay here?"

"Nothing I can't handle," Jack said.

"Good." Wade went on to ask him about the hands out on the range and the two men discussed ranch affairs until they reached the corral and everyone dismounted.

Julia didn't mind until it became clear to her that Wade's entire attention had been diverted to the coming ride with the Rangers. He barely said two words to her before huddling with Jack for more discussion. Brownie, not Wade, escorted her as she carried her carpet bag and the box with the revolver to the house. Though she wasn't sure what she'd expected from Wade, it hadn't been a total ignoring.

Her warm welcome from Adelina and Silver Wing made her feel better. "The twins, they sleep," Adelina said. "I tell them you come with presents in the morning."

Silver Wing nodded. "They never sleep if they know you come tonight."

"Did everything go all right while I was gone?" Julia asked, wondering if they could read on her face what had happened in Austin.

When neither answered immediately, she came to attention. "What happened?" she demanded.

Adelina laid a hand on Silver Wing's shoulder. "When she go out to feed Brownie, Jack Crain, he bother her."

Julia fixed her gaze on Silver Wing. "What did he do?"

Silver Wing looked at the floor. "He try to touch me, I say no, he don't stop."

"Me, I don't let her go out no more," Adelina said. "I feed Brownie today."

"I'll see to it he doesn't try that again," Julia promised. As soon as she spoke, she realized with a sinking heart that Wade would be riding off with the Rangers in the morning. Leaving Jack Crain in charge.

Leaving it up to her to see to it that obnoxious man was kept in his place. Jack Crain had paid no attention to her admonitions in the past, he wouldn't be any more likely to now. On the face of it, the task seemed impossible. She'd have to tackle Wade before he left and insist he warn Jack to behave.

Julia went to bed too tired not to be able to sleep but she lay awake for a time, plagued by unhappy thoughts. She understood why the Rangers were after Sam Bass and Company—she wanted them captured as much as anyone else. But why did Wade have to go with him? Why couldn't he send some of the hands—Jack Crain, for example?

Though she tried to convince herself she was being unreasonable, she couldn't halt her increasing belief that to Wade she was of secondary importance. How easily he put her aside to ride away and leave the ranch in the charge of a man he knew she mistrusted. In a sense, he was leaving her with Jack Crain.

Love had never been mentioned between them, nor had she expected it to be. Surely, though, their nights in Austin must have meant something to Wade. She took a deep breath and rolled onto her side. Maybe not. Maybe she was the only one who felt a new closeness, who thought something vital had happened to bring them closer together. Heaven knew Wade was important to her. Apparently, though, she wasn't of equal importance to him.

Or was she of any importance at all?

Chapter 11

Julia rose before the sun, dressed hurriedly, and was just in time to catch Wade going out the back door. Controlling her upset because he hadn't bothered to tell her goodbye last night and couldn't have this morning if she hadn't made it a point to rise early, she said, "I must speak to you before you leave."

He nodded, glancing around—to see if Adelina was still in the kitchen, she knew.

"Adelina is tactful," Julia said. "She's stepped out. Not that she couldn't have heard what I have to say. It has to do with Jack Crain."

Wade sighed. "You're perfectly safe here on the ranch with Jack in charge."

How could he be so dense? "No, I'm not. Neither is Silver Wing. He tried to molest her while we were in Austin. Luckily she got away."

"I told you the girl was a problem," Wade said.

"Silver Wing is *not* the problem." Julia spat the words out. "Jack Crain is. He's insolent to me, as well."

"That's just his way, always joking. As for Silver Wing, she has to stay away from the ranch hands."

"All she was doing was going out to feed Brownie!" Julia cried. "Jack Crain was waiting and ambushed her. You must tell him to leave her alone."

"He's riding out to the range this morning. I'll have a word with him when I get back. Meanwhile, keep the girl in the house so he won't be tempted."

Julia stared at him in frustration. He didn't even come close to understanding; she shouldn't have expected him to. Not where his old friend Jack was concerned.

"At least I have the revolver," she muttered.

His puzzled frown told her he didn't have any idea what she was referring to. Then the frown faded and he nodded. "You mean in case Sam Bass and Company arrive unexpectedly. Don't worry, they steer clear of the ranches. And this time we mean to get them for sure."

She resisted the urge to pound him with her fists and shriek at him. Couldn't he see she'd meant Jack Crain?

"I'll be back soon," he told her.

"I certainly hope so. Adelina leaves in a week and I don't believe you've found a replacement."

"I'm letting her arrange for one. She knows her people better than I do."

"You might have told me. Now there's bound to be a gap between her going and another housekeeper arriving."

He shifted position, obviously eager to be on his way. "I was hoping you'd stay around to hold things together until Adelina's replaced."

How touching. He needed her to stay so she could fill in as his temporary housekeeper, not for any other reason. Not because he, personally, wanted her there.

"I wouldn't abandon the twins. Or Silver Wing, either, for that matter," she said sharply. If he thought she was going to add his name to her reasons for staying on, he was badly mistaken. At the moment she wished she'd never set eyes on him.

"You look ready to shoot someone," he remarked.

His first accurate observation this morning.

"I got to git," he added. "The major's waiting."

"Give him my regards," she said coolly. "And by all means, git." She turned and stalked from the kitchen, not wishing him to see the glitter of tears in her eyes.

She returned to her bedroom, determined not to cry. Wade Howland wasn't worth a single one of her tears. After straightening her bed covers and tidying her room, she opened the wooden box and lifted out the Beaumont-Adams revolver. Wade had filled the five empty holders with new bullets he'd bought in Austin.

Remembering the twins' curiosity, for safety reasons she decided not to load the cylinder, but she certainly would do so if Jack Crain proved to be the problem she expected him to be. Perhaps facing a revolver would convince him she wasn't about to allow him to trifle with Silver Wing. Certainly nothing else was likely to.

She'd leave the question of whether she would actually aim at him and pull the trigger unanswered until that problem had to be confronted.

Putting away the revolver, she unpacked the twins' new clothes and laid them in two neat piles on her bed. On top of each she placed a small and colorful Mexican doll she'd persuaded Wade to buy from a woman selling them down by the river in Austin. Each girl also got a new pencil from the stationers. She was saving the books for a later surprise.

When Nancy and Susan woke and came rushing into her bedroom, their delight lifted her spirits. Once they were dressed and fed, she told them about the ponies.

"We'll go and look at them this morning, but no riding until Papa Wade comes back from being with the Rangers," she said.

To Silver Wing, she said in a low tone, "Jack Crain is riding to the range today so it's safe to go out."

Even Adelina traipsed forth to view the ponies in their

section of the corral. "That one's mine," Susan said, pointing to the bay with the white mark on his forehead, the showiest of the two ponies.

Nancy's lower lip trembled. At that moment the dapple gray walked over to the fence and snuffled at her. "This one likes me," she said, brightening.

"It's good when horse chooses you," Silver Wing said.

"I like him, too," Nancy said. "What's his name?"

"Yours is Cloud and Susan's is Star," Julia said.

"Sky ponies," Silver Wing told them.

Later, when the twins were playing on the porch with their new and old dolls, Julia told Silver Wing what Wade had said, editing it slightly.

"He doesn't blame you but he feels you'll be safer if you stay in the house while he's gone," she said.

Silver Wing nodded. "I don't like Jack Crain," she said.

"Neither do I, but, unfortunately he's an old friend of Mr. Howland's."

"That man's heart not good. Man with bad heart no friend." Silver Wing spoke flatly.

Julia, recalling Jamie's odd comment about friends as they were heading for Austin, decided that he must feel the same way. It was something to remember. Perhaps he'd prove to be their ally against Jack Crain if push came to shove.

But Jack wasn't around today, so there was no cause to be anxious.

Later in the day, she showed the books to everyone. The twins were captivated by the pictures in theirs and each took a book to bed with her for their naps.

Silver Wing kept staring at the book Julia had chosen especially for her as though she couldn't believe her eyes.

Adelina looked on with approval. "It is good to read and learn. When I go from here, me, I miss you and the twins," she told Julia. "Silver Wing, too. Maybe when you marry Senor Wade, I come and see you."

Julia shook her head. "Adelina, we don't plan to marry.

But I will surely miss you after you're gone. No one can ever take your place."

"Me, I find you good woman to come here," Adelina assured her.

Julia hoped so. If not, she was condemned to remain at the ranch indefinitely. She'd come to accept Texas, heat and dust and all, she loved the twins and, more and more Silver Wing was beginning to seem like the younger sister she'd never had. And then there was Wade . . .

She knew she'd never forget him. He'd remain lodged in her heart for the rest of her life.

"What is love?" she impulsively asked Adelina.

The older woman's dark eyes rested on her with compassion. Covering her heart with her hand, she said, "Love, you feel here."

"My father say he never love other woman after my mother die," Silver Wing put in. "He say love come one time."

"Una vez, nada mas," Adelina said. "One time, no more, come great love of man for woman, woman for man."

"But how do you *know*?" Julia asked.

Silver Wing shook her head. "I can't tell what I never feel."

"I feel it once," Adelina said. "Ramon, he wish to be matador, to fight *el toro*. The bull, he kill my Ramon." She sighed. "Then I meet Jose. He say we marry. We have two girls. Me, I come to love Jose, but not the same. He die, I cry long time. Miss Jose. But Ramon, he still here." Again, she touched her heart.

Involuntarily Julia's hand covered her own heart, where Wade was stored. Was it love? How could she be sure? If she was in love with him, it was obviously one-sided. She hadn't really expected a farewell kiss, but he could have at least touched her hand. Or given her a fond look. Or words other than, "Got to git."

"Senor Grant, he die for love," Adelina said. *"Muy malo,* very bad. No good to be jealous."

"Wade told me about his brother," Julia said. "How terrible and how sad." *Jealousy*—could that be what she'd felt about Monette? She hoped not. It bothered her to even think it might be.

The day passed quickly and pleasantly, for the most part. So did the following one and the next. But on the fourth day, Jack Crain rode back to the ranch. Jamie, who'd been left in charge during his absence, came to the back of the house where Julia was sprinkling a small patch of nasturiums with left-over water from washing her underwear.

"Little boss come," he told her. "Keep Apache girl inside."

"By little boss you mean Jack Crain?" she asked.

He nodded, turned away, and headed for the corral.

Julia shouted for Silver Wing who'd gone to feed Brownie and the girl came running, with Brownie at her heels.

"Jack Crain's on his way back here," Julia said. "I do hope Wade is, too."

But he wasn't. Two days later, in the afternoon, the hands who'd ridden with the Rangers appeared, claiming the boss had sent them back to the ranch. Julia went out to question them but either they didn't know where Wade was or they weren't going to tell her. Maybe by Ranger order? Julia had no idea.

Jack Crain intercepted her as she was heading back to the house. "Heard you talking to the hands," he said. "They ain't gonna talk."

"I discovered that." She started to walk past him but he held up his hand.

"I know where the boss is," he said in a low tone.

Despite herself, she hesitated, waiting to hear, even though she wouldn't give him the satisfaction of asking him.

"Ain't Sam Bass keeping him away. Old Sam got caught, he did, that's why the boys come home. The boss stayed over in Austin." He eyed her with a smirk. "Know who's

there, don't you? Purtiest gal in Austin, bar none, name
of Monette, that's what's keeping him away.''

With the utmost effort, Julia kept from betraying her
shock. "Thank you for the information, Mr. Crain," she
said coldly and marched past him toward the house, trying
to ignore his snickering.

He was lying, he must be, she told herself firmly. He'd
made it up from the whole cloth just to plague her. She
shouldn't give credence to anything Jack Crain might say.
Wade was undoubtedly still with the major, making certain
all the outlaws were behind bars.

The trouble was she couldn't convince herself. It did
little good to remind herself that Wade was not tied to any
woman, including her, and he had a perfect right to see
Monette if he wished. Was he with her or not? If only there
were a way to find out.

Once in the house, Julia was upset to find Silver Wing
crying in a corner of the main room. "What's wrong?"
she asked, putting an arm around the girl. "Are you feeling
bad?"

Her sobs easing, Silver Wing pulled away and put her
hand over her heart.

Alarmed, Julia asked, "Are you in pain?"

Silver Wing shook her head and began to wipe at her
wet face with the heel of her hand. Julia handed her a
handkerchief to use.

"Always I live outdoors, use cabin for shelter and for
sleep. With my mother's people, the same. Make my heart
sad I must stay in house." Silver Wing sighed.

"I'm sorry you have to," Julia said. "But it's just until
Mr. Howland returns and speaks to Jack Crain."

"I don't belong here," Silver Wing said.

"Well, neither do I, but here we both are for the time
being. Other people depend on us and so we must make
the best of it. Think how much the twins need you. A few
more days and Adelina will be gone, I couldn't get along
without you being here to help." She patted the girl's

shoulder. "I know you must miss your father. Wouldn't he be proud to know you've learned to read? Come, let's hear you read a passage from your new book before the twins wake from their nap."

That evening, Brownie's barking heralded the arrival of Adelina's son-in-law riding in with a friend. In the flurry of Spanish that followed, Julia couldn't make out what caused the change in plans. It took a while before Adelina, translating, told Julia that, yes, he'd come two days early because he didn't want to ride alone and it was the only time his friend could go. They both were very tired and, if possible, would like to rest a day before escorting Adelina to Austin. They'd sleep on the porch.

"There might be room in the bunk house," Julia said uncertainly.

Adelina shook her head. "Porch is better. No fights."

Julia didn't argue, aware Adelina knew more than she did about what went on at the ranch. She suspected, though, that it might have to do with Jack Crain being the foreman. "Tell them they're welcome to stay," she said.

As it turned out, the friend was more than tired, he was sick, running a fever. Adelina dosed him with a concoction of what she told Julia was willow bark and made him as comfortable as possible on the porch.

At dawn the next morning, Julia was dressing when she heard Brownie barking. For a moment her heart leaped in anticipation, but then she realized the dog wouldn't bark at someone he knew, so it couldn't be Wade. A stranger approached.

She finished dressing and hurried to the kitchen. Adelina was just letting a stocky older man who looked vaguely familiar in the back door.

He doffed his hat. "Howdy, Miss Julia," he said. "Bet you don't recollect who I be. Name's Tyson, Ed Tyson."

"The man with the puppies," she exclaimed.

He chuckled. "See the twins got theirselves a dog, after

all. They sure did like those pups. Ain't seen you since the day you got here, you planning on staying on?''

That was where she'd seen him before—at the wedding disaster. ''Just until Mr. Howland can find a new house-keeper,'' she said. ''Adelina is going back to Austin to help her daughter.''

''That so? Well, the reason I stopped by, folks hereabouts do that when they be going in to Austin 'cause maybe a neighbor needs something and you can save him a trip. Wade sent a hand over to ask me when he went in but I was okay then. Now I got to go myself. I know he's off with the Rangers, thought maybe I could pick up anything you needed. Going to be a quick trip. Can't afford to stay over.''

''That's very kind of you, Mr. Tyson.'' Julia gave Adelina a questioning gaze.

''About out of honey,'' Adelina said.

''I'll get some for you. Anything else?''

Adelina shook her head.

''Well, then, be on my way. Long ride.'' Mr. Tyson had his hand on the door when Julia was seized with an irresistible impulse. If Wade was in Austin, this was the perfect chance to find out why.

''Wait, please,'' she told him. ''I've a mind to ride in with you.''

Adelina gaped at her and Mr. Tyson looked somewhat surprised.

''If you'd be so kind as to have someone saddle Dodie for me,'' Julia went on, ''I'll be ready in a matter of minutes.''

In her bedroom, she threw a change of clothes into her bag, crammed in the box with the revolver and donned her old brown riding habit.

Mr. Tyson was no longer in the kitchen. Julia hugged Adelina in farewell, saying, ''I'll be back tomorrow evening.''

''Me, I stay till you come back, no matter what,'' Adelina told her. ''Why you go?''

''There's something I have to do in Austin.'' Which was

the truth. She couldn't rest until she discovered whether
or not Jack Crain had been telling the truth.

Impulsive, she knew, but she couldn't help it.

At the corral, Mr. Tyson helped her onto Dodie,
mounted his rangy buckskin, and they left the ranch,
escorted by Brownie.

"Not great on looks, is he?" Mr. Tyson commented.
"Had a dog looked a lot like him once—best dog I ever
owned. Smartest, too."

"Brownie *is* smart. Now that he's met you, he won't
bark when you come to the ranch again. And, watch, he's
reached the limit of how far he'll go."

Proving her words, Brownie turned and trotted back,
leaving them to ride on alone.

"Called my dog Spot," Mr. Tyson said. "Not 'cause he
had spots but 'cause he could spot a bad 'un quick's a
wink. Never made a mistake. If old Spot didn't like a man,
that man was just plain no good. Saved me a heap of
trouble with hands."

"Brownie doesn't like Jack Crain," she said, without
thinking.

Mr. Tyson gave her a quick glance. "Sounds like you
don't care much for the feller, either."

"I don't."

"Some men never do learn how to get on with the
ladies," he said.

Deciding enough had been said about the subject, she
changed it. "I have to confess I don't remember you from
that rather upsetting day I arrived."

"Ma and me wondered at Wade setting the wedding on
the day his bride was supposed to get here. Seemed kind
of hard on the gal. Your sister, I heard."

"Yes. Emma ran off and got married at the last moment
and so the Reverend Miller persuaded me I should come
to Texas and explain to Mr. Howland what had happened."
She sighed, "It was a poor idea. I can't blame Wade for
thinking I'd arrived in Emma's place."

"Don't know what your sister's like, but Ma and me thought old Wade couldn't do much better than you."

"He's not interested in marrying me," she said primly.

"Too bad. Must be out of his head."

"To be fair, I'm not interested in marrying him, either."

"You could do a lot worse, Miss Julia. He needs a wife."

"To take care of the twins, yes, he does."

Mr. Tyson shook his head. "Not what I mean. Twins need a mother, sure, but Wade needs someone, too. A gal like you, someone with a little spirit."

"What was his brother Grant like?" she asked. "And Grant's wife, Teresa Sue?"

"Guess you heard what happened. We all figured Grant was going to do some man damage sooner or later, never thought it'd go that far. His wife was a sweet little gal. Too bad she didn't have enough gumption to set him straight."

"Jealousy is hard to overcome," Julia said. Hearing her own words made her flush. Isn't that why she was making this rigorous trip? Because she was jealous of Wade's interest in Monette? For the first time she felt a modicum of sympathy for Grant. To be jealous was to be unreasonable.

What she should do was turn around and ride right back to the ranch, leaving Mr. Tyson to go on alone.

"Before I married my Nell," he said, "I couldn't stand to see her so much as smile at another feller and I got all het up if she talked to one." He chuckled. "Nell cured me dang fast. Said she weren't about to marry a man who acted like a born fool. Said she weren't no calf I was fixing to buy, she was her own self, thank you, and if I didn't want to trust her, then she wanted no part of me. Comes down to trust, in the end."

He was right. Still, what reason did she have to trust Wade? They weren't on the verge of marriage, far from it. He'd made her no promises. So why was she riding to Austin?

Because, she realized, those nights in the Lone Star had been, in a way, a promise, at least as far as she was concerned. Did Wade feel the same? That was the real reason she was heading for Austin. To find out.

Then why had she brought her revolver?

"Wade is teaching me to shoot," she told Mr. Tyson. "He gave me a revolver. I brought it along in case we encounter trouble." That *was* the reason, wasn't it?

"Can't be too careful. Crain told me the Rangers got Sam Bass and Company but you never know when you might run into Comancheros. They ain't likely to hang out so close to Austin, though, so doubt if you'll need to use your revolver."

Of course, she wouldn't use it. Not unless they encountered outlaws, which seemed unlikely. Dwelling on outlaws reminded her of Les Slocum.

"Did Jack Crain say anything about Les Slocum?" she asked. "I'm wondering because I know Wade shot and wounded him a few weeks ago."

"Ain't heard a word about Les. Nor his brothers. They never rode with Sam, but they're bad 'uns, same as Les."

By afternoon, she was on first name terms with Ed Tyson and had been invited to come and visit him and Nell.

"Bring the twins, if you want," he added. "Our boys are growed, one's married. No grandkids, yet, though. Ma misses having little ones around."

She talked about the twins for a while, then they both fell silent until the increasing abundance of trees showed they were nearing the Colorado River—and Austin.

"You got a place to stay?" Ed asked. "Reason I'm asking, I don't like to think of a young lady alone in a hotel. I sleep over to Ma's sister's place. She's got plenty of room. You'd be better off there than a hotel."

Julia, who'd hadn't considered where she'd spend the night until they were well on their way, breathed a sigh of relief. She had very little money left and, to tell the truth, she'd be nervous alone in a hotel.

"Thank you for the offer," she said. "If you think I

wouldn't be putting your sister-in-law out, I'd like to stay there."

"Minnie don't meet many ladies from the East, she'll take to you like a cat to butter. Talk your arm off, maybe a leg, too." He chuckled. "Be doing me a favor, I won't have to listen."

Texas was full of friendly folk. Coventry was friendly, too, but only to its own. Strangers weren't well accepted until they'd been around for a year or so.

"I'll take you to Minnie's first thing," Ed went on. "You can leave your things there and go about what you need to do tonight. Or wait till morning. We won't leave real early, I got some errands first."

She agreed. Minnie lived not far from Congress Avenue, on a cross street named Mulberry, in a two-story frame house. Having passed the Dynasty and Frenchie's on the way, Julia was careful to take note of how to get back there.

Now that she was actually in Austin, she regretted the impulse that had driven her here. But she hadn't ridden all this way to back out of what she'd come to do.

Minnie—Mrs. Ventor—greeted her with the enthusiasm Ed had predicted. Plump and graying, she was a cheerful, motherly woman. Once she'd been shown to the bedroom she'd be occupying, Julia refreshed herself as best she could.

She'd worn the old riding habit because she thought it made her look less conspicuous. Except, of course, for the white hat and she hoped that wouldn't draw too much attention to her. Perhaps Mrs. Ventor might be able to lend her a darker hat.

"I've just the thing," the older woman said when she asked. "A brown bonnet that'll match your costume just wonderful. 'Tis an old one, you may keep it, if you like."

Julia hadn't worn a bonnet for a long time but, tying it on, she felt comforted by the way it covered and concealed her hair.

"You sure you'll be all right alone?" Mrs. Ventor asked

as Julia prepared to leave the house. "Ed's off on some business already, but my husband'll be home soon. He'd be happy to escort you."

"I'll be fine," Julia assured her. "I managed to travel to Texas all by myself."

"I want you to tell us about that at supper. You'll be back by then, won't you?"

Julia forced a smile. "I hope so."

She set off, fervently wishing she were back at the ranch, or better still, had never left Coventry. How simple life had been there. The boys she'd known—they had been boys, not men—had never caused her the misery she was feeling now. Probably because she hadn't really cared for them, except as friends.

Her feelings for Wade were so wildly different that she wasn't even sure how to classify them. He made her angry. Miserable. Happy. And when he took her into his arms . . .

No, she wasn't going to think about that. Not when chances were he had those same arms around Monette at this very moment.

But what if she were wrong? Julia smiled. Then she'd have ridden many weary miles to have herself proved wrong—and she wouldn't mind at all.

Chapter 12

Wade leaned back in the tin tub, luxuriating in the warm water. One good thing about the Dynasty, if you asked for a room on the first floor, you could have a bath. You had to carry in your own water and fill the tub—though someone would empty it for you in the morning.

How good it felt to get clean after all the riding they'd done tracking down Sam Bass. Chalk another one up to the Rangers. The Bass gang were all behind bars now except for Les Slocum, and nobody seemed certain whether or not he was still alive.

Wade could have ridden home with his hands but there was one little matter in Austin he needed to take care of first. Picking up the bar of sweet-smelling soap, he lathered himself, then used the cloth to rinse. I'll come out all scented up like a New Orleans madam, he thought, smiling.

Might as well smell good for what he was going to do, though. Better than the stink and dirt on him when he registered at the hotel.

He heard the snick of a key turning in the lock and sat

up abruptly, sloshing water onto the floor. Reaching to the chair next to him, he grabbed his Colt, aiming it at the door.

The door opened and he let his pent-up breath out in relief. Should have known who it would be.

"What kind of greeting is that?" Monette demanded with a suggestive pout. "Do you intend to shoot me with your big bad gun?"

Wade replaced the Colt on the chair. "What did you do, bribe the clerk for the key?" he asked.

"Merely called in a favor. Everyone owes me." Her sultry glance told him very clearly what she expected from him.

Wade stood up, grabbed the towel on the chair back, wrapped it around his waist and tucked it in. He stepped out of the tub and faced Monette who was handsomely dressed in a gold silk gown cut low enough in front to take any man's mind off the cards she was dealing.

"We have some unfinished business," he said.

"We certainly do have, *mon ami,*" she purred, reaching for the fastenings at the top of her gown.

Julia stood outside the Dynasty Hotel for several minutes, working up her courage to go inside after she'd realized that, as an unescorted lady, she couldn't possibly walk into Frenchie's. She doubted if even escorted ladies entered the gambling hall very often. A hotel was different. While an unescorted lady might raise eyebrows, it wouldn't be unheard of for the occasional woman traveling alone to need a room.

She discarded her original plan—to claim Wade was her husband or her brother and ask if he was registered—as a better idea occurred to her. Now all she needed was to force herself to walk through the door of the hotel.

"Need help, little lady?" a masculine voice said from beside her.

She glanced at the smirking man who asked the question, saw him reaching for her arm and all but bolted into the Dynasty to escape him. Hurrying to the desk, she asked, over the noise drifting through the swinging door into Frenchie's, if a room was available.

The elderly clerk looked her up and down, finally nodding. As she'd known he would, he pushed the register across the desk for her to sign. She scanned it quickly while pretending to fumble with the pen.

Wade Howland. His signature was scrawled opposite room number 10. A mixture of triumph, because she'd tracked him down, and despair, because he was here, rocketed through Julia temporarily rendering her motionless.

"Something wrong, Miss?" the clerk asked.

Gathering her wits, she said, "Goodness, yes. This hotel is far too noisy. I've decided not to stay here, thank you."

Outside again, she was relieved to see the man who'd accosted her was gone. Evening shadows were lengthening, soon it would be dark. Somehow she had to make her way to number 10, a room she felt sure must be on the first floor. She dare not parade past the clerk, so she must look for another entrance. Deciding there was probably a rear entrance leading to the stables, she skirted the square, three-story building, heading for the back.

Finding the rear door unlocked, she eased inside, stepping into a small vestibule that led into a corridor with doors to either side. No one was in sight but she felt terribly conspicuous as she ventured along the hall. Lamps in sconces lit the numerals on the doors. Number 10 was approximately half way along the corridor, to her right.

Taking a deep breath, Julia lifted her hand to knock, then held. What if he called out, asking who was there? She curled her fingers around the knob and gently turned it. The door opened.

"Oh!" she gasped.

* * *

Startled, Wade looked over Monette's shoulder at Julia standing in the doorway of his room, her face white with shock. "What the devil are you doing here?" he growled.

Without replying, she turned and fled. Wade started after her, remembered he was naked under the towel, and lunged for his clothes, ignoring Monette's loud demand to know who the little brown wren was.

Once dressed, he told Monette that he'd talk to her some time later. He strode into the lobby and asked the clerk if a lady dressed in brown had gone past.

The clerk shook his head. "Someone like that come in a bit ago wanting a room but changed her mind and left."

Clever of her, Wade thought. Saw my room number on the register and then sneaked in the back. But what the hell was she doing in Austin? He rushed out the rear door and checked the stable, discovering Dodie wasn't and hadn't been there. Where was Julia staying? Must be the Lone Star since she didn't know anyone in Austin.

When he didn't find her at the Lone Star, he stood in front of the hotel, shaking his head. He had no idea where to look next. Since there was little point in aimless searching through the streets, he began retracing his steps to the Dynasty. Before he reached the hotel, Fred, Frenchie's Negro bouncer, intercepted him.

"Miss Monette say to warn you. Three mean hombres alooking for you. She got the clerk to say you'd up and gone. Ain't safe hereabouts—best skedaddle and lay low. Got your horse and gear." He jerked his head in an invitation for Wade to follow him.

Hand on the grip of his Colt, Wade trailed Fred through an alleyway until they reached Thor, hidden in a dark niche. The gray was saddled and ready to go.

"Tell her thanks," Wade said as he mounted. "I owe you, Fred. Adios."

He turned the opposite way from the Dynasty and rode

through the alley until it led into a side street, his mind sorting through possible enemies. Three men gunning for him. The number clicked. Slocum had two brothers—so old Les wasn't dead. Bad news. Now what?

Damn that woman to perdition. Les knew Julia, and here they were, both in Austin. She'd have no way to know what danger she was in. He didn't have much choice except to leave a trail for the Slocums to follow, leading out of Austin, away from the W Bar H. That'd give her a chance to get back to the ranch without Les spotting her. She must be going back and she must have an escort—there was no way for her to have gotten here without a guide.

Come to see where he was, had she? He turned that notion over in his mind. Monette, she'd figured he was with Monette, otherwise why come to the Dynasty? Anger clenched his jaw. None of her blasted business what he was doing with Monette, why would she think it was?

Couldn't be any other reason—if anything was wrong at the ranch, Jack Crain would have sent a hand to notify him. Julia was damn lucky he hadn't caught up with her in the Dynasty. The way he felt right now he might just have wrung her neck.

Julia ran most of the way back to Mrs. Ventor's, arriving, to her dismay, in time for the evening meal. Not wanting to cause the Ventors or Ed any distress, she did her best to don at least a semblance of normality. After acknowledging her introduction to the man of the household, she joined them at the table and forced herself to swallow a few mouthfuls of food.

As soon as she possibly could, she excused herself, saying she was extremely tired.

"You're pale as cottonwood down, Miss Sommers," her hostess said. "Ain't sickening or something, are you?"

"No, all I need is a good night's sleep," Julia assured her.

"I won't keep you from that, then," Mrs. Ventor said. "Good night and sleep well."

Once in bed, Julia prayed for sleep, anything to obliterate this desolate emptiness within her. Why could she never leave well enough alone? With her eyes closed, the image in the Dynasty flashed before her—Wade, virtually naked, and Monette with her top half-undone, her breasts all but falling out of an inadequate camisole. Her sigh turned into a moan of pain. How could he?

Did their nights together in the Lone Star mean so little to him? If only she'd been more circumspect, nothing would have happened between them, she never would have given in to her mad impulse to ride to Austin with Ed Tyson and right now she'd be in bed at the W Bar H with an intact heart. Instead, here she was in Austin with her heart ready to break.

Sleep beckoned from so far off she couldn't reach it, no matter how she tossed and turned. When she finally did doze off she plunged into a frightening dream . . .

Julia urged her mare into a gallop, fleeing from a faceless pursuer on a black horse. Terror rode with her. Whoever, whatever he was, if he caught her, she was doomed. No one knew where she was, she didn't even know, except that it must be somewhere in Texas because of the paucity of trees and the endless rises and dips.

Dodie was as frightened as she, nostrils flaring, foam flecks around her mouth. Faces flashed past her—Jack Crain, with an I-told-you-so smirk, Ezra Miller, sadly shaking his head. Brownie materialized, snarling and snapping at the heels of the black horse, then all were left far behind.

In the distance, she could see a row of trees. If only she could reach the river, she'd be safe on the other side. How she knew this wasn't clear, but she was sure it was the truth. But relentlessly, inch by inch, foot by foot, the black horse and its faceless rider gained on her.

Putting on a desperate spurt of speed, Dodie stayed ahead. They were almost to the trees now and beyond would be the river and

safety on the other side. As they came closer, she saw no water lay
beyond the trees. To her horror, it wasn't a river but a railroad
track. No train was in sight. On the other side of the tracks waited
four mounted men with bandanas covering their faces.

There was no escape . . .

Julia woke with a start to grayness and a tapping on her door. "Time to rise and shine," Mrs. Ventor called. "Ed's up already."

Shaking shards of the unpleasant dream from her mind as best she could, she rose and began to dress. The sooner she left Austin behind, the better.

Mr. Ventor was at the breakfast table talking to Ed when she sat down.

". . . so it seems Les Slocum isn't dead, after all," he was saying. "Londo swears he saw him yesterday riding down Congress, healthy and mean as a hog."

"Les Slocum?" Julia said, her voice rising.

"In the flesh, along with his two brothers," Mr. Ventor told her.

She swallowed, consumed by a fear akin to what she'd experienced in her dream. Thank God they were leaving today. With luck, Les Slocum wouldn't see her. If he did happen to, maybe he wouldn't recognize her with the brown bonnet hiding her hair.

"Don't you worry none," Ed told her. "The Slocums are looking for bigger game than you and me. Most likely figuring on robbing a train, now that old Sam showed Les how."

Once they were on their way, Julia breathed a sigh of relief when they reached the edge of town. No longer would she have to expect Les Slocum to come riding out of the next cross street. Though it was true he could be anywhere, she felt better out in the open where she could see riders coming.

She'd taken the precaution of loading her revolver and leaving it in an open saddle bag, where she could reach it quickly, and this helped to allay her fear to some extent.

Ed, too, was armed—every man in Texas seemed to be—and so they weren't entirely helpless.

It wasn't until the sun was half-way up to the zenith that it occurred to her there might be another reason why the Slocums were in Austin. Wade had wounded Les—were they after him? She tried to calm her spurt of fear by reasoning that they couldn't know he was there. For all they knew, he was still with the Rangers or home on the ranch. But she remained in a state of anxiety for the rest of the ride back.

The sun was lowering when Brownie came to greet them, escorting them to the corral. Ed Tyson said goodbye to her there.

"Got to git for home," he said. "Want to make it afore dark. Ma'll worry if I stay over."

She bid him farewell, dismounted, and removed her bag, carefully placing the revolver inside. She was hefting out the bucket of honey when Jack Crain sauntered up.

"I'll take care of the mare," he told the hand waiting to see to Dodie.

"Notice you got yourself a revolver," he said to her.

Ignoring that, she said, "Les Slocum and his brothers were spotted in Austin. Les may hold a grudge against Wade for wounding him."

Jack's smirk faded. "Nasty bunch. You tell Wade?"

"I didn't see him," she lied.

"Them Slocums shouldn't bother him once he gets home. Too many of us at the ranch. By the way, you got company." The smirk returned. "Old friend from back east, name of Ezra."

"Ezra?" she cried. "Ezra Miller?" He was the last person she expected to see.

"Real greenhorn. Them easterners don't know diddly-do." He spat in the dust by her feet.

She hefted the bucket in one hand, her carpet bag in the other. "Thank you for taking care of Dodie," she said coldly and marched toward the house.

Ezra ran out and met her half way. "Julia!" he exclaimed, taking both bucket and bag from her. "Thank God you're back safely."

"Hello, Ezra," she said, pleased to see his familiar face. "Whatever are you doing in Texas."

He didn't answer immediately and, when they reached the kitchen, he had no chance. Susan and Nancy rushed to throw their arms around her. "Papa Wade come home?" Nancy asked.

"Not yet. Maybe in a day or two."

"Ezra come," Susan said, pointing at him. "He can read."

They didn't have a chance to talk until after the evening meal, since Ezra ate with the hands. Silver Wing shepherded the twins off to read to them, and Adelina shooed Julia away when she offered to help clean up.

"Last time I do this," Adelina said. "Pablo's *amigo*, his friend, is better, we leave in morning."

Julia and Ezra drifted off to the front porch and sat on the steps. "Doesn't feel much like a summer night in Coventry," he said.

She moved directly to the point. "You haven't told me why you're here."

"I came to bring you home with me, of course."

Julia said nothing for a time. Here was her way out. But should she take it or not? "I'm surprised your father agreed," she said finally.

"Oh, he didn't. I left divinity school and went to work for a farmer—been cutting hay or I'd have been here sooner—to earn some money. Didn't make a whole lot, but Grandma Miller left me a little in her will and there was enough to pay for the trip here . . . and back, for both of us."

"You left divinity school?"

He nodded. "I don't have the call, so I decided God

had some other plan in mind for me. I thought about it and figured maybe He wanted me to come to Texas and find you."

She could leave with Ezra right away and be gone by the time Wade returned. Except that Adelina would be gone, too. She couldn't desert Silver Wing.

As if her thinking about the girl inspired Ezra, he said, "Silver Wing is awfully shy, isn't she?"

"She doesn't know you very well."

"I suppose. You know, she's the prettiest girl I've ever seen." Belatedly, he added, "other than you, I mean."

"Ezra," Julia said carefully, feeling her way, "what do you think about Silver Wing?"

"What do you mean? I just told you—she's shy and she's beautiful."

"Um—she is half Apache, you know."

"She told me. I think that's very interesting."

Julia eyed him. Ezra had always been easy to read and she could tell he was perfectly sincere now. His attitude toward Silver Wing was so entirely different from the ranch hands', she couldn't quite believe it. Perhaps she'd been away from Coventry too long.

"Adelina told me Silver Wing couldn't go outside because some of the men bothered her," he continued. "I mean to confront any man who so much as looks sideways at her. She's a lovely girl, sweet and innocent, and she shouldn't have to put up with that sort of thing."

Silver Wing had certainly made quite an impression on Ezra, in a very short time. "Um—the ranch hands are rough and ready Texans," she said. "I'm afraid they view her as a half-breed—which makes her, in their eyes, fair game."

"You can't believe that!"

"No, but they do. I'm just trying to explain the situation."

He clenched his fists. "No one better dare to touch so much as her little finger as long as I'm around."

Julia didn't bother to point out that he wouldn't be around long enough to make any difference. "Things are different in Texas," she said. "Both good and bad. How did you get here anyway. It's a long walk from the railroad station."

"I sent a telegram. Mr. Crain got it yesterday and came to the station and picked me up in the buggy today. He told me there was room for me to sleep in the bunkhouse."

Ezra in the bunkhouse? Julia knew well that Jack Crain didn't do anything out of the goodness of his heart. Not a drop of the milk of human kindness ran in his veins.

"I can tell you don't think I'll fit in there," Ezra said. "I've changed, Julia. When you work on a farm you learn a lot."

"This isn't the same as a farm back east," she said and then let it drop.

Ezra had always been bull-headed. If he'd made up his mind to sleep in the bunkhouse, that's what he'd do, no matter what she said.

"I can't leave until Wade—Mr. Howland—comes back from Austin," she said. "Even then, if he doesn't bring a housekeeper with him, I'll have to stay on until Adelina arranges for one to replace her."

She expected him to protest. Instead, he said, "You're quite right. We can't leave Silver Wing at the mercy of ignorant men."

Silver Wing again.

"The way she takes care of those two little girls tugs at my heart," he added.

Tugged at his heart? Ezra did tend to extravagant expressions of emotion—she'd forgotten about that.

"When I first set eyes on her," he said, "it was like getting struck by lighting."

Julia began to wonder just what Ezra planned for her if she went back to Coventry with him. Certainly not marriage, not if he could go on about another girl in this fashion. In any case, she couldn't marry him. It was too late and all Wade's fault.

"I take it you don't mind staying around for a few more days," she said dryly.

"Not at all. It'll give me the chance to find out how a ranch is run."

"You don't intend to go to work with the hands?" she asked in some alarm.

"Why not? I mean to earn my keep while I'm here."

"But you're a—a greenhorn." She used Jack Crain's word because she didn't know another as descriptive.

"I can learn. After all, Julia, I'm a grown man."

She still thought of him as a boy, but perhaps she was wrong. Defying his father seemed to be a step in the right direction.

"Emma sends her best wishes and wants you to write her," Ezra said. "She thought you might marry Mr. Howland so he wouldn't be too disappointed about her failure to fulfill her promise to him. I told her, not Julia, she's got a mind of her own. None of us could understand why you didn't write or return, though. Now that I'm here, I can see the problem. We knew nothing of the twins, of course."

As if his mention evoked them, Nancy and Susan spilled out onto the porch. "Ezra read," Susan said.

Silver Wing appeared in the doorway. "They won't go to bed," she said.

"After Ezra read," Nancy announced.

"At your service, girls," he said, his gaze fixed on Silver Wing.

Smitten, sure enough, Julia told herself, aware than he'd never looked at her in just that way. She felt a bit sorry for him. Nothing could possibly come of it, any more than could come from her being smitten with Wade.

Because she was, there was no denying it. Furious as she was with him—how could she ever forgive him?—leaving him would be a wrench she'd never get over.

And she'd have to leave once the new housekeeper got here. Then there'd be no possible excuse for her to stay any longer. Ezra had come to fetch her? Very well, she'd go back to Coventry with him.

Actually, boy or man, she was glad he'd arrived. Otherwise, when Adelina left tomorrow morning with her son-in-law and his friend, she would have been left alone with Silver Wing. Wade was still gone, so Jack Crain was in charge. She didn't trust the man as far as she could see him. True, she had the revolver, but if it came to shooting him—could she?

Ezra might be a slender reed to depend on, but he was on her side. Maybe a little more on Silver Wing's than hers, actually. She just hoped it wouldn't come to a standoff, Ezra against Jack Crain, because it was a foregone conclusion the bad guy would win.

Which reminded her of Les Slocum. Wade would be traveling back to the ranch alone. The thought frightened her. What if he didn't know the Slocums were around? Even if he had heard, he was one against three. What chance would he have?

Julia rose from the steps and went slowly into the house. No matter what he'd done, she couldn't bear to think of him being killed. And all because of her. It was her fault and hers alone that Les Slocum was gunning for Wade. If Wade died, it would be her fault.

She blinked back tears, suddenly aware of how much he meant to her. She'd rather die herself than see him shot down.

She stopped in her tracks, the truth shooting through her like a fiery arrow. Smitten was far from the right word. No longer did she have to ask about and wonder about love. Love had her by the throat and wasn't about to be shaken loose. Never mind what he'd done, never mind that she'd never been so angry at anyone in her life, she was in love with Wade Howland . . . and there was nothing she could do about it.

Chapter 13

Wade woke before dawn in his night camp along the Colorado. Not only was he still on the wrong side of the river as far as getting back to the ranch went but also some miles farther southeast than he should be. He'd spent the night hiding in the Mexican part of town down by the river and, early in the morning, succeeded in drawing the Slocums after him by parading along Congress, first up toward Capitol Square and then down toward the river as though he hadn't a care in the world. When he was sure they'd spotted him, he crossed the bridge over the river.

He'd fled west with them in pursuit. Thor could outrun any horse except maybe Sam Bass's fabled Denton mare. Much later, he'd lost them by hiding in a pecan grove until they thundered past. He'd then doubled back and circuitously began traveling north, taking care to keep to cover as much as possible.

When, exhausted, he'd stopped to sleep, it was evening and he'd gone past Austin, still on the east side of the river. He'd chosen a hill back from the river with a few trees straggling up it, a spot not as comfortable as flat land but more defensible. Reason told him the Slocums also must have camped somewhere for the night, but there was no way to be certain they hadn't figured out his ruse. If they had, they'd be tracking him again, figuring that sooner or later he'd have to cross the river to get home. There were no other bridges except the one in Austin, only fords, and damn few of those.

If I were the Slocums, he told himself as he chewed a strip of jerky for breakfast, I'd have one brother up a tree acting as lookout and the others waiting in ambush at a ford.

Which ford would they choose? And which side of the river were they on? Since he didn't know the answer to either question, the only solution, since he had to cross eventually, was to get himself on the other side now, while he still had the grayness of early morning for cover. Never mind that the Colorado ran swift and deep here, he really didn't have a choice.

As he cinched on Thor's saddle, he talked softly and affectionately to the gelding. Everything depended on Thor. While he let the horse pick his way down the rise, directing him toward the river, another thought occurred to him. If the Slocums were smart enough to figure he'd doubled back to go home, they still wouldn't know whether or not he'd used the bridge at Austin to get back to the west side of the Colorado. But if they decided he had, they'd surely have crossed over, too.

In that case, the ambush wouldn't be at a ford and he could go on to the next ford more or less safely. "To hell with it," he muttered. "We'll chance getting across here."

Thor plunged down the bank into the water, finding footing for a few moments, then struggling through deep water, fighting the current as he made for the opposite bank. At last the horse inched his way to the bank and climbed up onto firm footing some ways downstream. Wade let him rest, patting his neck and murmuring to him. They were on their side of the Colorado, now all they had to do was get home safe.

If the Slocums had crossed at Austin and were on this side, they might have camped for the night ahead of him. He scanned his memory for places where an ambush might be possible. He couldn't come up with any really good spots—once you rode away from the river, the land was too open to be able to hide well. They didn't really need an ambush, though, since there were three of them and only one of him.

He urged Thor out of the trees, heading away from the river toward the unmarked trail to the W Bar H. He didn't know they were ahead of him, they might not be . . . have to take his chances, he couldn't sit here all day.

Motion ahead of him sent his hand to his Colt. A better look showed a closed-in wagon pulled by a sway-backed gray horse. As he neared, Wade saw the wagon was painted white, with red lettering saying: PROFESSOR M.G. WILKES AND HIS CURE-ALL ELIXIR.

An idea striking him, Wade rode up to the wagon, then slowed Thor when he came even with the driver, a tall, thin man with a long black beard threaded with gray. "Howdy, professor," he said.

"Good morning, sir," the man replied, doffing his stove-pipe hat for a moment.

"Would you mind stopping?" Wade continued. "I have a proposition for you."

"If it means an increment in my sadly depleted funds, I shall be delighted," the professor said.

"If you can be of use to me, I'll be of use to you," Wade promised.

The professor pulled up his horse. Wade paused to scan to either side, in back and in front. No riders were visible. "I notice your wagon is set up for two horses," he said.

"Alas, old Ben gave up the ghost last week. Bess, here, does her best, but she's getting on, like all of us."

"Still have the second harness?"

"I do. Why do you ask?"

"My gray here's reliable and steady. Never pulled a wagon but if I hitched him up and coaxed him along, he'd do it for me."

The professor raised his eyebrows. "Are you offering to lend me your horse to help Bess pull my wagon?"

Wade nodded. "I have a reason."

"I suspected as much. Lay it before me, sir, and we shall try to reach an agreement."

Wade explained his problem as simply as he could. "And so, professor," he finished, "it looks like my best chance to stay alive. In return, you may set up on my ranch. I'll send some of my hands to the neighboring ranches and you'll have a chance to sell your elixir to those who come to see what it's all about. That's providing you can assure me it's not poisonous."

"Wouldn't harm a babe," the professor said. "Never has. I'd have been hanged long ago if anyone died from what I sell. Plus the Lord would not approve, not at all. I agree to your terms, sir. Shall we get to work?"

Thor was not enthusiastic about being hitched to a wagon. Bess's placidity as well as Wade's soothing murmurs helped calm him, but it was clear he didn't like what was happening. After the professor started off again, Thor realized he had to move with Bess or be thrown off balance, so he complied. Wade walked beside him until he could see Thor was resigned to this new chore.

Hurrying back to the wagon, he leaped onto the seat, opened the closed door behind the professor and entered the inside. He'd been shown a concealed niche when he hid his gear in here and now he made sure he could fit into the niche. Edging out again, he braced himself against the roll of the wagon to peer through the peep holes cut here and there.

Time passed slowly. He had no idea how long it was before he caught sight of a rider cutting across the wagon's path, shouting, "Hold up there, old man."

It wasn't Les but it could be a Slocum—he didn't know the brothers. Wade ducked into the niche as the professor halted the wagon.

"What may I do for you, sir?" the professor asked.

"Seen any riders along the way?" the man asked.

"I didn't pass any, not with this old rig," the professor told him.

"Asked ya if you seen any, not did ya pass any."

"Not any riders, no. Near daylight, though, I passed a man hunkered down in a night camp by the river. Might not have seen him if he hadn't hailed me, asking did I have salve for a lame horse. I offered him some of my elixir—wonderful for curing man or beast—but he didn't want any."

"What color horse?" the man said.

"I happen to remember that because the horse was gray like my pair, old Bess and Ben. A bit lighter in color, as I recall, but definitely a gray."

"Near daylight, you say?"

"That is correct, sir. Just enough light to see fairly well."

"Did he mount up?"

"He did, sir, just as I was pulling away. He appeared to be heading in the direction of Austin."

"Whatcha got in the wagon?"

"My elixir and the equipment for preparing it—also my living quarters as I have no other home."

"Mind if I take a look inside?"

"Not at all, sir. I'd be delighted to show you my elixir and, perhaps, sell you a bottle. I can assure you that any ill you might suffer will miraculously—"

"Yeah, okay, never mind. Where you headed?"

"I understand there's a small settlement up a ways along the river called Braxton. No doubt the folks there, being a good ways from Austin, have little chance to visit a doctor. I feel certain my elixir will prove to be a godsend to them. You have no conception how many diseases can be cured by the purchase of even one bottle of this marvelous concoction. Many folk swear by it. There was a man over in east Texas who—''

"On your way, professor," the man said.

The wagon started with a jerk and rolled on, but Wade stayed where he was until he was sure it wasn't a trap meant to flush him out. When he finally looked out one of the peep holes in the rear of the wagon, he couldn't see any riders following. Nor were there any in sight when he checked all the peep holes.

The driver's door creaked open and he froze, reaching for his Colt.

"They're not following," the professor said.

Wade made his way to the front of the wagon. "I heard only one man."

"I spotted two others, one to each side of the trail."

"Can't be sure they won't come back," Wade said.

"Then perhaps you had better remain under cover while you direct me to your ranch."

The professor had a point. Wade made himself comfortable and tried not to fall asleep. Despite himself, he kept dozing off and jerking awake, then looking out to see where they were, so he could keep the wagon on the right trail. He'd make better time if he unharnessed Thor and rode ahead but he didn't want to take any chances.

He was as brave as the next guy, but three against one were not good odds. At least Julia should have gotten back to the ranch safely—he'd given her a day by decoying the Slocums. He still didn't understand why she'd decided to track him down in Austin.

If she thought he was going to explain what he'd been doing at the Dynasty, she was badly mistaken. His affairs were not hers. It was past time she learned to mind her own business, not to mention control her wild impulses.

The professor's call of "Riders ahead," put him on alert again. "It seems to be two men and a woman," the professor added. "They look like Mexicans to me."

Wade eased his hand off his Colt and peered through

the front peephole. Mexicans, right enough. Something
familiar about the woman. He looked closer and shook
his head. Hell of a note to forget what was going on at
your own spread. It was Adelina Mendoza, heading for
Austin with what must be her son-in-law and an outrider.

"It's okay, professor," he said through the closed door.
"That's my housekeeper. Don't want her to see me in case
they meet the Slocums. You can't be forced to tell what
you don't know."

The Mexican men greeted the professor and rode past.

With Adelina gone, Julia had full responsibility for the
twins and all the work to be done in the house. If she was
there. She must be. Adelina wouldn't have left Silver Wing
alone in the house, would she?

The sooner he got there, the better.

Dusk was settling in by the time Wade, dozing again,
heard Brownie barking. He rose, pushed open the driver's
door and sat beside the professor, calling to the dog.
Brownie immediately quieted down. Instead of trotting
beside the wagon though, he suddenly perked up his ears
and streaked back toward the ranch buildings.

Tensing—was something wrong?—Wade concentrated
on listening. A woman screamed. A man shouted. He
leaped down from the wagon and ran toward the sounds,
hearing grunts and thuds as though men were fighting.
The sharp crack of a revolver startled him. What the hell
was going on?

The twins, playing on the porch with their dolls, took
it into their heads to go see their ponies, even though they
knew they weren't to go to the corral alone. The first
Julia realized what they were doing was when Silver Wing,
helping her in the kitchen, suddenly ran out the back door
calling, "Nancy! Susan! Come back."

Julia stopped stirring the pot of chicken soup and started
after her. At the door she hesitated, hurried into her bed-

room and came out with the Beaumont-Adams revolver. She'd loaded it after Adelina left that morning, putting it well out of reach of curious little hands. The reason wasn't so much that she knew Les Slocum was alive and on the loose as because she didn't trust Jack Crain.

Plucking a dish towel from the rack as she passed through the kitchen, she draped it over her arm to conceal the revolver. No point in appearing to be a fool. But she didn't intend to be anywhere near Jack Crain without it.

As she neared the barn, she saw that Ezra, who'd been working around the barn and corral all day, was collecting the twins. She also noticed that Jack Crain had cornered Silver Wing and was edging her into the barn.

Ezra saw what was happening at the same time she did and turned the twins loose. Silver Wing's scream scared them into running toward Julia and she turned, herding them ahead of her to the house.

"Go to your room," she ordered, "and don't come out until I say so."

Frightened, they obeyed.

Julia ran outside again, hearing Jack Crain's shouted curse as she rushed back toward the barn. She pulled up short when she saw Ezra and Jack pummeling each other while Silver Wing cringed against the side of the barn.

"Get in the house," Julia yelled at her. "Take care of the twins." Silver Wing didn't move, staring at the two men.

Julia crossed to her, grabbed her hand and pulled her away from the barn. "The twins," she cried, giving her a shove toward the house. "Go to them."

The girl blinked at her, took a few steps, then broke into a stumbling run. Satisfied Silver Wing would be safe in the house, Julia turned her attention to the fighting men. To her dismay, Jack had knocked Ezra down and was preparing to kick him.

"Stop!" she screamed, flinging aside the dish towel. "Don't make another move, Jack Crain, or I'll shoot."

He glanced at her, saw the revolver in her hand, and froze. As Ezra scrambled away from him, somehow her finger tightened on the trigger. The gunshot took her by surprise. She gasped, her gaze fixed on Jack Crain. Had she shot him?

At that moment Brownie ran up and began growling at Jack.

"You damn little bitch!" he snarled, to all appearances unwounded.

"Hold everything!" Wade's sudden appearance, on foot, startled them all. "Mind telling me just what the hell's going on here?"

"She shot at me." Jack said before Julia had a chance to speak. "No reason."

"I had a reason!" she cried. "You were molesting Silver Wing."

"I engaged him in fisticuffs, sir," Ezra put in, one hand to his bloody nose. "He had no right to harm—"

"Who in blue blazes are you?" Wade demanded.

"Ezra Miller from Coventry."

"The kid jumped me," Jack said. "I was just defending myself."

"Ezra was trying to protect Silver Wing," Julia cried, waving her arms in agitation. "Jack knocked him down and was starting to kick him."

"Julia." Wade's voice was low but firm. "Julia, calm down. Give me the revolver. Now."

Only then did she remember she was holding it. She did as he asked. He pulled the cylinder out. "Okay. Take Ezra to the house and tend to the bleeding. I'll—"

At that moment a closed-in wagon, sides and top painted white, rattled up to them and stopped. "Professor Wilkes, at your service," the driver announced.

Julia gaped at him and the wagon. If she weren't mistaken, Thor was one of the two horses pulling this remarkable contraption.

"The young man appears to have a nose bleed," the

professor said, stepping down to the ground. "Allow me, son."

He led Ezra to the wagon step, sat him down and made him tip his head back. "Now pinch your nose—hard, mind you—between your thumb and forefinger and hold it there," he ordered.

Glancing about, he asked, "Any more wounded? I do believe I heard a gunshot."

"She missed me," Jack muttered. "By a hair."

"I'll talk to you later," Wade told him. "Unhitch Thor and take care of him. "Julia, I'll talk to you now—in the house."

Leaving Ezra with the professor, Julia walked ahead of Wade to the house. In the kitchen, Silver Wing was stirring the soup with both twins clinging to a handful of her skirt.

"Papa Wade!" they cried in unison and flung themselves at him.

Finally gathering her wits enough to remember she was temporarily the cook and that Wade was probably hungry, Julia said to him, "I've made chicken soup. Would you like some?"

He was starved. Temporarily putting aside sorting out the melee, he nodded.

"Eat with Papa Wade," Nancy announced, Susan echoing her.

"Let them," Wade told Julia. "Silver Wing can serve us. You go put this away." He handed her the Beaumont-Adams.

He attacked the bowl of soup with relish and had a refill. Temporarily satisfied, he waved away offers of anything else, ordered the twins to finish their soup and, when Julia returned, led her into the main room.

"Let's hear it from the beginning," he said.

"The twins were on the porch—"

"Beginning in Austin," he interrupted.

"Oh, Austin. Um—I rode in with Ed Tyson."

"Why?"

He watched various expressions flit across her face before she finally blurted, "Because you didn't come home. Jack Crain told me where you were and I didn't believe him so I went to see for myself." She glared at him defiantly. "He was right."

"Believe what you wish."

"I believe what I saw!"

"I suppose you realize you put yourself in harm's way again."

She looked puzzled for a moment before saying, "You mean from Les Slocum? I didn't know he was even alive until I heard about it in Austin. I hope you didn't run into him."

"Why do you think I rode home in the professor's wagon? Another thing—what's Ezra Miller doing here?"

"He arrived before I got back from Austin. He came to take me back to Coventry."

Her words hit Wade like hammer blows.

"But I'll stay until your new housekeeper arrives," she added. "That is, if you promise to keep Jack Crain in his place."

"And just where is that?"

"As overseer, or whatever you call him. He has no business trying to molest Silver Wing."

As usual, she had him off-stride. "What was she doing by the barn in the first place? I thought I told you to keep her in the house."

"I started to try to tell you—she ran after the twins, who were heading for the corral all alone."

"How did Ezra get mixed up in it?" he asked.

"He's smitten with her. Not like Jack, in a nasty way. Ezra is a worshipper from afar."

He must be more tired than he realized, Wade thought, because none of this made sense. "I thought Ezra came to take you to Coventry to marry."

"I said take me back with him, not marry me. I have no intention of marrying him. Or anyone."

For some reason he suddenly was able to breathe easier.

"I still have to get a meal on the table for the hands," she reminded him.

"We'll feed the professor, too, while he's with us," he told her.

"Very well. About Ezra. He's sleeping in the bunkhouse and helping out in the barn and corral. The hands tease him but don't mean him any harm. How about Jack Crain, though? Won't Jack bear him a grudge?"

"Plan to have a talk with them both. Right after we settle the matter of what you do and don't do with a loaded revolver."

She looked him in the eye. "I know what I did wrong. I wasn't careful with the trigger and I pulled it without meaning to. I didn't really intend to shoot at Jack Crain, just scare him into behaving decently."

"You were also waving that revolver around without regard to where it was pointed."

Biting her lip, she said, "I guess I got excited. With cause."

"I want your promise that you won't touch this revolver again unless you need to shoot it to protect yourself or someone close to you against real danger."

"All right. I promise. But you have to do something about Jack Crain."

One thing about Julia, she never let up. "Told you I'd talk to him. Ezra, too. Can't have bad blood among the hands." He handed her the Beaumont-Adams.

"You've unloaded it," she said, "and I don't have any more bullets."

He handed her the four he'd removed. "I'll give you more later."

As he watched her leave the room, he couldn't help admiring the way she carried herself—straight and proud. Somehow it appealed to him more than Monette's deliberately provocative backside wiggle.

* * *

Outside, he found Ezra, nose bleed staunched, talking to the professor who was tending to old Bess.

"But if you're an ordained minister, sir, what are you doing selling this elixir?" Ezra asked.

"A man grows weary of preaching about the Lord to souls who won't listen," the professor said. "I find it refreshing to travel over the country seeing new places and meeting new people. If, on occasion, someone asks me to hold a service, I do so, but my living depends on my cure-all elixir." He turned to Wade. "If you're looking for your foreman, I believe he's taking care of your gray."

Wade nodded his thanks. "When the dinner bell sounds, you're welcome to join us for the evening meal," he told the professor before fixing his attention on Ezra and saying, "Want to talk to you. Let's take a little walk."

When Wade was sure the two of them were out of earshot of any possible listeners, he stopped. Ezra also halted, and Brownie, who'd been walking with them, trotted back toward the professor's wagon.

"Got a rule on the W Bar H," Wade said. "No fighting. Don't care what you do when you go into town but no fighting on the ranch. You get one warning, after that you're gone."

"He was trying to pull her into the barn," Ezra protested. "Silver Wing, I mean. She was screaming—someone had to protect her."

Wade had no doubt the girl was afraid of Jack, but that wasn't the point. "My rule still holds."

Ezra shifted position but didn't drop his gaze. "I'll try my best, sir. But if Silver Wing—"

God save him from these Coventry easterners. "Jack won't be bothering her again."

"Then you can count on me obeying your rule," Ezra told him.

Wade nodded. "Understand you came to take Miss Sommers home."

"I did. If you don't mind, I'll stay on until the new housekeeper arrives and Julia's able to go. I'll earn my keep doing odd jobs or whatever you'd like me to do."

"You're welcome to stay. I'm sure Adelina will be sending us her replacement very soon." He started to turn away.

"Uh, sir?" Ezra said, stopping him. "Would you mind if Silver Wing went with us?"

Wade raised his eyebrows. "To Coventry? She'd be more out of place there than she is here. Best place for her is with her own people."

"If you mean the Apache, sir, I beg to disagree. Julia tells me her father was a white man, one of us. So aren't we her people as much as the Apache?"

Wade sighed. "She's a half-breed, an inbetween. Truth is, she doesn't belong anywhere."

Ezra's face took on a stubborn set. "I can't accept that. She's a child of God, as we all are."

"No argument there, but some of us are more fortunate right from the day we're born than others. May not be fair, but it's true."

A light came into Ezra's eyes. "Yes," he murmured. "Yes. Now I know why the Lord chose to direct me here."

Chapter 14

Wade's talk with Jack didn't go well. Jack argued rather than agreeing to watch his ways.

"You been listening to that little blond bitch too much," Jack finally accused. "Softening you up, that's what she's doing."

"Leave Julia out of this," Wade ordered, his gorge rising. "And be careful what you call her."

Jack shrugged. "If you say so. Must be getting some off her to make you—"

"Shut your damn mouth!" With great difficulty Wade kept from taking a swing at his old friend. "No more discussion. Either abide by the rules or get out. Understand?"

Jack shot him a dark look before stalking from the barn. Wade slowly followed him out. Hell of a thing when a man can't have a reasonable talk with a friend. But Jack had no right to malign Julia, none at all.

* * *

The next day, Wade honored his promise to the professor by sending a couple of hands riding to neighboring ranches with invitations to attend an afternoon feed two days from now and hear Professor Wilkes discuss his cure-all elixir. Being a minister, the professor would also baptize babies if that service was needed.

Julia and Silver Wing were thrown into a frenzy of food preparation, even though the main course would be a steer roasted outdoors on a spit by the man who took care of the cook wagon on the roundups. Ezra proved of great help when he offered to teach the twins to ride their ponies, thus keeping them from underfoot.

The evening before the party, Julia, stepping out onto the porch in the early evening, came upon Ezra and Silver Wing sitting close together on the steps, holding hands. She retreated without disturbing them, certain the girl was perfectly safe with Ezra.

She checked the twins' bedroom to be sure they were both asleep, then eased out the back door, lifting her face to the the full moon. How beautiful these summer nights in Texas were. The lemon tree Adelina had planted in an old nail keg was in blossom and the sweet scent drifted on the warm breeze. She wandered over to the garden at the side of the house, where she leaned against the posts holding up the grape arbor.

She'd scarcely seen Wade since his return. Not that she wanted to see any more of him. His chastisement of her behavior with the revolver had been fully justified—she'd used it recklessly. Even though he'd been right, the way he'd spoken to her remained an irritation. Yes, she'd been wrong, but what about his behavior in Austin? What about Monette? While she certainly didn't expect an apology, he could have offered an explanation.

Or could he? Maybe there were some things better left unsaid.

Like love? Unsaid on her part, true, and always would be. On his part? But then, as he'd proved in Austin, he didn't love her. She sighed.

"Thought that was you," Wade said from behind her.

Julia started and turned to him, his face, like hers, shadowed by the grape vines overhead.

"Sound like you're tired," he added. "Sorry I'm working you so hard, but I promised the professor."

"I'm fine."

"A little cross with me, though?"

Had he heard it in her voice? "I don't mind at all about the party," she said truthfully. The source of her discontent had nothing to do with that.

"Is it Ezra?" he asked.

"Ezra?" She was genuinely confused.

"You know—Silver Wing."

"Oh, that. It does disturb me, though not the way I think you mean. I'm pleased they're happy with each other but I worry about what will happen when Ezra and I return to Coventry."

"He told me he wants Silver Wing to go back with the two of you."

"I doubt she will. If she did, I fear the result."

"All Coventry's not like you and Ezra—is that it?"

"I'm afraid so. Strangers are regarded with suspicion there. Especially if they're unusual in any way."

"Don't sound much different from Texas."

"It is, though. Texans are quicker to offer hospitality, to make you feel at home."

"Thought you didn't like any part of this state."

"I've gotten used to living here. I expect I'll find Coventry lacking in many ways on my return." Unexpected tears surprised her and she blinked rapidly, glad the darkness hid her face. She'd known all along she had to go back, so why did it upset her so much now?

"I'm thinking of getting Ezra to rebuild the gazebo by

Rose Creek before he leaves," Wade said. "Claims he's handy with a hammer and nails."

Julia swallowed, trying to clear her voice before she spoke. "I suppose he is—he often helped with church repairs. I'm pleased you've decided to see to the gazebo."

"You sound odd. Is something the matter?"

"No!" She spoke more emphatically than she meant to.

"The truth is, I've been doing some thinking," Wade went on. "The time has come to put the past where it belongs—in the past. My mother would be pleased to know her gazebo will be restored. As for Grant and Teresa Sue— it wouldn't matter to them. The place where the tragedy happened had nothing to do with Grant's jealousy."

"Jealousy is a terrible feeling." Julia spoke before she thought and was immediately sorry. Had her words revealed her reason for tracking him down at the Dynasty?

"Understand why you like Ezra," Wade said. "He's helped the professor out so much, the old man has taken to treating him like a son."

"Ezra would be better off with a father like the professor," Julia said fervently. "The Reverend Miller has little tolerance for anyone who behaves differently than he thinks they should."

"Like you."

"Like me. He must be beside himself since Ezra left, fearing he'll be saddled with me as a daughter-in-law."

"Can see he wouldn't exactly welcome Silver Wing," Wade said. "You, though . . ." His voice trailed off.

"You think I'd make a satisfactory daughter-in-law?"

"Not quite what I was thinking. Make some man one feisty handful of a wife." What was it she heard in his voice—amusement? Surely not wistfulness.

"I don't expect to ever marry," she said coolly. Again, she fought unwelcome tears. What was the matter with her? What with all her weeping at night she was turning into a regular leaky sieve.

He didn't comment and she was trying to compose herself when she felt his fingers on her cheek.

"You're crying," he accused. "Knew something was wrong. What is it?"

At that—didn't he know he was the cause?—her shredded composure deserted her and she began to weep in earnest.

Wade's arms wrapped around her, holding her to him. His hand stroked her back as he murmured soothingly. Julia, feeling as though she could dissolve into him with no effort at all, told herself she must pull away—and did not.

This was where she belonged, she knew it right down to the marrow of her bones. Her tears drying, she raised her face and his lips feathered over her wet cheeks to her lips where she tasted the salt of her own tears in his kiss.

The warmth of his mouth kindled an answering heat within her. Now that she knew what that heat could lead to, she yearned to travel that magic road with him, never with anyone but Wade. From the way he cupped her against his hardness, she knew he, too, wanted and needed more than kisses.

"Julia," he said with the telltale hoarseness of passion in his voice.

She began to melt, helpless against the wild flaring within her, until a stray thought dropped into her mind with the sharpness and coldness of an icicle.

Did he say Monette's name in the same way?

Struggling against herself as much as him, she fought free of his embrace. "No," she gasped. "No more."

He let her go, saying, "What's wrong?"

"You know very well," she told him, then spun away, fleeing into the kitchen and on to her room, where she flung herself on the bed and wept all over again.

* * *

The next day she was too busy with the many details for the party to be unhappy. People began to arrive before noon, many of the women bearing jars of preserves and pickles. One couple with three little girls brought a cured ham. No one arrived empty-handed. The twins, bashful at first, soon were enthusiastically mingling with the other children.

Silver Wing tried to stay in the background as much as possible even though, outside of a few questioning looks, no one remarked unfavorably about her presence. Some time ago, Julia, with Adelina's help, had altered several of Teresa Sue's gowns from the trunk to fit the girl and so she was dressed much like everyone else. But still she stood out. Perhaps if she hadn't been so pretty, it wouldn't be so obvious.

Two babies were presented to the professor for baptism in his role as minister. The crowd congregated to witness the ritual in a silence broken only by the howling of one of the babies who definitely didn't like being immersed in water. Afterward, the professor was cheered and had his hand shaken by every visiting male.

Julia, who hadn't realized he did sleight of hand tricks, was as fascinated as anyone there at the performance that followed, with Ezra as his assistant. When it was over, and the applause died down, the professor began an oration about the virtues of his elixir, convincing many of the guests to buy a bottle.

The tantalizing smell of roasting beef had teased appetites all day and, when the time came to eat, everyone was ready. Julia and Silver Wing were kept busy replenishing the long wooden tables set up under the trees near the house while Ezra trotted back and forth with plates of sliced beef.

"My," Ed Tyson's wife said to Julia, "I'd forgotten what a pretty girl you are. And Ed says you're every bit as nice as you are pretty. Can't think what's wrong with Wade."

"I guess we just don't suit each other," Julia said as brightly as she could.

Nell Tyson leaned close and lowered her voice. "I must tell you that today he's been watching every move you make. He's certainly not indifferent to you. How do you feel about him?"

Taken aback, Julia wasn't sure what to reply. She snatched up an empty platter and said, "Please excuse me, I must refill this."

Was Nell Tyson right? Julia had trouble believing it. Unless, of course, Wade had been watching her because he wondered if she'd be able to keep fulfilling the needs of the guests. That was probably the explanation.

Everyone appeared to be enjoying themselves. Some of the men kept disappearing into the barn for short periods and she suspected there must be whiskey—or red-eye as they called it here—inside. If she was right, at least none of them seemed to be overdoing their imbibing.

Later, when most of the neighboring ranchers had left, and the cleanup began, Ezra came into the kitchen where Silver Wing and Julia were busily scraping scraps off dishes.

"I have some alarming news," he said. "One of the ranchers heard the Slocums had rounded up a gang and were making plans to come after Mr. Howland. Do you think there can be any truth to it?"

His words made Julia's blood run cold. "I'm afraid it might be true," she said. "Les Slocum hates Wade."

Ezra shook his head and turned his attention to Silver Wing. Julia, occupied by fearful thoughts of what might happen to Wade, paid little attention. Only when he'd left the house did she realize she'd forgotten to give him the scraps for Brownie.

"I've been remiss," she said to Silver Wing. "I haven't yet taught you to shoot. If worse comes to worst, as it might with the Slocums, you should know how."

"I learned to shoot my father's rifle," Silver Wing admitted. "After he got sick and couldn't hunt, I had to."

"Good." Would it come to that? Julia wondered. Would she and Silver Wing find themselves having to defend the house? She doubted it. With most of the hands in from the range right now, any gang of outlaws would surely think twice before attacking the ranch.

With the dishes all scraped and stacked for washing, Julia eyed the mound of scraps intended for Brownie. "Why don't you go ahead and get the twins in bed before we attack the dishes," she said. "I'll run these scraps out to Brownie."

From the moment the dog came to the ranch, Adelina had insisted he not be fed near the house. "Not good, dogs begging at doors," she said. As a result, Brownie's food dish was near the barn.

Twilight cloaked the ranch, but it wasn't yet pitch dark. It would only take a moment to run over to the barn and feed Brownie. Gathering up the scraps in a cloth, she left the kitchen. Half way there, Brownie met her, trotting eagerly at her side, his nose aimed at what she carried.

She dumped the contents of the cloth into his empty dish and started back. As she came even with the stand of cottonwoods where the tables had been set up, a dark figure stepped from the greater darkness between the trees.

"If it ain't Miss Hoity-Toity," Jack Crain said.

Noting the slur in his voice, she realized he must have been one of those frequenting the barn. Without replying, she tried to skirt around him, but he grabbed her arm.

"Just a damn minute, here. Tried to kill me, you little bitch. Ain't gonna let no uppity—"

"Let me go!" she snapped, struggling to get away.

"You gotta pay the forfeit," he mumbled, yanking her closer, so close she could smell the whiskey fumes.

When she realized with disgusted dismay that he intended to kiss her, she fought harder.

"Damn wildcat," he snarled, his grip tightening until it hurt.

"Stop it!" she cried, doing her best to kick him in the shins as she turned her face away from him. He smelled even worse than she remembered from their first meeting.

Something thudded against her foot and she heard growling. Brownie? Jack let out a yell and suddenly she was free. "Bloody dog bit me," he shouted. "Gonna kill the bastard."

Poised to flee, Julia held. Brownie was circling Jack, growling. She saw to her horror that Jack now had a knife in his hand and was lunging at the dog.

"No, you can't," she cried, flinging herself at Jack.

As he left the corral carrying a lantern, Wade saw Brownie wolfing down what must be party leftovers. He came to attention when the dog suddenly abandoned his food and, snarling, took off toward the house. Alarmed, Wade followed him.

He heard a man yell, then shout that the dog had bitten him. Sounded like Jack. Then Julia cried out. Wade broke into a run and found them all three of them by the trees. Light from the lantern showed a distraught Julia wrestling with Jack, who had a knife in his hand. Brownie circled them both.

"Jack!" he yelled. "Drop the knife. Julia, get away."

Julia let go of Jack and retreated. Jack turned to face him. "Dog bit me," he muttered. "No reason, just up and bit me. Gonna do for him, ain't no one gonna stop me."

"He's drunk and he's lying," Julia snapped. "Brownie bit him because he was trying to kiss me and Brownie could tell I was trying to get away."

Rage enveloped Wade, coloring everything red. He set the lantern down hard and lunged at Jack who brought up the knife he still held. Wade grabbed his wrist and twisted. The knife fell into the dirt. Wade let go and started to step back.

"You son of a bitch," Jack howled and swung at him.

Wade blocked the punch and hit him hard across the jaw. Jack dropped like a stone and lay unmoving. Wade glanced at Julia who was staring from Jack to him.

"Go in the house," he ordered, still consumed by anger. "You shouldn't be out here provoking the men."

The color drained from Julia's face. Without a word, she turned on her heel and stalked toward the house. Wade knelt beside Jack and felt the pulse in his neck. Beating. Just knocked. cold.

The professor, with Ezra at his heels, came hurrying up. "Anything I can do to help?" the professor asked.

The redness was slowly fading from Wade's vision. He eyed Jack, sprawled in the dirt and said, "He'll sleep it off. Ezra can help me get him to the bunkhouse."

With his rage ebbing fast, shame began licking at Wade. He wasn't proud of clobbering a drunk. Should have stopped once Jack dropped the knife. Hell of a thing to do to a man who'd been his friend—been his friend till he touched Julia. He had no doubt her account was the truth. Drink might account for the insult, but he'd never feel the same about Jack, never trust him again.

"His leg is bleeding," the professor said, kneeling beside Jack.

"Brownie bit him," Wade said tersely. The dog, evidently realizing he was no longer needed, had vanished.

"A dog bite can be nasty," the professor said, rolling up Jack's pant leg. "Better let me cauterize it."

"Whatever you think."

Eventually, the bite treated, Ezra and Wade rolled Jack onto a blanket and dragged him to the bunkhouse. Jamie eyed them as they transferred Jack to his bunk but kept his mouth shut. Smart man, Jamie.

Wade walked toward the house, his mind roiling. Wasn't

enough he had to worry about what the Slocums were up to, looked like he'd have to replace his foreman, as well. Most disturbing was his own behavior. He'd acted like a blasted maniac. Bad as Grant. That thought froze him in his tracks. He took a deep breath and let it out slowly. Jealousy?

He shook his head and continued on. Not at all. He'd been a tad tough on Jack but no one on his ranch was going to molest women. And no man anywhere, ever, was going to lay a hand on Julia against her will.

Satisfied he'd solved one problem, he entered the house. The kitchen was clean but there was no sign of Julia. She must have gone to her room. Annoyed with him, he supposed, recalling his words to her. Words spoken in anger, as if the encounter had been her fault.

He turned toward his bedroom, stopped and changed direction. He wasn't ready to sleep. He headed for the front porch but halted again when he realized someone was sitting on the steps, in the light of the full moon. His heart speeded. Julia? As he came closer he saw the woman had dark hair and held. Silver Wing. What was she doing there?

He answered his own question easily. Waiting for Ezra. A doomed pairing, with grief sure to follow. But it wasn't up to him to try to separate them. Let them have their time together before the parting of the ways.

Retracing his footsteps, he wandered along the hall until he stood outside Julia's room. He had no business here, none at all. She had every right to be outraged if he tried to invade her bedroom. He must not bother her. Yet he didn't move, thinking of Silver Wing and Ezra.

He was no more ready to part with Julia than Ezra was to part with Silver Wing. He wanted her here with him, not in Coventry, but he knew she wouldn't listen. At the moment, though, she *was* here with him. He was still there, staring at her door, when it opened.

"Wade!" Julia exclaimed.

She wore the same white nightgown she'd had on that first night in his house, when she'd had that dream about an intruder in her room. Wait—Jack had hoisted a few that day, too. Was it possible—? Hell, maybe she hadn't been dreaming.

"Was it Jack?" he demanded.

She blinked at him. "Jack Crain? You mean tonight?"

"No. When you first came—in your room."

"I—I'm not sure. I thought it must be him at the time because when he picked me up at the railroad station he forced a kiss on me, claiming in Texas everyone kissed the bride. That was before he knew I wasn't . . . the bride, I mean. I found him repulsive, but I hated to accuse him of being the intruder, because I wasn't positive and I didn't wish to accuse an innocent man."

"No wonder you were afraid to be left alone at the ranch with him when I rode off with the Rangers. Never thought Jack would . . ." He shook his head.

"Is—is he all right?"

"He'll live." He'd been trying not to stare at her, with the lit lamp behind her in the room making the gown almost transparent, but his gaze persistently returned to her provocatively outlined body. "Wanted to say I got pretty het up and said some things I didn't mean."

"I heard someone outside my door and thought maybe one of the twins needed me. I never dreamed it was you coming to apologize—since you never do."

"Seldom, maybe. Not never." Time to leave now that he'd done what he meant to do—or had he?

She ran her tongue over her lips, her action focusing his attention on her mouth and testing his already fragile control. He could almost taste her lips, pink and warm and sweet as honey. He swallowed, longing to pull her into his arms, to feel her softness against him. That's where she belonged—in his arms. In his bed.

"I forgive you," she said. "I realize you were fighting

mad. And—thank you. She took a step toward him, put
her hands to his face and stood on her tiptoes to brush
her lips over his. "Good night," she murmured as she
stepped back and closed the door in his face.

Chapter 15

All was calm the next morning. Jack Crain didn't appear for work, nor for meals, which was just as well, Wade thought. Last night he'd handed Jamie a bank draft to give to Jack in lieu of wages owed, so he'd half expected Jack to be gone by now. The man must know he was no longer welcome at the W Bar H.

Before noon, Jamie confirmed that Jack had the bank draft. Later, Jamie, two hands, and the cook with his wagon headed out to take their turn on the range.

The following morning, no one appeared for breakfast except Ezra and the professor. "Where is everybody?" Wade asked.

"Mr. Crain rode out real early with the rest of the hands," Ezra said. "I mean those who didn't go with Jamie yesterday."

"Jack rode out? And took the hands? Why in hell would he do that?"

"I thought you'd told him to."

As Wade shook his head, it dawned on him what Jack had done to revenge himself. He'd quit and somehow he'd talked the three who normally worked at the ranch into going with him. Either because they weren't satisfied here or because he'd managed to dupe them in some way.

Damn. Going to have to replace those men. Meant he'd have to ride to Austin. Some friend Jack had turned out to be.

Yet he didn't dare ride to town. Bill Mokes had gotten in from Austin just in time for the party day before yesterday and talk was all over the town about the Slocums recruiting men for a gang.

"Hear it's to get even," Bill had finished.

Yeah. With him. Too dangerous to take a chance—what if he met them on the way? He couldn't leave here in any case with no men except the professor and Ezra to protect the women and the twins.

The problem was, with no hands to depend on for firepower, he didn't think the ranch was defensible against a gang of armed men. "Low-down, stinking son-of-a-snake," he muttered, meaning both Jack and Les Slocum.

Turning to the professor, he said, "Would you take the twins and the women in your wagon to Ed Tyson's ranch and stay there until I'm sure it's safe for them to return? Ezra will ride shotgun."

"I'm always happy to help," the professor was saying when Julia marched from the stove to the table.

Looking straight at Wade, she announced, "I'm not going anywhere."

"Be reasonable," he said.

"I agree the twins and Silver Wing should go to Ed's— and the professor, too," she said. "But I'm not."

"Look, Julia, the Slocums are out for blood. They—"

"You taught me to shoot. I can be of help."

Wade continued to argue with her to no avail. Finally he said, with some irritation, "We're wasting time."

"I agree," Julia said. "I'll help Silver Wing pack the twins' things."

The professor and Ezra went out to hitch up the wagon.

Wade had given the professor a retired range horse, an old but still healthy gelding, to replace Ben.

A sense of urgency drove Wade to the locked cabinet where he kept his guns. Besides the carbine he used when riding with the Rangers, he had Grant's rifle and one of his own. The Colt Grant had used in the tragedy was buried deep in Texas soil but the rifle had no family blood on it. He removed guns and ammunition and laid them on the bed. His Colt was in its holster, strapped on, as always.

He heard Nancy's piping voice coming down the hall. "Mr. Tyson got more puppies?"

"I don't know." Julia's voice was calm. "You'll have to wait until you get there to find out."

"Take Brownie?" Susan asked.

Silver Wing replied, "Mr. Tyson has dogs. He doesn't need Brownie."

"Take ponies. Ride ponies," Nancy insisted.

"You're going to get to ride in Professor Wilkes's wagon," Julia told her. "That'll be fun. And maybe Mrs. Tyson will make a gingerbread boy like the one she brought for the party."

Wade started down the hall, arriving at the twins' bedroom as Susan was saying, "Take books."

"One apiece," he told them. "Hurry up and choose, because the wagon's about ready to go."

They had to have a hug and a kiss from both Julia and him. He lifted a girl into each arm and carried them from the house to the wagon. "You do what Silver Wing and Mr. and Mrs. Tyson tell you," he said as he helped them through the door into the wagon.

Silver Wing climbed in after them, the professor swung onto his seat and clucked to the horses. The wagon, creaking and groaning, began to roll with Ezra, already mounted on the buckskin that had belonged to old Hank, riding by its side, wearing a holstered revolver Wade had given him.

Julia's hand crept into Wade's as they stood watching

the departure. He wished she was in the wagon and, at the same time, admired her stubborn courage in staying with him. Hand in hand they walked back to the house.

"The Slocums don't know Jack Crain rode off with the hands. Maybe they won't risk any attack," she said.

He shrugged. There was no way to tell what the Slocums did or did not know. Or whether or not they'd attack. Or when.

She nodded her head at Brownie who'd chosen to escort them rather than the wagon. "He'll give us fair warning if they do attack."

Once you got used to the mutt he didn't look so ugly, Wade thought. He'd proven to be no trouble and the ranch had acquired a good watch dog.

"I've only heard him growl at two people," Julia added. "Jack Crain and Les Slocum."

"Guess he's a better judge than I am," Wade said. "About Jack, I mean."

"I didn't like Jack Crain, but I never dreamed he was scoundrel enough to desert you and persuade your men to go with him at a time when he knew you were in danger."

A man he'd sworn was his friend. Yet here was Julia standing by him whether he wanted her here or not. "We'd best go in and review how you shoot a rifle," he said.

The guns were still on his bed. Julia hesitated in the doorway but came on into his room. "I've never been in here before," she said. She smiled slightly. "You've been in my room, though—that first night I spent in this house."

"And almost last night," he said. "Tell me, I've always been curious. Did you really faint that day?"

She blushed and he wondered if she had any idea how charming she looked when she did.

"I tried to will myself to, but I never actually have fainted and I couldn't then. I've watched other girls do it, though, so I imitated them." She glanced at him. "I was at my wit's end, it was the only way out I could think of."

"If you hadn't faked that faint, we might be married by

now." He held her gaze for a long moment, till she finally looked away.

"But my name wasn't Emma," she said, leaving him wondering exactly what she meant as she picked up one of the rifles. "Does this work the same as that carbine you showed me how to use?" she asked.

Julia was a good pupil. Using what he'd told her about the carbine, she loaded the rifle and aimed it correctly. She remembered exactly how how to fire it and what not to do. When the two rifles and the carbine were all loaded, he handed her the carbine.

"We'll leave that in the main room and I'll put a rifle in the kitchen," he said as they left his bedroom.

Gun in place, he joined her in the main room. "What do we do now?" she asked.

He shrugged. "Wait till Brownie barks."

"Would you like to read?" she asked.

Reading wasn't what he wanted. She was. "You could read to me," he said. "What do you have in mind? Mother Goose?"

She made a face at him. "I bought myself a book of poetry in Austin," she said. "Do you like poetry?"

"Wouldn't know. Never tried it."

"It's never too late." She swept from the room, leaving her words echoing behind her.

Never too late.

She returned in a moment with a small leather-bound book with gilt-edged pages. "We'll have to sit down," she said.

"Only if we sit together so I can read over your shoulder if I feel like it."

She eyed him dubiously before she sat on the sofa next to him. He felt as though he was coaxing a wary filly who believed he was up to no good to trust him.

"What would you like to hear?" she asked.

"Something lively."

"I'm afraid this book has only odes and such, nothing lively."

"You choose, then." He watched her flip through the book, pausing, then shaking her head and going on. "What's the matter?"

"They're all so—so romantic."

He leaned closer and looked at the pages. "There's a name I know—Shakespeare," he said. "Read that one." He pointed.

She cleared her throat and began:

> *Take, O take those lips away,*
> *That so sweetly were foresworn;*
> *And those eyes, the break of day,*
> *Lights that do mislead the morn:*
> *But my kisses bring again, bring again;*
> *Seals of love, but seal'd in vain, seal'd in vain.*

Julia closed the book with a snap, wishing she'd never mentioned reading.

"I liked the part about the kisses," Wade said.

She felt him touch her lips, tracing their outline with his finger. "I'd rather you didn't take those lips away," he said softly.

"Sealed in vain," she murmured. A mistake because, when her mouth was open, he leaned over and kissed her.

Wanting more of his Texas taste, she slipped her tongue inside his mouth, resulting in him tipping her sideways so she lay across his lap, his arms around her, holding her close. The kiss intensified, offering and claiming on his part as well as hers.

She offered her love, she knew. Whatever he offered, she was willing to accept.

Julia shouldn't be here with him, Wade thought. How could he keep her safe against who knew how many armed men bent on killing him? He didn't want her to die with him. We'll live! he vowed. Somehow we'll come through this despite the odds.

With her in his arms, he came close to believing they might survive. Holding her like this, he could believe in almost anything—in happiness, even.

Stubborn, wrong-headed, wonderful Julia. His Julia, who preferred to stand by him no matter what the danger, rather than flee to safety. His arms tightened around her. How could he bear to lose her?

He took his lips from her to murmur against her mouth, "You shouldn't be here."

"I'm where I belong," she whispered.

He'd closed and locked the doors but left the windows open at the top. A warm breeze blew through the openings carrying the sweet scent of flowers. Julia had weeded and watered the little garden his mother had planted, neglected since Teresa Sue's death. Her tender heart couldn't bear to see even plants suffer.

"There's no other woman like you," he told her.

She stirred, pushing away from him and sitting up. "What about Monette?"

What brought that on? he wondered, both annoyed and frustrated. "Don't imagine there are too many like her, either," he admitted. "But she doesn't matter."

"Monette matters to me." Julia started to get up from the sofa.

He caught her arm, keeping her sitting there. "You think you know why I was with her in the Dynasty. What if you're wrong?"

She eyed him incredulously.

"You are, you know," he added.

"Impossible!"

"Calling me a liar, are you?"

Julia caught her lower lip between her teeth.

"I've made wrong judgments, but I've never lied to you," he told her.

Could she believe him? Julia asked herself. Certainly she

could think of no other explanation for the scene she'd witnessed in room number 10, but *was* there another one? Was Wade telling her the truth? It would take a tremendous leap of faith for her to accept this.

She rose from the sofa and walked to the window, peering out as though making certain no intruders approached. In reality she hardly took in what was outside, so intent was she on what Wade had said.

Could you love someone without trusting him? That was a question she couldn't answer.

"The Slocums can't be coming—Brownie would have warned us." Wade spoke from so close behind her that his breath stirred a tendril of her hair. His arms slid around her, holding her to him, making her feel his need.

Julia felt herself melting, started to make an effort to twist away, then held. If years stretched out ahead of them, Monette would make a difference. But she had to face the fact they might have only hours.

His hands cupped her breasts, causing her breath to catch. What mattered was the here and now. She chased all thought of Monette from her mind and gave herself up to what she and Wade both wanted.

She turned in his arms, embracing him, lifting her face for his kiss. When he covered her lips with his, she dissolved.

Wade didn't know what conclusion Julia had come to about believing him, but her eager response told him it didn't matter right now. He wanted her so much he could hardly wait. But first he had to feel her need, to have her quivering against him, traveling with him toward beyond.

He was a plain man, he'd never thought of making love in such fancy terms—her and her poetry—but that was before he'd made love with Julia. Everything was different with her, from a single kiss to the joining. She took him past anywhere he'd ever been. Beyond.

He meant to be sure he took her there with him. And he refused to believe it might be for the last time.

Much as he longed to hold her naked body against his, he abandoned the idea. Not the right time. But they still could make love to each other. Come to think of it, they'd always been naked before. This would be a first. The idea made him even more eager to feel her soft warmth surrounding his hardness.

He lifted her off her feet, holding her against him as he edged over to the nearest seat, a straight-backed side chair without arms.

Bemused with desire, Julia watched as Wade sat down, letting her go. Almost immediately his hands slid under her skirts, finding and releasing the ties of her drawers so that they slipped down her legs to the floor. He opened the front of his trousers and caught her to him, murmuring huskily, "Sit on top of me."

As she did, he eased himself inside her and she moaned with pleasure, wriggling to increase the indescribable sensations spiraling through her. The faster she moved, the more intense the feeling became until she clung to him, gasping his name, flying apart, somewhere beyond herself.

He groaned, thrusting upward, holding her tightly, her name on his lips.

Later, collapsed against him, she whispered, "Oh, my. I had no idea that was possible."

"Now you know." His breath was warm against her ear.

"I thought you had to lie down."

He chuckled. "Looking forward to showing you other possibilities, Julie girl."

She sat up far enough to look at him. "Nobody ever called me Julie before."

"Good. Then it's my name for you. Mine alone."

His words warmed her heart.

Later, after she'd gotten to her feet, retrieved her drawers and made herself presentable again, they wandered into the kitchen to find something to eat.

"Maybe the Slocums won't show up," she said as she

sliced the bread she'd made yesterday, offering it to him with the honey jar.

He shook his head. "They will. Sooner or later. In the meantime—" He paused suggestively, grinning at her.

"We can eat," she finished for him.

"That's not all I had in mind."

"Heavens, we're lucky Brownie didn't start barking in the midst . . ." Her words trailed off.

"Of making love?"

"Why is it called that? I would think, well, love isn't always involved, is it?"

"Can't say it is. There are other words not meant for your ears."

"Women aren't as fragile as men seem to think. I admit I don't like to hear bad language, but it certainly wouldn't make me faint. The language the man who painted Great-aunt Polly's house used was enough to blister Emma's and my ears—but we survived. And memorized every word. Not that I've ever used any of them."

"He used language like that in front of young girls?"

She shook her head. "He was on the ladder outside and the windows were open because it was summer. He had no idea we could hear every word. Interestingly enough, we couldn't find some of them in the dictionary. Maybe I'll ask you about one or two of them sometime."

"Don't count on me to tell you what they mean. I might not know."

"Oh, you Texans know everything."

"Guess maybe we sound like we do. Finding out I got a tad more to learn than I figured."

"Like what?"

"Can't say I understand women yet."

She laughed. "That's easy. We just want to be loved." The moment the words were out, she regretted them. Her laughter vanished and she looked away from him. Why couldn't she learn to think before she spoke? She knew

he didn't love her and now he'd think she was trying to
force him to say he did.

"I'd better feed Brownie," she said, rising from the
kitchen table.

"Call him," Wade ordered, "Won't hurt to have him
eating by the kitchen door until this is over."

Brownie came running and gobbled up the scraps she
gave him, obviously not caring where he was served. He
lapped at the water she set out and trotted back toward
the barn.

"You realize this could go on for days," he said, standing
by the door watching the dog.

At first she thought he was talking about feeding
Brownie, then he turned to look at her and she saw the
telltale glow in his eyes. Her treacherous heart began to
pound in anticipation.

"We can't possibly—" she began, then paused, not certain how to put it.

He smiled. "We can try. Been thinking that the Slocums
can't be sure how many men are on the ranch so likely
they'll hit us at night. Till they do, figure we've got every
day, all day. If I'm wrong, we still have Brownie to let alert
us."

"But—"

"Thought you wanted to learn all the other ways. Change
your mind?"

"Not exactly. But don't you dare try to back me into a
corner, Wade Howland—which is what you're trying to
do."

"Want to play hard to get, do you? Don't mind that
game, we can have fun with it."

She didn't know what she wanted. Well, that wasn't true
because she did want to make love with Wade again. "It's
just that I find it difficult to talk about . . . about . . ." Again
she couldn't find the right words.

"Sharpens the anticipation."

"Maybe for you."

"Can see that pulse beating at your throat. Going pretty fast and hard for someone who's standing still." He bent and touched her throbbing pulse with his lips.

"Wade!"

He ran his hands over the curves of her hips. "Like it better when you whisper my name in my ear," he told her.

Heat flowed from his words, from his touch, through her clothes to center deep inside her. Then he pulled her to him and kissed her.

Already aroused, Wade's desire increased when Julia's lips parted under his. The first tentative touch of her tongue sent a thrill through him. With Monette, when the coupling was over, it was over. With Julia that wasn't true. He couldn't get enough of her.

Maybe he never would. That thought took him aback for a moment, but with her in his arms it was impossible to keep focused on anything but the way she made him feel. "Beyond," he whispered against her mouth.

She made an inquiring murmur.

"That's where we're bound for," he told her as he lifted her into his arms and carried her into her bedroom. "Way beyond. May never return."

Chapter 16

Early the next morning, Julia, who'd volunteered to stay awake for the second half of the night, was sitting on a kitchen chair, not asleep, but not fully awake, either, when she was startled by a tapping on one of the kitchen windows. She leaped to her feet and stared—at Silver Wing gesturing toward the locked door.

Alarmed—had something happened to the twins?—Julia let her in. "Are the twins—?"

"Twins are happy with Tysons."

"Why have you come back?"

"My mother's people use wolves—watchmen—to protect their villages," Silver Wing said. "I come to be your wolf."

"But that's dangerous."

"I know how. I ride, Brownie comes with me."

Looking at Silver Wing's determined face, Julia realized she wasn't going to be able to talk her out of it. Before she could decide what to do next, Wade appeared in the kitchen.

"Thought I heard something," he said, staring at Silver Wing.

"She wants to be our wolf—that is, a look-out," Julia said. "I told her it was too dangerous."

Wade rubbed his eyes, yawned and ran his hand through his hair. "Think you can stay alive?" he asked the girl.

She nodded.

"Know how to shoot a gun?"

"Rifle, yes."

"Good. I'll give you one to take along. When you saddle up, get the right gear to hold the rifle." He left the kitchen, returning with one of the rifles, which he handed to Silver Wing, along with extra ammunition.

"Don't try to shoot unless it's to save your life," he ordered. "If you spot the gang, hightail it back here and hole up with us. And don't forget to being the rifle back inside with you. We'll need it. Good luck."

Silver Wing turned toward the door, paused and looked back to say, "Ezra rode from the Tysons. Don't know where." She left the house, heading for the corral, Brownie trotting alongside her.

"You let her go," Julia said, trying not to sound accusing.

"We need all the help we can get. I wonder where the devil Ezra went?"

Julia couldn't even speculate about Ezra. It was bad enough that Silver Wing insisted on risking her life, the good Lord only knew what Ezra might have decided to do. But she could do nothing to keep any of them safe. All she could manage to do was deal with the moment, which meant fixing breakfast. She started to busy herself at the stove.

Wade left the kitchen, came back with the rifle and the carbine and set them on a cupboard counter along with ammunition. "Never mind what you're doing," he ordered. "Sit down." When she did, he seated himself at the table. "I've been thinking."

"What about?" she asked.

"Grant and me, we never were much alike, I always figured. Was right—but wrong, too. When I came home from Austin the other evening and saw Jack manhandling you, everything turned red. Lost control, just like Grant. Didn't know what I was doing—could have killed Jack. Because he'd dared to touch you. Scared me down to my boots when I came out of it."

"You didn't even injure him badly," she said.

"Could've. Just like Grant."

"No. Seeing red or not, you stopped once you knocked Jack down. You didn't try to kick him the way he meant to do to Ezra. You didn't take a knife to him like he was trying to do to Brownie. And you never once pulled your gun. You're not your brother, you're yourself. Wade, not Grant."

He sighed. "His was jealousy. Don't know what to call mine."

"Anger?" she suggested. "You didn't want me hurt but you weren't jealous of me. Why should you be?"

"Guess you've never given me any cause."

"Like you gave me." Again she'd spoken too quickly. Would she never learn?

He shot her a startled glance. "Jealous? You were jealous?"

In for a penny, in for a pound. "Why else would I make that tiresome trip to Austin? It was foolish of me, but there it is."

"Jealous because of Monette?"

Julia bit her lip, then stopped and looked him straight in the eye. "Didn't I have cause? Whether I had the right to be jealous or not is beside the point—I was."

"And there I was, just as you figured."

She nodded.

"Guess it must have looked pretty incriminating to a jealous woman."

That was so obviously true she didn't bother to reply.

"Want to hear the real story," he asked, "or have you set yourself not to believe any other explanation?"

"You have a right to explain whether I believe you or not."

"Always knew you were hard-headed. Here goes, take it or leave it. Stopped off in Austin to talk to Monette. She and I'd been seeing one another pretty regular for the past few years. Thought it was only fair to tell her she didn't have to wait for me to show up anymore. So there I was all dirty and dusty—a bath sounded like heaven. Monette found out I'd registered, got an extra key from the clerk, and surprised me." To his annoyance he felt himself reddening. Shouldn't rightly have to explain anything like this to a lady.

"Monette being like she is and thinking I'd come to see her for—another reason—she sort of naturally undid her top. Was trying to get her to stop but, it ain't easy when all a man's wearing is a towel. That's what you walked in on—and why the door was open to begin with. Don't leave my hotel doors unlocked. Ever."

Julia stared at him with such a blank expression he couldn't tell what she was thinking. "You weren't going to show up anymore to see Monette?" she asked finally.

"That's what I said."

"Why?"

He shifted in the chair. "You know."

"Maybe not. Tell me."

" 'Cause of what happened in the Lone Star. Didn't seem right after that." It was the blasted truth. He hadn't wanted any other woman but Julia after having a taste of her.

"But you don't love me."

"How the hell do I know?" he all but shouted. "Look what happened to Grant on account of love. Scares the bejesus out of me. How can I be sure I won't go crazy like he did?"

"Why should you? You're not your brother."

"Get to seeing red like I did with old Jack, can't be sure what might happen."

"Don't upset yourself. You don't have to love me." Julia rose and walked to the stove and began preparing breakfast.

He watched her, half-aware what he felt for her was a close kin to love. He didn't want to go any further, even if he was beginning to understand just how dreary life would be without her.

He finished the meal she set before him and was starting on his second cup of coffee when he heard the pound of horse's hoofs outside. Jumping to his feet, he ran to the window. Seeing Silver Wing pulling up her horse, he unlocked and threw open the back door.

She grabbed the rifle from the saddle holster, then she tried to coax Brownie inside with her, saying, "I'm afraid they kill him when he bark."

Wade hoisted the surprised dog into his arms and lugged him into the house. With Silver Wing safe inside, he locked the door again. Brownie crept under the table, the picture of misery.

"How many?" he asked. "How far away?"

"Six men. Be here soon. Not see me."

"I'll take the kitchen." Handing Julia the carbine, he told her, "Take your bedroom. Silver Wing, the main room. Don't expose yourself to their fire."

The women hurried off. Wade checked his rifle to make sure it was loaded, then crouched by a window, out of sight but able to see them when they came. One man and two women against six outlaws. Even if one of the women was half-Apache and the other stubborn enough to stand up with him in what she must realize was a losing battle, he didn't hold out much hope. Which didn't mean he'd give up easily.

Tamping down his anxiety about Julia—he couldn't afford to be distracted—he set himself to wait. He noticed the horse Silver Wing had ridden was wandering back toward the corral. Just as well. Might save the poor beast from being shot.

Keyed up as he was, it seemed to take hours before any riders appeared. His first warning came when Brownie, still huddled under the table, began to growl. "Shut up!" he snapped. "No barking."

The first man he spotted was a stranger wise to the ways of cover. Wade tried his best to get a clear shot but wasn't able to so he held his fire. Somewhere out of his sight, the man must have dismounted because the next he saw of him was on foot, evidently checking out the bunkhouse.

In her bedroom, Julia, careful not to make herself a target, crouched beside the window, peering warily around the edge. Tracking one rider with the carbine, she tensed when another rider appeared among the trees. How had he gotten so close to the house without her spotting him? She switched to cover him because he was closer, at the same time trying to remember what to do after she fired. She'd expected to feel frightened but she wasn't. At least, not yet.

Though tempted to call on God for help in aiming straight, it didn't seem right when her purpose was to kill a man. She'd have to depend on herself, as Great-aunt Polly had always advised. Her loaded Beaumont-Adams revolver lay within reach in case she had to use it.

When the first shot came, she started. Not from outside, she realized quickly, but from the main room. Silver Wing had fired her rifle. Presumably the house was surrounded.

That single shot unleashed a fusillade of bullets aimed at the house, concentrating, as nearly as Julia could make out, on the front of the house, where Silver Wing's shot had come from.

The first rider she'd seen had disappeared but the one in the trees had dismounted and was now ducking from tree to tree, never in the open long enough for her to aim at him. At first she'd thought him a stranger, but now she'd about decided he might be Les Slocum. Could she kill him if she had the chance? Julia grimaced. A better question might be even, if she tried to kill him, was she a good enough shot to so much as wound him?

Thank God the twins were safe at the Tysons'. She wondered if Silver Wing was okay after all that shooting, but she didn't dare leave her post to find out.

How had Les got so much closer to the house? Never mind trying to kill him, she'd better fire off a shot in his general direction to make him back off. Aiming as best she could from her crouch, Julia pulled the trigger of the carbine. The roar of her gun made her ears ring and the recoil jarred her. She knew she hadn't hit Les, but she had the satisfaction of seeing him dart back, retreating into the grove. Scared the scoundrel, she told herself.

After making certain none of the other outlaws was near, she laid the carbine on the bed and dashed to the main room. Silver Wing crouched by a window, rifle in hand, broken glass at her feet. A trickle of blood ran down her arm.

"You're hurt!" Julia gasped.

"Shots break window. Glass cut my arm. Not hurt bad." She smiled without humor. "Before battle my mother's people say, 'This is a good day to die.' Not afraid, like me."

"Did you hit any of them?"

"Maybe."

"If you're sure you're okay, I'd better get back to my post." Julia handed the girl her handkerchief and hurried to her room.

Once again crouching by the window, she wondered if something was wrong with her. Silver Wing admitted to being afraid and yet she wasn't. Why not? Wouldn't any sane person be terrified? She'd been frightened enough when Sam Bass captured her. Had that experience made her immune to fear? On the other hand, she didn't think it was a good day to die.

A gun blast from the kitchen set her teeth on edge. She waited for return shots but none came. Presumably Wade was all right.

Where could Ezra have gone? If he was trying to locate the range hands, from what Wade had told her, that would be a lost cause because the range riders separated when they were out there, each doing a different job. He'd have trouble finding any of the three.

Yet Ezra wasn't stupid and he was no longer as green as he'd been when he arrived. He did tend to believe the Lord had sent him on a mission, but she didn't see how that notion could have anything to do with why he'd ridden away from the Tysons'. Silver Wing had, too—she'd come to help them. But where was Ezra?

Winged the bastard, by God, Wade told himself. Sent him skedaddling with no return fire. How long would this devil's crew besiege the house? He'd heard Julia shoot the carbine and Silver Wing the rifle. With shots fired from three different parts of the house, could be the Slocum gang thought there were too many armed men in here to risk their necks.

If that was true, the gang might back off for now and come back under cover of darkness, making it a lot tougher to spot them. Peering cautiously from another window, he caught a glimpse of a rider disappearing around the barn. Every one of the six, he suspected, had dismounted to begin with. Now at least one was back on his horse. Regrouping?

Ducking from window to window, he spotted another

rider, took quick aim and snapped off a shot. Damn.
Missed.

Julia appeared in the kitchen doorway. "I saw Les Slocum riding away," she reported. "He's the one I scared
off with my shot earlier."

"That's three for sure," he muttered. "Go ask Silver
Wing what's happening on her side of the house."

Moments later Julia was back. "She spotted two of them
leaving. She got cut by glass when they shot at her, though,
and she's still bleeding."

"Better see to that."

Julia nodded and left. Wade tried to decide if the gang
had left one man hidden nearby to watch the house and
decided, since that's what the Rangers would have done,
the Slocums probably had, too. Their lookout shouldn't
be a danger unless any of them ventured outside. He
glanced at Brownie, still huddling unhappily under the
table.

"Sorry, you old mutt," he told the dog. "I know you
don't like it in here but you'll have to stick it out with us."

Julia led Silver Wing into the kitchen, a handkerchief
saturated with blood tied around the girl's upper arm.

"Sit her down," he said. "We're safe enough for the
moment, let's take a look at that arm."

Julia brought water in a pan from the kitchen pump and
some clean cloths while he untied the bloody handkerchief
from the girl's glass cut. After Julia swabbed away some of
the blood and he got a good look at the injury, he swore.

"Hell, that's not from glass," he muttered. "There's a
bullet in there."

"What are we going to do?" Julia asked.

"Can't be very deep or the bone would be shattered.
Must have been a ricochet. Get me a clean knife, and we'll
dig out the bullet."

Julia stared at him wide-eyed but did as he asked. He
glanced at Silver Wing's face. Though her color was ashen,
she showed no sign of fear or pain.

"Going to hurt some," he told her, "but it's got to come out."

She nodded.

Julia handed him a short and narrow knife and he nodded his approval. "You hold her arm steady," he ordered.

When he was sure Julia had a good grip, he set his jaw and poked into the bullet hole with the point of the knife. Silver Wing made a tiny sound but didn't move. The knife tip almost immediately grated against metal. As he'd thought, the bullet hadn't penetrated far. Thank God.

"We'll have it out in a minute or two," he told the girl, aware he was going to have to hurt her more than he had already. He'd seen grown men pass out in similar circumstances.

With a quick slice of the knife he widened the hole enough to get the knife point in behind the bullet and then pried it out. He thought the gasp of pain came from Silver Wing but belatedly realized it was from Julia.

"You can let go," he told her, "and get me the jug of whiskey from the top shelf of that cupboard." He gestured with his head. "Bring a cup, too."

As Julia dragged a chair over to climb on to reach the shelf, he dropped the bullet onto the bloody handkerchief. "Good girl," he told Silver Wing. "The worst is over. The whiskey's going to sting some, that's all."

First he used the water to wash the hole, then poured a couple fingers of whiskey into the cup and drenched the wound with the fiery liquid. He thought Silver Wing flinched a little but he wasn't sure.

Taking one of the clean, dry cloths, he wrapped it around her upper arm to cover the wound, tying the ends to keep it in place. "If I was an Apache," he said to her, "I'd honor you with an eagle feather. You're a brave warrior."

"Maybe I hit one enemy." Her voice trembled as she spoke.

"That's even better. What's going to happen is you'll run a fever for a few days, can't be helped. The wound ought to heal okay. Us Rangers have pretty good luck using whiskey."

"Adelina left some of her infusion of willow bark she used for fever," Julia said, her voice not much steadier than the girl's.

"You okay?" he asked her.

"If Silver Wing could stand it, I can," she told him. Turning to the girl, she said, "Let me help you to the sofa so you can rest."

"Think I'd better carry her," Wade said and proceeded to do so.

Once on the sofa, Silver Wing insisted on having him lay the rifle next to her, saying, "Next time, I kill him." She spoke calmly but what he heard in her voice made him glad she wasn't his enemy. Apache, sure enough.

He and Julia returned to the kitchen where he helped her clean up the mess and stow away the jug of whiskey.

"There's some dried beef," she said, "and two eggs left of those I gathered from the chickens day before yesterday. Do I have time to fix some food before they attack us again?"

Smart gal. Knew they hadn't given up. But then Julia was smart as all get out. Hadn't fainted on him, either, when he was digging out that bullet. He wouldn't have any other woman.

"Go ahead," he told her. "Doubt if they'll be back before dark. Can't go outside, though. One of them's bound to be watching, hoping to pick us off one by one."

"Do you know," she said to him, "I was more afraid watching you do that to Silver Wing than I was when the Slocums were creeping up on us?"

He nodded. "You're mostly scared ahead of time, that's the way it is. When you're in the middle of it, you're too busy."

She smiled. "I was afraid I was some kind of freak. I think you deserve an eagle feather, too, for taking care of Silver Wing the way you did."

He shrugged. "Had to be done. Saw it done more than once, figured I could if I had to. Just as soon not have to do it again, though."

He watched her bustling around the kitchen, getting things ready, amazed at her coolness under fire, so to speak. He wondered if she knew she had a smear of dirt on her forehead. For some reason it made her look even more desirable. Too bad they couldn't risk making love.

"You can do pretty much everything," she said. "Nothing daunts you."

"Can't say you're right. No one ever asks me to cook more than once after they taste what I turn out."

"That bad?"

"Worse. Even I can't eat it. Brownie'd probably turn up his nose, too." He glanced through the window, seeing nothing alarming. "Going to take a turn through the house so I can look out all the windows," he told her. "Learned in the Rangers to always make sure."

The grounds, in the sunlight, had never looked more peaceful. There was no sign of the Slocums or their lookout. While he was at it, he swept up the broken glass from the shattered window in the main room. Silver Wing, he noticed, had her eyes closed. He hoped she slept. Nothing comfortable about a bullet hole in your hide, even with the bullet dug out.

He was sorry it happened to the girl but if it had to be one of the women, better her than Julia. He couldn't bear to think of anything hurting Julia.

Odd Ezra took off like that. What in hell was he up to? If he'd managed to skirt around the Slocum gang and was riding to Austin for help, they'd never get here in time. The kid would've done better to ride back with Silver Wing and help them out here. Come night, they'd need all the help they could get.

He'd been trying all along to convince himself they'd come out of this alive but he knew it was a pipe dream.

Taking one more turn through the rooms, he returned to the kitchen. Julia turned from the stove and smiled at him.

Wade's heart turned over in his chest. Striding to her, he pulled her into his arms, holding her close.

"Somehow," he murmured. "Somehow."

Chapter 17

The rest of the day passed slowly. Wade and Julia took turns napping, fearing they'd get no sleep in the night to come. True to Wade's prediction, by late afternoon Silver Wing grew feverish. Julia dosed her with willow bark and hoped for the best, but the girl didn't improve. Soon she was out of her head, babbling in a mixture of English and what Julia knew must be Apache.

"Ezra!" Silver Wing kept calling. "Come back!" Then she'd try to struggle up off the sofa.

Finally, in desperation, Julia took the bottle of cure-all elixir the professor had given them and coaxed a dose down the girl with difficulty because Silver Wing didn't seem to know who she was.

An hour later, as the long shadows of evening began to appear, Silver Wing's confusion abated and her skin was cooler to the touch. "I dream I was Yu-Ti," she said. "Yu-Ti is *Ndee*, one of Dream People. Apache. She live many, many moons ago." She pushed herself up to a sitting position. "Yu-Ti search for her warrior, killed in battle. She never find. Brother Wind and sister Rain bury all dead warriors. Great Father take pity on Yu-Ti. He put color of fallen warriors' shields in flowers and change her to butterfly. Spring and summer she search yet.''

Silver Wing's expression was so sad that Julia's heart went out to her. "You called for Ezra," she said. "Is that who you searched for in the dream?"

"Never find," the girl whispered.

"Maybe not in the dream, but Ezra isn't a fallen warrior. Wherever he rode to, he'll return."

"Dreams tell what comes," Silver Wing insisted.

Wade, who'd come into the room during the story, said, "I've heard the Apache have vision dreams. Yours wasn't that kind. You had a fever dream. Fever dreams don't have anything to do with the future . . . or Ezra."

Silver Wing gazed at him as if wanting to believe his words, but couldn't quite.

"Put aside the dream and think about how we can stay alive," he went on. "You can't use the rifle with that injured arm. Know how to shoot a revolver?"

Silver Wing shook her head.

"Julie, get yours," he ordered. "We'll teach her how."

Julia came back with the loaded Beaumont-Adams and, sick as she was, the girl had no difficulty managing the revolver.

Wade hauled the sofa to one side of the broken window. "We need you to man this post, Silver Wing. Remember what I told you about the short range of this revolver—it doesn't shoot as far as a rifle. But it'll kill a man at short range just as dead as a rifle can."

Julia, realizing she would have to take up her own post in her bedroom, thus leaving the girl alone, handed her the bottle of elixir, saying, "If you get feeling real sick again, take a swallow from this."

Wade put a hand on Silver Wing's uninjured arm. "In your dream, you were a butterfly, but here and now you're a brave warrior."

The girl raised her head. "A warrior of the *Ndee*," she said proudly.

Straightening, Wade put an arm around Julia's shoulders and led her from the room into the kitchen. "I wish—" He broke off, leaned to her and brushed her lips with his.

"I wish, too," she murmured as she left him, heading for her bedroom.

Because lighting any lamp would give the Slocums an unfair advantage, Julia crouched by the window, carbine in hand, in the gathering darkness. She'd never felt so alone in her life, not even during the wee hours of last night when she'd stood watch while Wade slept.

During the day, with the sun shining, it hadn't seemed possible that any of them might be killed. With night on the way, though, dark thoughts crowded into her mind. Silver Wing wasn't dead, true, but she'd been wounded by a ricocheting bullet meant to kill.

Wade hadn't yet been fired on nor had she. What would happen when the Slocums returned? For the first time fear trickled through her. She couldn't bear it if Wade died.

In the kitchen, Wade strained his eyes to see into the thickening darkness, trying to spot the slightest movement. When Brownie, still under the table, suddenly gave a half-bark, half-growl, he started.

"Hear them, do you?" he muttered. "Wish I had your ears." A moment later he spotted a flare of yellow light that quickly vanished. His heart sank. A torch. He'd tried his best not to think of the possibility the Slocums might fire the house, trapping them inside.

"Come on, Brownie," he said, unlocking the back door and easing it open a tad. "No sense in you being trapped with us. You're safer out there in the dark."

The dog needed no coaxing. Slithering through the opening, he ran into the night, barking his head off.

Wade thought they might fire at the dog to shut him

up but no shots came. Smart. Any shot would provide those in the house with a target to aim at.

He tried to decide whether to risk it inside or get out while the getting was good. Once the house began to burn, the flames would highlight them if they attempted to escape. They'd be sitting ducks.

Rifle in hand, he ran to Julia's bedroom. "Bring the carbine and come with me," he ordered. Not waiting to see if she followed him, he hurried to the main room and urged Silver Wing off the sofa. "Hang onto the revolver," he told her.

He could feel the increased heat of her skin and her trembling, so he supported her as they crossed to the front door. With his hand on the lock, he shook his head. Not the door, you damn fool. Like as not they'll be waiting.

He guided Silver Wing along the hall to his bedroom, hearing Julia behind him. Easing a window up as quietly as he could, he peered into the now inky darkness. If he couldn't see them, they couldn't see him.

Whispering to Julia, he told her to crawl out first and then he'd hand out Silver Wing. This accomplished, he handed Julia the carbine and the rifle, then crawled out himself. When he touched Silver Wing she leaned against him and he understood she was at the end of her strength. He'd have to carry her. And where in hell was he going to take them to hole up?

"Root cellar?" Julia whispered into his ear.

He was about to dismiss her suggestion—the root cellar could prove to be a trap for them if the Slocums found it—he held. Silver Wing was a liability. He couldn't carry her and shoot, he had to find a safe place to stow her. The root cellar offered the only possibility he could come up with.

After whispering his plan to Julia, he told her to hold onto his belt so they wouldn't be separated. He scooped up Silver Wing and led the way as best he could toward the slanting tunnel dug into the ground where they stored root vegetables. The layer of clouds he'd noticed on the horizon in the afternoon had spread up the sky, hiding the moon, so that it was as black as the inside of a steer.

He stumbled several times, then tripped over something he couldn't see and had to struggle to stay on his feet. He fumbled around for awhile, cursing silently, before his groping hand finally brushed across the wooden door to the cellar.

As quickly as he could, he deposited Silver Wing inside on the dirt floor. Leaning to her, he whispered, "Do you still have the revolver?"

Her, "Yes," was so faint he scarcely heard her. He hoped she'd be all right.

Easing the door shut, he felt around for Julia, encountering nothing but open air. Where was she? He risked a whisper. "Julia?"

No answer.

Where in hell was she? He knew she'd been gripping his belt to begin with because he could feel the tug. When had he stopped feeling it? Must have been when he tripped and fought to keep his footing. The belt probably jerked from her grasp and she couldn't locate him again. Why hadn't she whispered his name? Damn, he had to find her.

Julia shifted the rifle and carbine she carried and groped ahead with her free hand. After she'd lost Wade, she hadn't panicked because she knew where he was headed and thought she could find the root cellar on her own. Hadn't she made the trip from the house to the cellar often enough? In daylight, though. This utter darkness had her turned around until she didn't know where she was going.

Because she was no longer sure where she was, she feared to whisper his name. What if one of the Slocum gang heard her?

She stopped where she was and turned in a circle, peering all around, hoping to see the white bulk of the house to orient herself. Even without moonlight, shouldn't she be able to spot the house?

She couldn't. Was it possible she'd changed direction and wandered into the grove of cottonwoods and now the branches were blocking her view of the house? Or was it just too dark to see anything? She fought down panic.

If only she'd stayed where she was after losing Wade, he probably would have found her by now. That's what the old woodsmen back east always advised—if lost in the woods, stay put, you'll be easier to find.

Shunting aside the thought of laying the guns down, she told herself that once Wade found her, and he would, they'd need the guns. Figuring it was too late to "stay put" she blundered on.

Suddenly, off to her left, a light flared. She stared in amazement, belatedly realizing she was looking at a torch. and, judging by its height, carried by a man on a horse. Wade hadn't explained why they'd left the house—she'd assumed they were taking advantage of the dark to sneak out and hide, eventually getting to the horses to escape. It took a few moments to filter through to her that the torch might mean the Slocums intended to set the house on fire and Wade must have suspected this.

The rider was coming toward her. Julia set down the rifle and carefully aimed the carbine, using the torch as a guide, remembering what Wade had told her about aiming slightly ahead of a moving target. She pulled the trigger and felt the recoil of the gun.

The torch vanished. As she bent to grope for the rifle she'd laid on the ground, a shot rang out and she heard something whizz over her head. A bullet? She'd almost been shot! Terrified, she dropped onto her hands and knees, hoisted her skirts and, awkwardly lugging the carbine with her, crawled away from the spot where she'd stood to shoot, expecting at any moment to hear another shot.

* * *

Wade, staring at the torch, heard a shot, saw the torch disappear, then another gun cracked. What the hell was going on? Was Julia involved? He altered his course toward where he thought the first shot came from. Damn this blundering around in the dark. Trying to be quiet was an impossibility. Where was she?

He tripped over something that sent him to his knees, his hand closing over the barrel of a gun. Running his fingers along it, he recognized his rifle. Though he groped all around the area, he didn't find the carbine. Which meant, he hoped, that Julia still had it, even though she'd dropped the rifle.

A flare of light startled him into a crouch, rifle at the ready. Not a torch, a fire. But it wasn't the house. Seemed to be the dead pine he hadn't gotten around to cutting down that was burning. Was the fire on purpose or a result of a dropped torch?

Taking advantage of the light and at the same time trying to stay concealed, he looked about for any sign of Julia but didn't see her.

Julia saw flames reach up and heard the crackle of burning. The house? No, the firelight showed her that's not what was aflame. It also showed a landmark. Directly in front of her, so close she'd almost crawled into it, was the big old stump she used to pass on her way to the root cellar. Afraid to stand erect for fear she'd be seen in the light from the fire, she eased up into a crouch and made her way cautiously toward where she now knew the root cellar was.

If Wade wasn't there, she'd wait. No more of this stumbling around.

As she neared the cellar, a dark figure loomed ahead of her. Thank God, she'd found him. Throwing caution to the winds, she stood up straight and hurried toward him, barely suppressing her urge to call his name.

When she saw him reach for the cellar door, she was close enough to risk speaking in a low tone. "I'm not in there," she told him. "Here I am."

He whirled to face her, not speaking. The firelight, blocked by the cottonwoods between it and the cellar, was too faint to show her his expression, or even his features.

"I'm so glad we've found each other," she whispered.

"Me, too." She could hardly hear him. He reached and grasped the barrel of the carbine, pulling it toward him. She let it go, surprised he was violating one of his never-do-this rules. *Never pull a gun toward you by the barrel.*

This was Wade, wasn't it? Suddenly unsure, she began to edge backward. At that same moment, he swiped the barrel of the carbine at her, missing her by a hair.

He was the enemy! Julia turned to run but he caught her before she had a chance, twisting her arm up behind her back, rendering her helpless with pain.

"Remember me?" Les Slocum asked.

"Let me go!" she gasped.

"We got unfinished business," he snarled. "That there root cellar looks like a good place to get to it."

She opened her mouth to scream but, before she could, he clapped his hand over her nose and mouth, almost suffocating her.

"Noticed the cellar yesterday when I was on this side of the house," he said. "Figured some of you might use it for a hidey-hole."

When she tried to struggle he twisted her arm higher and the pain stilled her attempt. The next she knew he had the cellar door open and was shoving her inside. It was then she remembered Silver Wing. Had Wade brought the girl here as he'd planned or was Silver Wing still with him?

It was too dark inside the cellar to see anything but, as near as she could tell, no one seemed to be in the small

opening. Les Slocum flung her onto the dirt floor so hard
the breath whooshed from her lungs. He dropped down,
levering a leg between hers as he tried to pull up her skirts.
Released from the pain of her twisted arm, she fought him
and, as soon as her breath returned, she screamed.

He wadded a smelly cloth into her mouth, making her
retch. His one-handed grip of both her wrists prevented
her from removing the cloth or striking him. Though not
quite helpless, she was no match for his strength.

He got her skirts thigh-high, cursing as he fumbled with
the ties to her drawers. She tried to writhe away from him
but could not. Gagging from the cloth in her mouth, she
despaired. How could she bear to have this vile man violate
her? He must not! With renewed strength, she did her
best to throw herself to one side. In vain. He kept her
pinned on her back.

She felt the ties on her drawers give way as he yanked
at them in frustration. Down they came, removing the last
barrier. And then he was on her, his hardness pressing
against her. She closed her eyes and braced herself for the
awful assault.

A woman screamed, the sound distant and faint. Wade's
head jerked up, listening, but the scream wasn't repeated.
He hadn't a clue where it had come from but the root
cellar crossed his mind. That would explain the muffled
sound of the scream. Silver Wing? Where was Julia? He'd
best take a look.

Before he could move, a high-pitched, ululating yell split
the night. Rebel yell! Who the hell could that be? He'd
been told the Slocums were from Pennsylvania originally.
Maybe one of their recruits had been a Confederate. A
volley of shots rattled off, so many it sounded like a battle.
But between what forces?

"Gotcha, you slavering son of bitch," a man shouted.

He'd swear the voice was Jack Crain's. He'd served with the Rebs. Was it possible—?

Whoever had arrived, they were on his side, leaving him free. Wade raised up to his full height and, in the dying light of the burning tree, hurried toward the root cellar.

As Julia struggled in vain against her captor, a sharp crack blasted her eardrums, echoing in the enclosed space. He jerked upward, then fell heavily on top of her and lay unmoving, his weight leaving her temporarily helpless.

With numb fingers, she pulled the nasty wad of cloth from her mouth, gagging as she did it. With the cloth gone, her mind begin to work again. Someone had fired a gun and killed Les Slocum. At least she was pretty sure he was dead. Who? Not Wade or he would have have hauled Les's body off her by now. Who else—? There was only one other person.

"Silver Wing?" she said hoarsely, the words rasping against her throat.

No answer.

"Silver Wing, are you there?"

No reply. She grew aware of the rattle of gunshots from outside. Though her attention remained fixed on getting out from under this tremendous weight, she was dimly aware she was hearing too many shots. To make her predicament worse, what she suspected must be Les's blood was oozing onto her, saturating the top of her dress.

Fighting nausea, she told herself there was something to be said for being able to faint under duress. How could a dead man be so heavy? Who'd shot him? And where had they gone?

"Wade, that you?" The call came from behind him.

Wade whirled, Colt aimed at a man carrying a lantern.

"It's Ezra," the man said. "Is Silver Wing all right?"

"Left her in the root cellar," Wade said, holstering the Colt. He hurried on with Ezra at his heels. "What's happening?" he called over his shoulder.

"Pretty much over. I found Jack Crain and the hands, called him a cowardly yellow dog and told them all what was going on. Turns out the hands thought they were following your orders, relayed through him. Once we got that straight, we hightailed it back here. Jack, too."

"Thought I heard him."

"Two riders got past us, heading for Austin, looked like. We shot three deader than doornails."

"Leaves one unaccounted for." Wade increased his pace, his anxiety mounting. Where was Julia?

"Silver Wing is all right, isn't she?" Ezra asked.

"Alive when I left her," Wade told him.

Reaching the root cellar, he flung open the door, grabbed Ezra's lantern and peered inside. He stopped breathing.

A mass of blood smeared bodies lay piled on the dirt floor of the cellar.

"Silver Wing!" Ezra cried, pushed past him and lifted the top body into his arms, carrying her into the open. The one underneath was a man, face down. Below him, Wade could see Julia's bunched-up skirts.

Wade set the lantern down. Red coloring his vision, he grabbed the man's arm and hauled him from the cellar. The body flopped onto its back outside and despite the smeared blood from a bullet hole in the temple, he recognized Les Slocum's face. Unaware he was cursing, he reentered the cellar, intending to lift Julia's bloodstained body into his arms.

To his amazement, he found her sitting up. "Such language," she said weakly.

He picked her up as gently as he could and brought her outside. Ezra had laid Silver Wing down and was kneeling beside her, tears running down his face.

"Hand me the lantern," Wade ordered, "and then bring her into the house."

His only concern was for Julia so he paid little attention to what Ezra had done with Silver Wing. Once inside, Wade carried Julia to her bed and eased her onto it. She promptly slid off the bed onto her feet.

"I'll get the bed all bloody," she protested, her voice a mere rasp. "Help me take off these stained clothes."

"But you're hurt," he said. "You shouldn't be—"

She grimaced. "It's his blood, not mine."

Finally understanding, Wade breathed a sigh of relief and set to undoing the buttons at the back of her dress. Between them, they stripped her down to the skin.

"My right arm hurts when I try to use it," she said. "Would you mind washing the blood off me?"

Under any other circumstances, he would have found it wildly arousing to bathe her naked breasts, especially when her nipples puckered under the cool water on the cloth. But all he could think of was that she was alive and not injured. Unless that bastard . . .

"Did he—hurt you?" Wade demanded as he dried her off.

"He twisted my arm up behind my back something fierce," she told him. "It still hurts. And my throat's sore from that nasty rag he forced into my mouth to shut me up."

"That's not what I mean. Did he . . . ?" His words trailed off.

"Oh, that. No. He tried, but someone shot him before he—before he—" She paused, shuddering.

Wade gathered her into his arms and she snuggled against him.

Ezra interrupted them. "Please," he said from the doorway. "I'm sorry to disturb you but please help me with Silver Wing. I put her on her bed." He turned and left.

Julia pulled away from Wade, took her robe from the hook and slid into it, doing up the fastenings as she walked toward Wade. "Was it Silver Wing who shot him?" she asked. "I forgot she had my revolver."

"Must have been," he said, "because that's where I left her—in the root cellar."

In the room Silver Wing shared with the twins, Ezra had lit the lamp on the wall. The girl lay on the cot, her clothes blood-smeared, the cloth missing from her arm wound, her color a frightening gray.

"I've asked God not to let her die," Ezra said, "but I don't know how to help her otherwise."

"Why don't you men leave while I get her into clean clothes," Julia suggested, heartsick at the girl's appearance.

As she stripped and washed Silver Wing, who responded only with a slight moan when she was rolled over, Julia distracted herself from the thought that the girl was dying by murmuring to her as she worked.

"Great-aunt Polly says cleanliness is next to Godliness. She's usually right. Ezra's asked God to save you, do you know that? You saved my life. I know Les would have killed me after he—did that horrible thing. So it's only right that God should save you."

Choosing a short sleeved nightdress that once had been Teresa Sue's, Julia slipped it over Silver Wing's head and eased it down over her. She examined the bullet wound on the girl's arm and shook her head. She'd cleansed it as best she could but perhaps more whiskey should be swabbed into the hole. After pulling a cover over the girl, she called to Wade, telling him to bring the jug.

Ezra immediately appeared in the doorway, asking, "How is she?"

"She has a fever," Julia told him. "I think we left the professor's cure-all elixir in the main room. It helped her before. Could you please fetch it, along with a cup of water and a spoon?"

She let Wade doctor the wound with the whiskey before wrapping a clean cloth around the girl's arm. Because she knew how much Ezra yearned to help, she had him raise Silver Wing's head while she tried to coax a teaspoon of the elixir down her, then a few spoonfuls of water. "I wish she'd swallow more water," Julia said as much to herself as to him.

"I'll stay with her," Ezra offered. "I'll spoon as much water into her as she'll tolerate."

Julia nodded. It seemed to be the best plan for all concerned, having him watch over the girl. As she started to leave the room with Wade, she heard men's voices in the kitchen and paused.

"The hands," Wade said. "I told them to go ahead and fix their own grub."

"I don't wish to be seen in my robe. Or seen at all right now."

He followed her to her room. "You need to rest. Go to bed. It's over. Ezra found Jack and the hands and they all came to the rescue. The three Slocums are dead, they won't trouble anyone again. One of their recruits died, too. The two remaining men must be half-way to Austin by now."

"Silver Wing saved my life," she said. "She mustn't die. I hope Ezra can will her to live."

"I thought you were dead." His voice was bleak. "Thank God, you're not." He pulled her to him and kissed her forehead. "We're all safe," he said. "Sleep well."

After leaving Julia, Wade stood outside her door for a few moments before joining the men in the kitchen. If she'd died . . . But she hadn't. He'd wake in the morning and she'd still be here, brightening the day. Making him glad to be alive.

As he passed the door to the room where Ezra watched over Silver Wing, he paused, remembering how grudgingly he'd let the girl come with them after her father died. He'd never begrudge her anything again. Because of Silver

Wing, Julia lived. He hoped Ezra had found a pipeline to the Lord, because the girl deserved to survive.

To his surprise, he found himself bowing his head—something he hadn't done in years—and sending up his own prayer for her, along with his heartfelt thanks.

Chapter 18

When Julia pulled up Dodie by Rose Creek, she saw that Ezra was putting the final coat of paint on the gazebo he'd been working on for the past two weeks. Though he'd salvaged some of the curlicued carvings, most was new wood.

Silver Wing was sitting on a stump, her bare feet dabbling in the creek as she watched the twins wading in the shallow water. Her wound no longer required a bandage. Though a puckered scar would remain, the hole was healing rapidly. Whether this was due to the professor's cure-all elixir, Wade's treatment of the wound with whiskey, or Silver Wing's own sturdy constitution wasn't important. She'd survived.

In her hair she wore a feather Wade had found for her on a head band she'd contrived from a length of red cloth—a hawk feather rather than one from an eagle, but it symbolized her courage.

Julia admired her unorthodox appearance at the same time as she wondered how Ezra could ever bring the girl home to Coventry and expect her to be accepted there.

She dismounted and tied the mare next to Cloud, the dappled gray pony hitched to a cart Ezra had clobbered together from an old, unused wagon he'd found in the barn. With the pony cart, Silver Wing could take the twins on short excursions. Like this one to Rose Creek.

Every hand on the ranch knew the girl had shot and killed Les Slocum—and not from afar with a rifle, either. Up close, with a revolver. Since that night, no one had bothered Silver Wing.

Of course, Jack Crain was no longer at the ranch. Though he and Wade had parted fairly amicably, Wade hadn't offered to take him back, had, in fact, promoted Jamie to Jack's job.

Julia wandered over to the creek, shook her head at the twins' invitation to join them in the water, and sat down beside Silver Wing, who smiled at her but didn't speak.

"I bet I could build an entire church if I tried," Ezra said to them. "I'd like to do it sometime."

"You said you didn't have a call," Julia reminded him.

"Not to be a minister, no." Ezra said. "But I mean to help God when I can, so maybe I have been called to do that. The professor says not every man who becomes a minister does hear a call from God. He didn't, but his father wanted him to be one and so he tried, but finally had to give it up. At least for the most part. He still obliges when folks need him to. I sometimes wonder about my father."

Julia had often wondered about the Reverend Miller's narrow-minded way of viewing people and events, but she didn't think that was what Ezra was referring to. Great-aunt Polly's belief in a reasonable God who helped people who helped themselves was easier to choose than the Reverend Miller's blaming and punishing God.

"For example," Ezra went on, "my father disapproved of you, Julia. I could never understand why."

She'd not been too sure why, either, unless her impulsiveness alarmed him. If Julia Sommers had proved too difficult for his approval, she hated to think how he'd feel when faced with Silver Wing as a prospective daughter-in-law.

"Do you plan to go back to Coventry?" Ezra asked her.

She evaded the question by saying, "I can't make any plans until Adelina's replacement arrives."

"Silver Wing and I are waiting for that, too, aren't we, dear?"

The girl smiled at him. "My warrior speaks, I listen."

Ezra grinned at her, evidently this was some sort of private joke they shared. "Some warrior, when you wear the hawk feather," he said.

"You carry bravery in your heart," she told him.

Their obvious closeness made Julia begin to feel like a third wheel. "Time I got back to the house," she said, rising. "The gazebo looks really beautiful, Ezra."

"I meant it to. Buildings should delight the spirit, don't you think?"

"If Rose Howland's spirit is able to understand what you've done, I'm sure she's delighted."

Ezra came over to help her remount Dodie and she set her course for the house. All the way back, his question nagged at her—did she mean to return to Coventry?

The closeness she'd shared with Wade before and during the Slocum attack had faded away like smoke in the wind. In fact, she had the feeling he was avoiding being alone with her.

When she reached the corral, one of the hands took the mare and she walked toward the house, pausing when she saw the professor sitting on the steps of his wagon. He'd returned to the ranch with the twins as soon as the Tysons got word that the danger was over.

"You seem deep in thought," he said to her.

"I have to make a decision soon," she said.

"Yes, we all must. Whether to do this or do that. Or whether to do neither and, instead, venture onto an unknown and uncertain path into the future."

"You have your wagon with you no matter where you go," she said.

"True. And you have yourself along with you whatever you decide to do."

Julia blinked, unsure of his meaning. Brownie, sleeping under the wagon, stirred, wriggled out, stretched, and yawned.

"I'm boring the dog," the professor said. "Too much pontification, a fault of mine."

"I like to listen to you," she insisted, "even if I don't always understand."

"There are several homely sayings such as, 'To thine own self be true.' Perhaps one more fit for the moment is this: An apple has the choice of remaining on a twig waiting either to be picked or to wither. The apple's other choice is to fall to the ground and rot."

"But I'm not an apple," she said, more confused than ever.

"Precisely my point. You are a young woman with a mind of her own, something an apple lacks."

"It seems to me we're back where we started, with me trying to decide what to do."

"Not quite." He smiled at her. "You are now the recipient of my wisdom and advice. No charge."

Julia smiled back at him. "Thank you, kind sir."

"Ah, a smile for my reward," he said. "More than adequate compensation."

She went into the house feeling cheered. The professor had a way of taking you out of yourself for the moment.

At the evening meal, Silver Wing, as usual, ate with the twins in the other room while Julia, acting as cook, served Wade and the hands before eating herself. Either that, or she had to eat hurriedly ahead of time. It wasn't the best arrangement but she didn't feel comfortable sitting at the table with them. The fact that Wade hadn't insisted she

eat with them made her all the more conscious of her
uncertain status in the household.

He lingered in the kitchen when the meal was over. She
waited, but he stayed there so she finally dished herself up
a plate of food and sat down at the table. Before she was
wounded, Silver Wing participated in the cleanup but Julia
had told her to wait until her arm wound healed completely
before helping.

Wade turned a chair around and sat on it backward. "I
didn't realize you were waiting to eat until we finished,"
he said.

"That's what Adelina always did—either ate before or
after. I never have time before. Which reminds me. Do
you have any idea when her replacement will be here?"

"One thing at a time. You're not my housekeeper. You
don't have to wait to eat."

"What am I, then?" As usual the words were out before
she thought.

"A guest?" He sounded uncertain.

"Hardly. I do believe I'm earning my keep."

"You'll eat with us from now on," he announced, leaving
her position still unnamed.

She opened her mouth to inquire about the replacement
once more but he spoke first.

"Thought we might ride to Rose Creek before dark.
Ezra tells me he's finished the gazebo and I'd like to take
a look."

Tempted to tell him she'd already been there once
today, she held back the words. He was offering her something and it would be foolish to turn him down before she
knew exactly what it was.

"As soon as I clean—"

"Now," he said. "Since Ezra spends all his free time
with Silver Wing anyway, he can help with the cleanup as
well as with the twins."

As they set off on the horses, heading for the creek,

Dodie turned her head to look at Julia, as if to ask, "Again?"

"Having trouble with her?" Wade asked.

"Not really. Dodie likes to remind me she has a mind of her own and that she's doing me a big favor by following my orders."

"Something like you, in other words."

Julia couldn't deny the truth of that. "I'm trying not to be an apple," she told him.

"What's an apple got to do with anything?"

"Something the professor said. You'll have to ask him."

"Don't rightly understand the man half the time."

"He's like the Bible, he tends to speak in parables."

Wade nodded. "Comes from him being a preacher, I suppose."

They rode in silence for a time, until Julia said, "You once mentioned knowing Shakespeare. From where?"

"Went to school in South Carolina. Teachers had us take different parts and read some of his plays out loud. Can make a lot more sense out of his words when you hear them than you can seeing them on paper."

"Which plays?"

"I remember *MacBeth* the best."

A boy would, she thought, all that fighting and murdering. "I liked *Romeo and Juliet* the best," she confided.

He grinned at her. "You would, being a girl."

"There's nothing wrong with romance."

"Suppose not. But that play didn't end happily, as I recall."

"Not all romances do."

"Some end with both of them dying." His bleak tone made her realize what he was referring to. Not *Romeo and Juliet,* but his brother and Teresa Sue.

Determined not to let him wallow in grief and regrets, she turned the conversation back to the here and now. "You still haven't told me when Adelina's replacement will be coming."

"Can't 'cause I don't know. Figured somebody'd be showing up by now."

"I have a suggestion."

He looked at her in mock apprehension. "Spit it out."

"There's that little house by the cottonwood grove no one is using. It needs fixing up but Ezra's good at that. Why don't you ask Adelina if her daughter and her husband and the two little boys would like to live here on the ranch. Pablo could work with the hands and the boys would be company for the twins. That way you'd get Adelina back. You have to admit she's an excellent housekeeper."

"That's not a bad suggestion. Problem is, I was thinking the same about the house, only I figured Ezra and Silver Wing might want to live in it—after they get married, that is."

"You think they will marry?"

"Foregone conclusion. Plain to see they're smitten with one another and, being the son of a minister, he's too honorable to have it any other way. I owe Silver Wing— she can stay at the ranch for the rest of her life if she wants."

"You don't think he'll decide to bring her back to Coventry with him?"

"Ezra doesn't strike me as a fool."

"He hasn't said a word about wanting to stay on here." As she spoke she realized he hadn't mentioned returning to Coventry lately either, just asked her if she was going to.

"Ezra has already agreed to fix up the little house once the gazebo is finished," Wade said. "If he decides to move on after he gets done, I'll sound out Adelina's family."

"And in the meantime?"

"Do you dislike the work so much?"

"It's not the work, it's the uncertainty."

He didn't reply until after they'd made the descent down to the creek and dismounted.

"Ezra does a fine job," Wade said. "Told him he could find work anywhere building and fixing up."

"Silver Wing calls him her warrior."

Wade smiled. "She'll turn him into an Apache yet."

He took her hand and together they strolled over to the gazebo. "Paint's still a tad tacky," he said. "Be careful."

"I can't help thinking your mother would be happy to see her gazebo beautiful again."

"It is, isn't it? Never really noticed that when I was younger."

They wandered over to the creek and stood watching the trickling water.

"I'm glad you decided to bury the past," she told him. "This is too lovely a spot not be be enjoyed."

"Trouble with the past, it lies uneasy in the grave. Don't want to stay buried." He let go of her hand, picked up some pebbles, and began plinking them into the water.

"Why?"

He shrugged. "None of my doing. I don't want it resurrected. Grant's been on my mind a lot lately. Seems to me he'd be alive yet if he'd never met and married Teresa Sue."

"Ed Tyson told me she was a sweet girl, a real homebody."

"That's just it—she was. Grant had no cause for what he did."

"So what you're saying is that your brother should never have married?"

Wade sighed. "Or else maybe married some gal he wasn't so crazy about, someone not so pretty."

Though Julia sympathized with how he felt about the tragedy, she was beginning to lose her patience. "Your brother chose to marry Teresa Sue," she said. "It might have been the same no matter who he picked. You can't second guess the past."

"You're right. Better not to marry at all."

She eyed him narrowly, wondering exactly what he was getting at. "We're talking about Grant?"

He blinked. "Yeah."

"Yet you're promoting marriage between Ezra and Silver Wing. Is Ezra so different?"

"Minister's son," he muttered.

Julia rolled her eyes. "The sons of ministers are no different from any other men. Ezra is no saint. His father would have had a fit if he'd known Ezra had kissed me on the church sleigh ride."

Wade stared at her. "Ezra kissed you?"

"On that sleigh ride once and once in Great-aunt Polly's parlor. Why?"

"You never told me that before."

"Why on earth would I have?"

Wade took off his hat and ran his hand through his hair. "See? That's the trouble."

"I haven't the faintest notion of what you're talking about."

He jammed his hat back on and glared at her. "I'm jealous, damn it. I don't like to hear about other men kissing you."

Irritation sharpened Julia's voice. "Heavens, you didn't even know I existed at that time. Besides, what's so awful about a little jealousy? I've already admitted jealousy drove me to track you down in Austin. But I certainly didn't feel like killing either you or Monette. And I'm willing to bet you have no intention of shooting Ezra. Or me. Admit it."

"I suppose I don't," he muttered.

"Then why are you carrying on?"

He turned to face her, his hands fastening on her shoulders. "What if it gets worse? How do I know it won't? Grant's didn't come on full-blown, he worked his way up to the rage that made him kill."

Julia's anger erupted. She jerked away from him and put her hands on her hips. "How do you know you'll be alive tomorrow? Or I will? Great-aunt Polly used to say, 'Life's too short to worry about the day that hasn't come.' She—"

"To hell with your great-aunt and her folk wisdom," he growled. "I got reason to worry and you know it."

"Don't you go putting your feelings onto me," she snapped. "If you want my opinion, here it is. You've let what your brother did eat at you to the point where you can't think straight." She turned away and would have started for the horses if he hadn't grabbed her arm.

"I'm not through."

"Well, I am!"

"Julie, be reasonable. I brought you here to try to explain."

Hearing him call her Julie diluted her annoyance but enough was left for her to say, "Explain what? All I've heard is the same old story of how you fear you'll be another Grant if you ever decide to love a woman."

Again he gripped her shoulders. "Loving's not a matter of decision. Only what to do about it is."

She could see pain in his eyes but she hardened her heart. How well she knew falling in love was not a matter of will. If it had been she certainly would have chosen another man to love, rather than this—this Texan who didn't want to love her in return.

"My God, Julie, you're driving me mad," he muttered, pulling her against him so hard she lost her breath.

In a moment, she knew, he'd kiss her and she'd lose her will as well as her breath. Refusing to let that happen, she put her palms against his chest and pushed. "Let me go!" she cried.

"I wish I could," he said, but released her.

Julia whirled and stalked to the horses.

They rode back to the house without speaking.

Wade watched Julia walk from the corral to the house, head held high. When she vanished inside, the professor, who'd been on the other side of his wagon, came around and said, "That young woman is troubled, my friend."

"Hard-headed," Wade muttered.

"As we all are at times."

Sighing, Wade had to agree. "I guess I don't understand women real well."

"Most men don't, which is fortunate. The few men who do tend to be charlatans who prey on the weaknesses of women."

His interest caught, Wade leaned against the side of the wagon. "You don't say."

"It's true. I once knew a man who called himself Count Alphonius Nagy. Phony was the right word for this man whose specialty was fleecing rich widows. They never seemed to catch on until too late. One finally did and threatened to call in the authorities. He killed her to keep from being exposed and buried her under a tree in her own apple orchard. Spring came, the frost heaved out of the ground, bringing part of her body to the surface. Since she still had his diamond stick-pin clenched in her fist, that was the end of the so-called count."

"Quite a story. You've led an interesting life. Your mention of the apple orchard reminds me of something Julia said about not being an apple. She wouldn't explain, told me I'd have to ask you."

The professor nodded. "I explained that an apple's only choices were either to stay on the tree and wither while waiting to be picked or to fall to the ground and rot."

"That's it?"

"Not quite. I believe you just said Julia told you she wasn't an apple."

"Yes, but—" Wade broke off as the significance of what he'd heard sunk in. He stared at the professor who raised his eyebrows but said nothing more.

After a moment, Wade started for the kitchen door, not quite sure of what he meant to do or say, but determined not to let the matter rest. Brownie, at his side, stopped abruptly and began to bark, his muzzle pointed toward the trail to Austin.

Stranger coming. Wade's hand drifted to the handle of his Colt as he glanced around to make sure the twins weren't outside.

Jamie appeared from the bunkhouse, rifle in hand, backed up by two more of the hands. Ezra emerged from the house, buckling on his holstered revolver. No more sitting ducks, Wade told himself with satisfaction.

When the three riders appeared, one obviously a woman, and the others not at all menacing, the men glanced at one another rather sheepishly and all melted away except for Ezra.

"We bring Senora Ramirez," one of the Mexican men said. "My mother-in-law send her to help you."

Wade advanced toward the riders who'd pulled up near the wagon. "You must be Pablo," he said. "You're welcome to spend the night and I'm happy to see Senora Ramirez."

He asked Ezra to help the men settle the horses and escorted the older Mexican woman to the house.

"Julie!" he called as he entered the kitchen. "Come and meet the new housekeeper."

Chapter 19

Maria Ramirez was older than Adelina and slower, but she proved to be a good worker in her unhurried way as well as an excellent cook. You couldn't fault Maria. With a capable housekeeper at the ranch, it was plain as plain could be to Julia that her time was up and she must go.

The problem was she didn't want to go.

In the evening, a week after Maria arrived, Julia reluctantly began to look through her clothes, deciding what to bring with her and what to leave behind. No use to take everything, Great-aunt Polly's house would be crowded enough with Emma and Floyd living there. She could stay only temporarily, until she found a way to support herself.

Julia saw Silver Wing hovering in the bedroom doorway and invited her in. "Ezra say you go back to Coventry," the girl said. "No good."

"I have to. There's no need for me here any more."

"Is need. Ezra and me marry. You stay to see."

Julia dropped the dress she'd been examining onto her bed and hugged Silver Wing. "You're getting married! I'm so happy for you both."

"Professor marry us, then we go."

Julia stepped back to stare at her. "Go where?"

"California." Silver Wing pronounced the name carefully, obviously not yet used to the word.

"You and Ezra are traveling to California?" Julia was flabbergasted.

"With professor and his wagon."

"The professor's going, too?"

Silver Wing nodded.

"Not one of you mentioned a single word about your plans," Julia said. "I had no idea. That is, I thought you might get married—but California!"

"Tell you first," Silver Wing said. "Ezra say you come along. No good Coventry. Better California."

"I'll have to think it over. But tell Ezra thanks."

After the girl left, Julia sat on her bed, her mind in a turmoil. California? She couldn't deny she was tempted. Almost anything sounded more promising than Coventry. Except for the fact she wouldn't see her sister or her great-aunt, maybe for years, California seemed the perfect solution.

But how could she bear to leave Wade? Or the twins? She fought the threatening tears by reminding herself she was not an apple, she had other choices than to wither on a branch or rot on the ground.

She rose and began reviewing her belongings in another light. If she were to go to California it might be best to take everything along.

The next morning Wade stopped to talk to Ezra, who was working on the small house on the far side of the cottonwood grove. "Coming along," he commented.

"I haven't found any rot," Ezra said. "The main problem is neglect. Luckily the frame itself is still sound."

Deciding it might be time to broach the subject, Wade began with, "You planning to stay on here?"

"If you mean long enough to finish fixing up this house, yes, I do. It'll take me another week at the most."

"You do plan to go back to Coventry, then."

Ezra shook his head. "Not on your life. After the professor marries us, Silver Wing and I are off to California with him. We'll be taking the two horses Silver Wing brought when she came here and, if you don't mind, the clothes you offered her from your sister-in-law's trunk."

"Take the trunk and all—welcome to it. Why California?"

"I've always dreamed of going there. My mother's younger brother rode out to California in the early fifties, after gold. Instead, he wound up driving mules with supplies for the miners. He met a widow who owned a hotel and married her. Between the two of them, they've done well. The letters they write to my mother are full of the wonderful climate and great opportunities for a young man like myself. But my father always pooh-poohed that possibility."

Wade thought over his words and nodded. "Might be the best place for you and Silver Wing. I'm pretty sure no one in California worries much about Apaches."

"My uncle claims the Indians out there aren't warlike. But, sir, Silver Wing is not an Apache."

"Not entirely, no. I'm pleased you two are marrying. When's it to be?"

Ezra reddened. "Right after I finish this house. I thought maybe Silver Wing and I could—well, have our honeymoon here before we start off on the trip."

"Was going to offer the house to you and your bride to live in anyway," Wade said. "Stay in it as long as you like."

"Thank you, sir. Silver Wing will be as pleased as I am. She's trying to persuade Julia to come with us to California, you know."

Wade stared at him. "Julia? To California?"

"Don't you think California would be a better destination for her than Coventry? If she goes back there, she'll probably wind up working in the mill to support herself. In my opinion, the mill's not the place for Julia. In California anything is possible.''

"Why in hell does she think she needs to go anywhere?''

Ezra eyed him levelly. "You'll have to ask her that yourself, sir.''

Wade muttered to himself as he walked back to the corral to saddle Thor. Why a man had to get himself mixed up with a woman was more than he could understand. His arrangement with Monette had been uncomplicated but that was over—because it wasn't Monette he wanted. No, he'd somehow gotten entangled with this eastern filly who looked like butter wouldn't melt in her mouth. Looks were sure deceiving.

Julia might appear to be all sweetness and light but she reminded him of horses he'd seen who'd rather die than be broke to the saddle. Spirited, with a mind of her own.

Going off to California was she? Well, let her go! He was better off without her complicating his life.

As he was about to mount Thor, Ed Tyson showed up, bound for Austin. "Anything you need, neighbor?'' he asked Wade.

Yeah, something no one could provide—peace of mind. "Nothing I can think of, Ed,'' he said. "Thanks for stopping by.''

Ed was about to ride on, when Julia came running out of the house, waving to him. "You remember Adelina Mendoza?'' she asked when she neared.

Ed nodded. "Sure do. Never forget a good cook.''

"Could you look her up in Austin and give her a message from Silver Wing and Ezra?''

"Be glad to.''

"You see,'' Julia went on, "they're getting married next Sunday and they'd like to invite Adelina to their wedding here at the ranch.''

"I'll be danged! So the boy's gonna tie the knot. What do you know?''

"You and your wife are invited, too," she added.

"You can count on us coming. And I'll do my best to pass on the message to Mrs. Mendoza." Ed touched his fingers to his hat and clucked to his horse.

As he rode off, Julia started to turn away.

"Hang on a minute," Wade ordered. "Want to talk to you." He tied Thor to a post and jerked his head toward the cottonwoods. "Over there."

"I'm quite busy at the moment," she said coolly. "Maybe later."

"Busy, hell. You're afraid to face me."

She made a disapproving sound. "I certainly am *not* afraid."

"Prove it by coming with me." Without waiting for agreement, he grasped her hand and pulled her with him, aware she had to half-run to keep up with him but past caring. Damn it, he intended to hammer this out once and for all.

When they stood under the shade of the big trees, she jerked her hand free and crossed her arms over her breasts. The pink dress she wore had a lower neckline than most of her gowns and her folded arms pushed the tops of her breasts into view, distracting him.

Apparently aware of where his gaze was directed, she dropped her arms and tugged at her neckline. "Teresa Sue and I did not have similar tastes," she muttered.

He suppressed a smile. "I enjoy the effect."

"You would."

"Nothing wrong with looking at a pretty woman if she isn't spoken for."

"Did you haul me away from my chores just to tell me that?"

This woman could irk him beyond any he'd ever met. Didn't she like to be admired? Most of them did. Trouble was, Julia wasn't most of them, she was one of a kind.

"Ezra tells me you're going to California with them," he accused.

"I'm considering it, yes. I believe it may prove to be a better choice than returning to Coventry."

Just like that, cool as you please. "You might have mentioned it to me."

"I've told you I can't stay on here, told you more than once. Don't you listen?"

"Didn't think you really meant to leave," he admitted. "You're so fond of the twins and all, I sort of figured you'd stay on."

"You're right, I love Nancy and Susan. It will break my heart to leave them."

"Then why even consider going?"

"With Maria here, you don't need me any longer."

Words jumped onto his tongue—he'd always need her, didn't she know that? Not just because of the twins but because he . . . Wade caught the words back before they poured from his mouth, shaken by what he'd almost told her. He couldn't afford to feel anything of the sort, much less say it.

"And so, when Ezra offered me the chance to go to California," she went on, "I realized I did have another choice besides Coventry."

"Unlike the professor's apple," he said.

She shrugged. "If our conversation is finished, I really should get back to my chores."

There she stood before him, tempting as a ripe apple, an apple he longed to make his. But she wasn't likely to permit him to so much as touch her. How different she'd been, warm and loving, when they'd been threatened by the Slocums. Now the Slocums were dead and she was going away from him.

He sighed. Maybe it was for the best. Once she was gone, he need never again worry about following his brother's course. No other woman could make him feel the way Julia did, so there'd be no danger.

"I'm going, then," she told him and walked away.

As he watched her, he couldn't help but think that all

too soon she would be going, she'd be walking away from him and never coming back.

Ed Tyson stopped by the ranch two evenings later with the news that he'd passed on the invitation to Adelina and she'd be coming to the wedding. Wade said he'd tell the others.

Ed nodded. "Mrs. Mendoza asked if I was sure there'd be only one wedding. Said I was." He shot Wade a sly look. "Couldn't figure out what she meant. You got any idea?"

Wade's "Nope" was curt.

"Too bad," Ed said. "Be seeing you on Sunday."

Disgruntled, Wade went to find Ezra to tell him Ed's news. He'd been avoiding Julia—let Ezra carry the message.

Ezra came into the kitchen to let Silver Wing know Adelina and the Tysons would be guests at their wedding. Julia and Maria were also working there and heard the news.

"Bueno," Maria said. "Good. Adelina and me, we have much to talk over."

Julia glanced at her in mild puzzlement. Maria must have seen Adelina in Austin before she left and not that much time had passed since then. Perhaps, though, she wanted to ask questions about housekeeping duties.

Maria turned out to be as good a needlewoman as Adelina, so she and Julia had been altering Teresa Sue's wedding dress which they'd found carefully wrapped in muslin at the bottom of the trunk. Silver Wing would not only be a beautiful bride, but a properly attired one. Ezra had a presentable "Sunday best" ensemble he'd brought from Coventry and never worn at the ranch, so the groom would be worthy of the bride, as far as clothing went.

The twins, having never seen a wedding, were full of questions. Nothing had been said to them yet about any

departures. Julia dreaded telling them when the time
came.

"Papa Wade says our real mama and papa were married," Susan told Julia that night as she put the girls to
bed.

"He said they got married so they could have babies,"
Nancy chimed in. "That was us."

"Us," Susan echoed. "Papa Wade says he remembers
when we were tiny, little babies."

"Silver Wing and Ezra gonna have little babies, too?"
Nancy asked.

"If they do, likely it'll be one baby at a time. You and
Susan are special. Twins don't happen very often." She
hugged Nancy, then Susan. "You're very, very special."

"Babies are funner 'n' puppies," Susan said. "Mrs.
Atkins got a little baby. At the party, he tried to suck my
finger."

Nancy giggled. "Silly baby."

"Babies do like to suck on things," Julia said.

"I'm gonna tell Silver Wing to hurry up and get a baby
so we can play with him," Susan said.

Julia suppressed a sigh. They'd sorely miss Silver Wing.
And they'd be losing her at the same time, as well.

When she went to bed, she couldn't sleep. After turning
and tossing for what seemed hours, she rose, opened her
door, and peered into the hall. One lamp, turned down,
was left lit in one of the hall sconces so people wouldn't
have to stumble around in the dark if they got up in the
night. Though it cast very little light, it was enough for
her to see no one else was stirring.

She padded down the hall to the main room where, to
her surprise, she found the front door ajar. Easing it open
enough to peer out, she saw no one on the porch so she
slipped through. As she stepped out, the warm night breeze
stirred her hair. She gazed up at the crescent moon and
one bright star near it. Back in Coventry, Ezra had once

told her some of what looked like brilliant stars were really other planets like Venus or Jupiter.

"So which one are you?" she asked softly. "Venus, maybe?"

" 'Fraid I can't qualify." Wade's voice, coming from off to her left, startled her.

"Oh!" she gasped. "I didn't see anyone on the porch. I didn't mean to—"

"If anyone is Venus," he interrupted, "you are."

Flustered, she tried to retreat, but he'd gotten between her and the door.

"I've been thinking," he said. "You can't go."

"Do you mean now or ever?" she asked, pretending to be calm and collected when her heart was hammering at his nearness.

"Not now, not ever. I can't get along without you."

Without warning, he reached for her, pulled her into his arms and kissed her. She'd fought against this happening for days and in the back of her mind she knew she should continue the fight. But she wanted the kiss so badly. Her need to feel his hard strength against her was so overwhelming, any thought of resistance was no match for it.

How could she get along without him? At the moment the very idea of attempting to was beyond her. They belonged like this, locked together in an embrace that transported her into some other world. There was no porch, no sky, no ranch, no Texas. Nothing existed except Wade and her.

Brownie began to bark.

Wade pulled away, cursing. "Get dressed," he ordered, pushing her ahead of him into the house. "Might be nothing, but better load that Beaumont-Adams."

Julia hurried into her bedroom and threw on her clothes. Taking the revolver from its box, she shoved the bullets into the cylinder, snapped it into place and eased cautiously into the hall.

She found Wade dousing the lamp in the sconce. She noticed he carried a rifle.

"You ought not to—"

"Don't tell me to wait in my room," she cut in. "Two armed is better than one. Besides, nothing can be worse than facing the Slocum gang."

"Stay behind me, then, you stubborn female."

She trailed him into the kitchen and out the back door. The moon was too thin to cast a decent light. Brownie was still barking and she could hear the thud of horses' hoofs.

A man cursed the dog with words similar to those the Coventry house painter had used. She recognized them without being exactly certain what some of the words meant.

"Hell, that's Jack," Wade muttered.

Jack Crain? Julia stiffened, raising her revolver.

"What the devil you doing here, Crain?" Wade shouted.

"Come in peace, I swear," Jack called back. "For the love of God, don't shoot, I got my wife with me."

Julia almost dropped the Beaumont-Adams in surprise. His wife? Hadn't Wade said they were divorced?

The professor emerged from his wagon carrying a lit lantern and called the dog to him. Brownie stopped barking, but, instead of going to the professor, he came to Julia.

"Send the woman into the light," Wade ordered.

A rangy bay walked into the illuminated ring cast by the lantern. On his back was a woman riding sidesaddle. "Please help me down," she said to the professor, who obliged.

Julia drew in her breath. The woman's cloak had opened when she dismounted, giving Julia a view of a rounded abdomen. Unless she was badly mistaken, the woman was with child.

Seeing her sway, impulsively, Julia hurried to her, ignoring Wade's order to halt. She put an arm around the woman, saying, "You must be exhausted. Let me help you into the house."

"I'm Celia," the woman said. "Thanks." Leaning on Julia, she allowed herself to be led toward the back door.

"You got some explaining to do, Crain," Wade growled.

Leaving the men to sort it out, Julia ushered Celia into the kitchen, found a chair by touch and guided her into it. She fumbled for a match and lit the lamp. The first thing she saw was Silver Wing staring from her to the stranger and back.

"Her name's Celia—Crain?" When the woman nodded, Julia went on. "This is Silver Wing, Celia. I'm Julia."

"Jack told me about you all," Celia said.

"Are you hungry?" Julia asked.

"If'n I could have a cup of tea?"

Silver Wing took a lid off the range, poked up the fire and added a chunk of wood. She moved the kettle from the back to the front burner and then went to the cupboard for the tea.

"I don't mean to be inquisitive, but I'd heard that you and Mr. Crain were divorced," Julia said.

Celia shook her head. "We just got married. Maybe he had another wife he never told me about. Wouldn't put it past him."

She seemed to have Jack's number. "I guess you must realize by now that your husband is not exactly welcome at this ranch," Julia said. "Which has nothing to do with you, of course."

"We didn't have nowhere else to go. Got no money and Pa wouldn't give us house room after the wedding." Tears filled her eyes. "Jack never would've married me if'n Pa hadn't prodded him to the minister with his rifle on account of . . ." Her voice trailed off and she rubbed her belly.

Not knowing how to respond to this tale of woe, Julia turned to Silver Wing and said, "Celia will have to sleep on the sofa."

Nodding, the girl left—to fetch bedding, Julia knew.

"I guess Mr. Howland ain't gonna let us stay here neither," Celia said, wiping her eyes.

"We'll find some solution," Julia assured her, uncertain just what Wade would do.

He could hardly take Jack on again as foreman and it'd be difficult, if not impossible, for a man like Jack to work under someone he'd formerly bossed. She suspected Wade would refuse to hire him at all.

"I sure hope so. Jack acted so sweet to me when we was courting back in Austin. I never figured—" She stopped and sighed. "Should've listened to Ma. She never did like Jack."

"Things have a way of working out." Julia didn't believe her own words, but she hoped they'd reassure Celia.

After the tea was made, Celia was persuaded to eat some bread and cheese with it before she retired to the couch. By then, Wade had brought in her bag, so she was able to don her nightgown.

Silver Wing went back to bed, leaving Wade and Julia sitting in the kitchen finishing up the pot of tea.

"Sent Jack to the bunkhouse for the night," Wade said. "Couldn't turn him away in the dark. But he and his wife leave tomorrow."

"Celia's in a family way, they have no money and her folks turned her out," Julia told him.

Wade muttered something under his breath that she thought it was just as well she couldn't hear.

"Damned if I'll hire him back," he growled. "Can't trust the bas—him."

"Sleep on it," she advised. "Maybe something will come to you."

"Hope you're working on an answer 'cause I sure don't have one."

Julia set down her cup and rose, yawning. "I'm going to bed. It's late."

"Maybe not too late," he said.

She studied him. "Too late for what?"

"For us. No good talking about it now, what with strangers in the house. We will, though."

Julia was too tired to argue, even though she had no hope that talking could change the way things stood between them. "Good night, then," she said.

Without rising, he caught her hand. "Promise me you'll listen."

She saw no harm in that. "I promise."

"Without interrupting."

That made her smile. "I guess I do that a lot. But so do you."

"Two of a kind. Good night, Julie." He released her.

She carried his words with her to bed. *Two of a kind?* Were they really? The idea had never occurred to her. She was still turning it over in her mind when sleep overtook her.

Chapter 20

At breakfast the next morning, Wade took Julia aside and told her he intended to send Jack out on the range for the time being so he could earn some money and yet not be underfoot. "Don't care to see his face anywhere around, and that's the truth," he added. "Won't turn away an old comrade, though, even if I can't call him friend any longer. I made it clear they couldn't stay here long."

Julia smiled at him. She'd known Wade would come up with a solution, even if it was temporary.

"Get his wife to helping around the house," Wade went on. "It'll give her something to do. Feel sorry for the gal, saddled with Jack."

Later, when she went out to feed Brownie, she saw Jack talking to the professor. He didn't look her way for which she was grateful.

Back in the house, she found Celia admiring Silver Wing's wedding gown. "Wish I'd've had the chance to get married right and proper," she said wistfully. "Guess I'm lucky to be married at all, though. If'n Pa hadn't spotted Jack riding down Pecan Street and followed him to find out where he was bedded down, likely enough I still wouldn't have a husband.''

She fingered the white silk and sighed. ''Ain't something a girl cares to remember, her man being forced to the minister at the point of a gun. ''Like as not, he never did care for me.''

''He must have,'' Julia said. ''Otherwise he wouldn't have courted you.''

''If'n you can call it true courting. Ma warned me he was out for only one thing.'' Celia took a deep breath and let it out slowly. She touched her abdomen with gentle fingers. ''But now that I got Jack roped and tied, I mean to see he stays that way on account of we're gonna be this un's pa and ma.'' She glanced at Julia and smiled slyly. ''Ma give me her pa's horn-handled hunting knife for my wedding present and Jack knows it. Never hunted, don't expect to. The knife's to remind Jack what'll happen if he don't stick to them vows we made.''

Julia swallowed, unsure what to say. Did Celia intend to kill him if he misbehaved? She was surprised to see Silver Wing nodding in approval.

''My father do that one time to man who try to force me,'' she said.

''You mean your father killed him?'' Julia asked.

Celia and Silver Wing exchanged a knowing glance that made Julia feel left out.

''Better you don't know,'' Celia told her.

Maybe it was at that, Julia thought, as an uneasy speculation began to trouble her. Whatever was meant by Celia's threat, though, it was plain that she was no one to be pushed around. Jack had met his match.

As the days passed, it became clear that Celia enjoyed children. The twins took to her, leaving Silver Wing free to get on with the wedding preparations. Celia's tales of how her younger sisters and brother got into one scrape after another held Nancy and Susan spellbound, making

Julia realize more than ever that the twins needed to be with other children more often.

But she wouldn't be here to do anything about that—nor anything else.

On Thursday, Wade rode into Austin with Ezra. Julia told herself it was no longer any of her affair—if ever it had been—whether or not Wade visited Monette. But she couldn't stop thinking about it.

Adelina arrived Saturday evening with not only her son-in-law as escort but Wade and Ezra as well. Pablo was relegated to the bunkhouse and, with Jack Crain gone, didn't refuse. Adelina shared her former room with Maria. The twins were so excited by all the company that Julia despaired of ever quieting them down enough for bed.

Ezra had bought Silver Wing a wedding ring that he showed to Julia in private. On the inside of the gold band the jeweler had etched EM & SW and tomorrow's date. "Do you think she'll like it?" he asked. "It's a surprise."

"It's lovely," Julia assured him. "She'll treasure it forever."

He beamed, stowed the ring back in its case and went off.

Celia had the twins firmly in tow. Maria shooed her away when she tried to help clean up after the meal and Silver Wing was preoccupied with Ezra, leaving Julia at loose ends. She had packing to do if she planned to leave for California in a few days—but she didn't feel like it. Restless, she wandered outside and found the professor sitting on the wagon steps.

"I've been thinking how fortunate it was for all of us that you came along when you did," she told him.

"Fortunate for me as well. I've made friends with some fine people as well as acquiring a strong, dependable horse in place of old Ben. I fear I'm a fiddle-foot, though. I've never been one to stay long in a place and California has always been a siren calling to me. I've hesitated to make the long trip alone but, with two armed, men, I—"

"Two?" she broke in to ask.

"Why yes. Jack Crain and I had a talk on the morning before he rode out to the range. He and his wife will join us on the journey."

Julia stared at him, speechless. Was she to be forced to travel with Jack Crain?

"I believe you have reservations," the professor said. "You should not. I've also spoken to Celia. Jack made a fine choice there; she's a singularly level-headed young woman and not in the least frightened of him."

"I agree she's capable, but I don't think he had any real choice."

"Perhaps the Lord lent a helping hand. In any case, with Celia watching him and Ezra on hand, Jack isn't likely to misbehave on the trip. Once in California, I suspect we shall have a parting of the ways."

"No doubt," she said dryly.

"Celia will also provide companionship for Silver Wing," the professor added.

Julia blinked. "What about me?"

"My dear young woman, do you really believe he'll let you go?"

"If you mean Wade, he has no choice," she said. "I make my own decisions."

"Ah, well, life is full of surprises, which is why every day is so interesting." He rose to his feet and patted her shoulder. "It's been my pleasure to know you. Now I must bid you good night as tomorrow will prove busy for all of us. Besides, someone awaits you."

Julia glanced around. In the rapidly fading light there was just enough left for her to recognize Wade standing a few feet away. She had no idea how long he'd been there.

He lit the lantern he'd been carrying. "I'd like you to help me make a final inspection of the little house Ezra's fixed up," he said. "Want to make sure everything is in order for their wedding night. Being a woman, you might see something I'd miss."

She could have asked him why it couldn't wait until morning but she didn't, even though she suspected his reason might not be the true one.

"I'll be happy to," she told him and fell into step beside him as they walked toward the cottonwoods with Brownie as escort.

"Seems to me the dog's taken a fancy to you," he commented. "He follows you around more than he does Silver Wing."

"She wants to leave him behind. Actually, he was her father's, not hers. And I've been feeding him lately. Maybe that's why he favors me."

"Homely old mutt that he is, he's got good taste in women."

She smiled at Wade's comment. "Am I supposed to say thank you for the compliment?" she asked.

"Surprise me if you did. You don't much cotton to compliments."

"Maybe because so many are false."

"Not mine."

"All right, I won't argue. I'm delighted you think Brownie has good taste."

"Don't sound like you mean that."

Julia laughed, feeling more light-hearted than she had in days. She enjoyed being with Wade and was determined to treasure every moment she had left of his company.

"Did the professor tell you Jack Crain and his wife are joining us for the trip to California?" she said.

"Heard something of the sort. Might prove a good move on Jack's part and I'll rest easier knowing there's two armed men to protect the women."

"I'm certainly not enthusiastic about traveling in his company."

"I wouldn't worry about it," he told her.

"Why? Do you really think Jack's changed that much?"

"Wasn't what I meant."

She was still puzzling over that when they reached the

house. He opened the door and ushered her inside, holding the lantern up so she could see the inside more clearly.

"Couldn't scare up much furniture," he said.

The house consisted of one main room, which doubled as a kitchen and living room. A wood/coal range occupied one corner, with a pump and sink beside it. Ezra had built in cupboards. A table and two chairs looked rather lonely set in front of a fireplace. Tucked into a corner, a spiral staircase led to a sleeping loft.

One smaller room opened off the main one and Julia saw a bed had been installed there.

"They have everything they need for the short while they'll be here," she said.

"Be mostly occupied with each other anyway," Wade added.

Understanding what he meant, Julia flushed, remembering all too well how preoccupied she and Wade had been while making love.

"It's a cozy place," she said, turning toward the door, suddenly needing to be out of there, away from where another couple would spend happy hours.

"Wait," he ordered. "I haven't shown you the sleeping loft."

Suppressing a sigh, she walked toward the stairs. The flickering light of the lantern cast shifting shadows on the walls and peaked roof as they climbed. She focused on the shadows, hoping to blot out any recollection of Wade's embrace.

At the top of the stairs, he stopped her and set the lantern down on the floor. "Heard you talking to the professor," he said. "You went on about deciding for yourself."

"Why shouldn't I?" she challenged.

He shrugged. "Heard him warn you life was full of surprises. Close your eyes."

"Whatever for?"

"Always a question, that's my Julie. Just do it."

Since there was no reason not to go along, she shut her eyes.

"Don't open them till I say to," he ordered, taking her arm.

With his hand on her arm, he guided her steps, then his hand fell away. "You can open your eyes now," he said.

She blinked in the lantern-light for a moment until her gaze fell on a white dress suspended from a top bunk so that it hung almost to the floor. All silk and lace, it dazzled her eyes. It was the most beautiful gown she'd ever seen.

"Why—why it's a wedding dress," she blurted, belatedly realizing what she was looking at. She stared at Wade. "But Silver Wing already has the one we made over for her. You didn't have to buy her this. Though it was certainly generous of you."

"I'm aware Silver Wing has her wedding gown," he said. "I didn't buy this for her."

Julia's mind raced. For Emma? No, he'd been all set to have the ceremony the moment Emma arrived. She'd have been married wearing whatever she'd traveled in.

"Another thing," he said. "I went to see Monette while I was in Austin. What with the Slocums gunning for me, I never did have the chance to tell her I wouldn't be coming to see her anymore. I took care to do that this time. You know what she said?"

Still confused, Julia shook her head.

"Monette said, 'Not to that little brown wren.' Wherever would she get such an odd notion?"

A picture flashed in Julia's mind—number 10, Wade wearing only a towel, Monette staring at her and, as she fled down the hall, demanding, "Who's the little brown wren?"

"She meant me," Julia told him. "I had on a brown bonnet. But I don't understand. What about me?"

"Guess I'm doing this all backward," he said. "Ain't easy for a man to admit he's been a fool. Never did mean to fall in love, but I did. For keeps. With you. Damn it, Julie, you must know I love you.''

"Not until this moment," she said, trying to collect her wits.

"Maybe not for sure, but I bet you suspected, the way I've been acting. Could hardly bear to let you out of my sight. Anyway, I bought that wedding dress for you, hoping you'd marry me.''

"You—you're asking me to marry you?"

"Yeah. Should've done it a long time ago. Fought against love like it was some kind of dangerous critter. It ain't. What love is . . ." He paused and held his hand toward her. "I found out love is you, Julie.''

She lay her hand in his, blinking back tears of sheer joy. "You have it wrong," she informed him. "From my point of view, Wade, love is you.''

He caught her to him, murmuring, "Going to get me a stubborn wife, I see." He held her away, gazing into her eyes. "You do mean to marry me, don't you?"

"I'd like to see anyone try to stop me," she told him. "I always wanted a stubborn husband.''

His arms gathered her close and they blended together in a kiss of affirmation, of promise, and of passion.

Sunday dawned bright and beautiful—a perfect Texas day. Nancy and Susan darted here and there among the guests like little pink butterflies. Julia, inside the house, watched them from an open window, obeying, with Silver Wing, the stricture that the grooms mustn't see the brides before the ceremony began or bad luck would follow.

"We're flower girls," Julia heard Nancy confide to Mrs. Atkins.

Susan held up two fingers. "For this many weddings.''

"Told Wade 'twas gonna be a double wedding," Ed Tyson said to his wife. "Honored to escort Julia, I really am. Always knew Wade was gonna do the right thing.''

"Took him long enough," Nell Tyson said. "That's a man for you."

Julia smiled. Wade was certainly the man for her.

"Happy for you," Silver Wing told her. "Happy for me, too."

Julia restrained an impulse to hug her, not wishing to crush either gown.

Adelina beamed on them both. Her son-in-law, Pablo, had been pressed into service to escort Silver Wing, pleasing her.

"Maria my good friend," Adelina said. "Me, I ask her to come here to help you till I find good woman who want to work on ranch. Maria, she don't want to stay long but she agree. Senor Wade, he talk to Pablo, say he and my daughter and boys come live in that little house you got mended so nice. Pablo, he work on ranch. Me, I come back and be housekeeper again and help my daughter when she need me."

"I do hope you said yes," Julia cried. "I can't think of anything I'd like better."

"Good for us all here, Pablo say. Me, I agree."

"I'd hug you if it weren't for my gown," Julia said. "What a wonderful wedding present."

"Senor Wade say you think up plan. *Muchas gracias.*"

"You're helping us as much as we're helping you. You're even bringing two little boys for the twins to play with."

Adelina rolled her eyes. "Some fights come, I think."

One of the neighbors had brought his violin and now struck up his version of a wedding march. Julia took a deep breath, remembering how she'd fought against this very happening on her arrival.

Allowing Silver Wing to precede her, she emerged from the house, walked to where Ed Tyson waited and put her hand on his arm. "Smile," he whispered.

She could not. A fluttering akin to fear troubled her insides. It was, she realized with dismay, much the same sensation that had gripped her on her arrival, after she realized a wedding had been planned.

Though aware of Silver Wing with Pablo as escort walking beside her, Julia felt as though she were enclosed in a space alone, traveling back in time.

As before, the crowd parted to form an aisle leading to the flower-and-ribbon-draped arch erected the day before. The professor, in his office as the Reverend Wilkes, waited there, facing her. The two other men under the arch had their backs to her. Ezra turned first, his smile for only Silver Wing.

The second man, dressed all in gray, turned toward her and she saw his shirt was open at the neck, increasing her sense that she'd been transported back in time. His skin was tan, his hair black, and he was scowling. She hesitated, but Ed kept her moving toward the wedding bower.

Wade's gray gaze fastened on her face and the scowl vanished. His lips curved into the beginning of a smile, warming her, banishing the strangeness. He was Wade, the man she loved. Would always love. Perhaps the beginning of love had been at that moment of arrival, when he walked along the aisle formed by the crowd to meet her.

When she reached him, he leaned and whispered familiar words in her ear, words he'd said on her arrival, "You're not what I expected, not at all." New words, loving words followed. "You're more. So much more. I plan to keep you forever."

Julia smiled at him, joined her hand with his, and together they faced the minister. And, she thought, the future as well. Always together.

Chapter 21

Late spring in Texas was a beautiful time of year, Julia thought as she sat on the front porch in a rocking chair. The faint shouts of the twins, playing in the cottonwood grove with the Mendoza boys, mingled with the chirps of birds perched on the roof of the house. The sweet scent of blossoms drifted on the breeze.

Last fall's cattle drive had gone well and the spring roundup was over. There'd be no shortage of money this year. Wade had already promised to put an addition on the house so they'd have space for a schoolroom as well as a nursery.

Once she'd thought she wouldn't have the patience to be a teacher and certainly she'd never had the training for it, but she'd found she thoroughly enjoyed teaching reading and writing and arithmetic to the twins and the Mendoza boys. When the addition was finished, she'd promised to add the Atkins's older girl, going on seven, and the Moyes's five-year-old son to her list of students.

She must be doing something right, because Adelina bragged proudly about how well her grandsons could read.

"Me, I never learn," she'd add. "Not even in *Español.*
My daughters, they never learn. Pablo, he learn to write
his name, that's all. Now the boys, they read to me. Maybe
they read to their baby sister when she gets older."

Adelina had recruited Esperanza, a sixteen-year-old girl
cousin of Pablo's to help her daughter and also help with
work in the ranch house when needed. Already it looked
as though there'd soon be another wedding in the offing
as Jamie was courting Esperanza.

As for the nursery, it was high time little Polly Rose had
her crib moved from her parents' bedroom to her own.
Julia smiled down at the baby sleeping in her arms. Polly
had blond hair but it was already clear her eyes would be
gray rather than blue.

Brownie, who'd been sleeping by the porch steps, raised
his head, looking toward the corner of the house. A
moment later Wade strode around the corner with what
looked like letters in his hand.

"Ed Tyson dropped the mail by," he said, climbing the
steps and leaning over to kiss her. He handed her two
letters, ran his hand gently over his daughter's head, then
sat in the chair next to Julia.

"Good news in both of those," he said.

"You may as well tell me what it is because I don't want
to disturb Polly by shifting around to read them."

"One's from Ezra. He and Silver Wing are settled on a
rancho near a little town called Los Angeles. They left the
professor in the village of San Diego."

"How about Celia and her husband?" she asked, refusing to mention Jack Crain's name.

"Celia had a little girl—seems to be the season for
girls—and they're living in San Francisco."

"What about the other letter—who's it from?"

"Our daughter's namesake, your Great-aunt Polly.
Seems she's decided to visit the great state of Texas. Emma
would like to come as well, but she's about to make Floyd
a proud papa so will have to postpone her trip here."

"Who would ever have thought I'd have a baby before Emma did?"

Wade slanted her a look that warmed her down to her toes.

"When is Great-aunt Polly planning to come?" she asked hastily before he could go on to tell her exactly why a Howland had been born before a Biddescomb.

"In July. She wants to make certain the baby arrives there before she arrives here. Says she won't be needed to help after that 'cause Floyd's mother is all set to take over. As she put it, the woman was 'hovering over us like a hungry vulture.' "

Julia rolled her eyes. "I can imagine. You're going to like my great-aunt, I know you are. Once you get used to her, anyway."

"Had the feeling she'd take some getting used to. But I've already met up with one plain-speaking, hard-headed Sommers woman so I doubt it'll take much effort to get along with another. She's welcome to stay as long as she wants. Might even make a match for her while she visits. Old George Lawless in Austin's been a widower for some time now. Could invite him to the ranch and see what happens."

"She'd never marry. She's said so many times."

"Might be 'cause she's never come up against a Texas man before. Young or old, we're something else."

"I certainly don't plan to argue with that."

"Good. Now, if you're real careful, maybe you can put young Polly down in that cradle in the main room without waking her."

"All right." She was about to ask him why, when she looked into his eyes and saw the reason glowing there.

Her breath caught and her insides melted, but she retained enough hold on her mind to murmur, "It's not yet noon—don't you have work to do?"

"When a man puts work before anything else, he's either on his last legs or he's one bullet short of a full cylinder."

Julia smiled at his words. She'd got herself a real Texas man, all right. As she laid Polly gently in the cradle, a name popped into her mind—the isolated train station where she'd first disembarked to plunge headlong into the greatest adventure of her life.

She put her hand in Wade's, gazed up at him and murmured, "This is Loveland."

ROMANCE FROM JANELLE TAYLOR

ANYTHING FOR LOVE   (0-8217-4992-7, $5.99)

DESTINY MINE   (0-8217-5185-9, $5.99)

CHASE THE WIND   (0-8217-4740-1, $5.99)

MIDNIGHT SECRETS   (0-8217-5280-4, $5.99)

MOONBEAMS AND MAGIC (0-8217-0184-4, $5.99)

SWEET SAVAGE HEART   (0-8217-5276-6, $5.99)